S!NG
LIKE NO ONE'S
LISTENING ♪♫♪

Other books by Vanessa Jones

Dance Like No One is Watching

S!NG
LIKE NO ONE'S LISTENING

VANESSA JONES

MACMILLAN

This edition published 2021 by Macmillan Children's Books

First published 2019 by Macmillan Children's Books
an imprint of Pan Macmillan
The Smithson, 6 Briset Street, London EC1M 5NR
EU representative: Macmillan Publishers Ireland Limited,
Mallard Lodge, Lansdowne Village, Dublin 4
Associated companies throughout the world
www.panmacmillan.com

ISBN 978-1-5290-6169-7

1 3 5 7 9 8 6 4 2

A CIP catalogue record for this book is available from the British Library.

Printed and bound by CPI Group (UK) Ltd, Croydon CR0 4YY

MIX
Paper from
responsible sources
FSC® C116313

To my three pals,

*and also to you, if you've ever
felt so nervous you couldn't.*

CHAPTER 1

If this was the opening sequence of a musical, I'd be stepping up to these doors with a leather suitcase in each hand and a smile on my face, about to break into song about what a wonderful morning it is, or the fact that the hills are alive, or something equally as cheesy.

But it's not a musical.

There's no orchestral swell, no birds tweeting. Only the grumbling underscore of traffic on Old Compton Street, a faint whiff of car fumes and bacon and, given that I came here alone, the excruciating absence of anyone to sing to. Only the *thud-thud* of my terrified heart to keep me company.

The vast, pale brick building sits elegantly on a corner of Soho Square. My ears pick up a mixture of classical piano and hip-hop beats from within, making me shiver with excitement. To my right there's a steel plaque, which reads:

Duke's Academy of Performing Arts
Formerly The King's School
Founded 1854

In smaller writing underneath I can just make out another sentence:

It was only in the theatre that I lived.
Oscar Wilde

1

No pressure, then.

OK, time to focus. This is not just the audition of my life. I'm auditioning *for* my life. Checking the time on my phone, I take a breath and step through the tall doors.

Omigod, it's *huge* in here. There are students everywhere, milling around, stretching, gossiping . . . they're even on the walls – adorning the white painted atrium in signed, framed ten-by-eights ranging from the 1920s to the present day. There are some names I recognize; lots I don't. A wealth of writers, directors, actors and dancers look down at me gloatingly with their glassy half-smiles.

I guess only the best students make it on to the Duke's Wall of Fame. Seeing their success makes my throat contract in an actual gulp.

How long have I got? Four minutes. Just time to slip to the toilet and go through my song. There's a student at the front desk waiting to sign people in.

'Name?'

'Er, Nettie.'

She scans the register.

'Sorry – it's Antoinette,' I correct myself. 'I don't really use my full name.'

'No worries.' She finds my name and looks back up in a double take. 'I'll change it.'

I thank her and squeeze past before she has a chance to ask me anything else that might make her realize who I am.

There are doors leading to enormous studios on each side of the foyer. I pass two on my left: one housing a street-dance class and the other a musical theatre lesson. I pause at the second studio window just as a boy is hitting the last few notes of 'Bring Him

Home', the rest of the class watching, spellbound. Wow. He's *amazing*. Proper jaw-droppingly good. I can't help wondering if that'll be me one day, here at Duke's, learning my craft, owning it, being generally brilliant . . .

OK, enough. Daydreaming won't get you a place here.

I tear myself away from the studio window and make my way through to the changing rooms. The adjacent toilet is white-tiled and clean. It's deserted. I lock the door and sing full out at my reflection. It goes OK, but God, I'm nervous. Maybe I should sing the other one. It's probably easier.

I start to gather my things together.

My phone bleeps with a voicemail. Absent-mindedly I put it to my ear and haul my bag over my shoulder.

'*Hi, Nettie. I'm in town—*'

The tiles on the toilet wall go blurry.

'*Did you say you needed shower gel?*'

The shock of her voice makes me retch.

'*Call me if you think of anything else. I love you.*'

Mum.

My knees buckle. I wildly grab the sink for support, dropping my phone on the hard floor in the process. It lands with a loud crack.

Mum . . .

I double over and throw up into the toilet.

. . . How?

I scrabble on the floor for my phone. The screen is a spider web of smashed glass but I can still see the list of voicemails, and there she is, right at the top. This isn't possible. This *isn't possible*.

I go to swallow but it kills. My head's too full of blood. I'm sure it's going to explode. I'm going to self-decapitate and bleed

3

to death here in the loo, like some sort of teen horror movie opening sequence.

I try to steady myself.

It doesn't make any sense. Mum died over a year ago. Why have I got a voicemail from her?

Is she . . . ?

Maybe it's all been a mistake. Maybe she recovered somewhere in secret. Maybe it's all been a long, hideous dream. Maybe . . .

This is ridiculous. Maybe-ing doesn't help – it just makes it worse when you come back to reality. God knows, I'm the expert.

Get a grip. You can't go to pieces – not here, not now.

I look in the mirror, struggling to take a deep breath as I wipe vomit from my lips. It's just some sort of technical blip – a mistake by the phone company. It's got stuck in the ether and been delivered late – like, fourteen months late. That's all.

I *cannot* let this affect me. Not today. It's too important. Just breathe.

I can't, though.

I *can't* breathe.

I was doing so well. Today was going to be difficult without Mum, I knew that. But I was holding it together – at least I was until I heard her voice. Now I'm winded, mugged. My throat's swollen with raw emotion and acid-burn and my eyes are stinging.

Oh no, not now. Don't cry now. Get it together, Nettie.

I press the corners of my eyes with shaking fingers and head back into the foyer, where a man in a spotted cravat pokes his head out of the audition room.

'Ah, Antoinette. Here you are. We called you a moment ago.'

'Sorry, I—'

'Not to worry. We'd like to see you now, if you're ready.'

4

I follow him into the studio, barely able to focus.

'So, what have you brought to sing for us?' says the man. He leaves me in the centre of the room and goes to sit down with the rest of the panel.

'Er . . . I've got "I'm Not Afraid of Anything" . . .' I falter. I'm surprised no one laughs. I must look literally afraid of everything right now. The room spins.

'Haven't you got anything else?' says a woman next to him.

I try to focus on her face, which right now is just a white blur inside a blackish-grey bob.

'We've heard that one seven times already today.' Her voice is cold and clipped.

'Oh. Um, I've got—'

'Well, whatever it is, let's hear it. I need a break from the mind-numbing tedium,' says the voice. I notice the echo it makes through the vast studio. Good acoustics, Mum would have said.

Mum.

I freeze. My feet won't move; I'm stuck in some sort of awful spotlight I can't step out of.

'Everything all right?' asks the man.

'Uh, sure.' Dazed, I force myself over to the pianist to give him my sheet music. As I walk slowly back to the centre of the studio and wait for the introduction, I know something's still not right. I'm unsteady on my feet and my throat's small, like I can't get enough air to my lungs.

Mum should've been here today. I wore that dress she gave me for my seventeenth – the one with the flowers. I picked her favourite song. I *needed* her. But . . . not like this. How could this happen, now of all times?

The first line is audible, but only just. My voice is thin; reedy.

5

With every breath it gets worse.

By the end of the first chorus, it's down to little more than a whisper. What's happening to me?

'*You'll never get in.*' My grandmother's last words to me as I left the house this morning float up to the forefront of my mind. '*I don't know why you're bothering. You'll never make it. Look where show business got your mother.*'

'*I don't care. It's what I want. Mum wanted me to go. She was proud of me – not that you'd ever know.*'

Mum.

I don't even have the energy to be angry any more. I'm drained of everything right now, except the overwhelming grief throbbing through my chest.

The pianist comes to a halt and I realize I've stopped singing altogether.

'Nettie, would you like a glass of water?' says the man.

'I—'

'Is there a problem?'

'No, I'm fine. I just—'

I just heard my dead mum on a voicemail and now I can't sing is the problem. But I can't say that, can I? Tear tracks prickle my jawline and I rub them away violently. The panel must think my nerves have got the better of me, standing in the middle of the studio and weeping silently with no explanation.

'Nettie?'

I mouth '*I'm sorry*' and run out.

The envelope sits on the table for a good half an hour before I have the courage to approach it. The gilt lettering on the back glares at me, daring me to rip it open.

There's no way I've got in after my fiasco of an audition, but this moment is the last time I'll ever *not know* for sure. Until I open that envelope, I can still imagine how my life would be if I got in, still hope for that chance to start building my life again.

There's no plan B. I didn't apply for uni because I was so set on musical theatre, so busy grieving for Mum that I forgot to make a backup plan. I'll be stuck living with Auntie – I have to call her 'Auntie' because apparently 'Grandmother' is ageing – until I'm as old as her and she's even older, rotting in this decaying townhouse in south-east London forever.

I pick up the envelope. It's only small – surely if I'd got a place there would be loads of information inside? I tear it open, bracing myself for the inevitable. When I read the first sentence, I can barely breathe.

Dear Miss Delaney-Richardson,

We are delighted to be able to offer you a place at Duke's Academy of Performing Arts on the Musical Theatre course, commencing this September.

I see the word 'delighted' and the rest of the letter is a blur.

Please see our student portal for a list of all available accommodation, local information and a list of your uniform requirements.

I've lost concentration. The letter goes on, I think. Something about Miss Duke requesting that places be accepted immediately and some more info on how to pay deposits.

Delighted.

But . . . *how?*

My audition was terrible. I mean, truly awful. I didn't even stay long enough to do the dance and drama classes, and my singing . . . I hastily turn over the page, wary there might be some kind of addendum to the letter saying that it's all been a joke. But that's it: the letter, a list of useful links and a couple of maps marked with all-night chemists and emergency dentists.

Did I get in because of Mum? She trained there as a dancer years ago. Maybe they recognized my name and thought I must be some shit-hot prima. They'll be disappointed.

Look. Who cares *how* I got in – I got in. I'm *free*. I get to leave this place and all the horrible memories and start a new life doing what I love.

I'll prove myself worthy of a place when I get there. I'm going to make it as a singer.

Except for one small problem.

I can't sing anymore.

CHAPTER 2

My new room in the halls is small and basic. There's a tiny bed, a miniscule wardrobe, a desk, a chair and a chest of drawers, all in the same pale beech veneer. The walls are a bland off-white and the only light comes from a single central bulb with a spherical paper lampshade. Not exactly the Palladium, but to me the stark, colourless room is a blank page. A fresh start. A New World.

I reach inside the open suitcase on the bed and pull out a single red rose pressed in a frame. It's the first flower Mum ever received onstage. Leaning it up against the wall on the desk, I'm transported, my mind watching from the wings as she curtseys to the roaring crowd and scoops it up elegantly. It's weird – lately I only seem to be able to see her from behind. I can't seem to picture her face. It's like I've tried so many times I've worn out the memory.

Mum died in May last year. It was a complete shock; well, to me, anyway. She never told me she'd had cancer before. This one was secondary. And it shot her down in six weeks. *Six weeks.* We'd barely had time to get over the diagnosis before she was gone and I was suddenly organizing the funeral, clearing out the house so it could be rented and moving in with a grandmother I didn't even know. Without realizing it I'd become this adult with a load of responsibilities, when what I felt like was an orphan without my mum. My family.

It had been just Mum and me for as long as I can remember.

No one else. Being without her was devastating. But I was coping. I thought I was, anyway.

Until the audition.

My voice didn't come back for three weeks after that awful day. A rush of shame hit me every time I thought about it, all wrapped up in a grief that felt as new as the day I lost Mum. The four walls of my room were all I saw; surviving on the breadsticks and raw vegetables that my grandmother left outside the door (God forbid she'd ever give me *real* food), unable to speak, unable to leave. I passed the time by watching old MGM movies on my phone, or staring out of the window at Crystal Palace Park, trying to remember the view from my old window in Woodland Road that looked down the steep hill towards the city. My grandmother's townhouse in Sydenham couldn't feel further from home, despite being just on the other side of the park.

At night I put Billie Holiday on the record player and curled up on my bed and cried; big, silent sobs that started in the pit of my stomach and shook my whole body as they escaped.

My friends tried calling, messaging; I even heard them turn up on the doorstep one day; but I didn't talk to them. Eventually they stopped trying.

I *couldn't* talk. Every time I tried, my throat went hard, just like it did in the audition – like muscle memory or something. I was terrified I'd never make another sound.

Ironically, the one thing my grandmother did do for me was bring my speaking voice back. After three weeks in my room, I managed to get dressed and go downstairs, only to find her sitting there calmly like it wasn't strange to see me out of my room for the first time in nearly a month – like there was *nothing wrong*. I almost laughed.

CHAPTER 3

I'm awake at 4 a.m. After trying to get back to sleep for an hour, I eventually get up, shower, dress myself and pack every possible thing I might need for my first day. I can barely lift my bag and it makes negotiating the escalators at the tube station tricky, but I arrive at Duke's on time.

This is it. This is the start of the rest of my life.

No sooner have I stepped over the threshold than a tall, leggy white girl comes tearing past me, dressed in a pair of tiny hot pants and a strategically placed scarf doubling up as a crop top, with a huge mass of blonde hair and more make-up than the cast of *La Cage*. She trips over my bag, which I've just let drop to my side, and falls flat on her face. A few people laugh.

'I'm so sorry – I didn't mean—'

The girl stands up. She snaps her head back razor-sharp, her hair whipping her face, and looks me up and down like Baroness Schraeder eyeing Maria von Trapp's homemade curtain-clothes. Then she tosses her mane, glares at the rest of the surrounding people as if daring them to laugh again, and disappears into one of the studios. I stare after her.

'You've made your first college enemy, then,' drawls a silky male voice beside me. 'Must be a record. Congratulations.'

I turn and find myself face-to-face with (and I'm not exaggerating when I say this) *the* most beautiful creature I've seen, like, ever.

13

Tall and muscular, *tick*.

Eyes like sapphires, *tick*.

Hollywood nose, *tick*.

Mouth like . . . OK, you get it.

As my eyes swoop over his athletic, tanned physique, I notice his incredibly expensive taste in clothes. I clock his shoes.

'Prada, darling. You like?'

I nod.

He puts his hand out.

'Alec Van Damm. Gorgeous boy dancer and all-round *mangenue* about to take Duke's Academy and the rest of the world by storm. Thrilled and delighted.'

He pulls me in for a couple of *mwah-mwah* air kisses. There's a pause while he looks at me expectantly.

'Holy Gwen Verdon.' He's already exasperated with me. 'What's your freaking name?'

'Oh, er – Nettie,' I say.

'A one-word name. I like it.' He adjusts his hair in the reflection of the window. 'Like Cher.'

'No, er – sorry. I mean, it's Nettie Delaney-Richardson,' I say. Right now I could heat the whole college with my outrageously hot cheeks.

Alec's hand stops mid-preen. His eyes flicker over my black hair and pale skin.

'Fuck me. You're not—' he begins.

'You reckon we'll have registration soon?' I say it quickly, before he can wander any further down *that* particular path. 'Maybe I should be stretching. Everyone looks so . . .'

'*Loose?*'

'I was going to say comfortable. You know, in their

14

surroundings. Are we meant to be doing that?' I glance around at all the ballerinas rolling around on the floor with their legs wrapped around their necks.

'Who cares? It's our first day. Cheer up. You must have *some* talent to be here. Who knows – maybe it's in your blood . . .' He throws me a sideways glance but says nothing else. Hopefully it was just a throwaway comment.

'Seriously, darling,' he says. 'They wouldn't have let you in if you were total crap. Old Duke's got a reputation to maintain. Come here. I want to get this moment up on my Instagram story.' He pulls me in for possibly the most awkward selfie of my life.

At that moment, the college secretary comes out of the office. She's got a mushroom of white curly hair and full stage make-up, reminding me of Madame Morrible from *Wicked*, only way less fabulous in a plain tweed skirt and blouse. An ex-dancer, for sure. I'd recognize one anywhere.

'Everyone into the studio theatre, please,' she barks in clipped tones.

Alec winks and pats me on the arse in the direction of the door.

Inside is rammed. Students everywhere, some dressed in leotards and pointe shoes, others fully clothed and clutching folders or musical instruments. There's so much to take in. But what I notice first is the *noise*. It's overwhelming.

A group in the corner is singing a song from *Rent* in full four-part harmony at the top of their voices. Someone else is tinkering on the piano at the far end, oblivious to the singers. A boy nearby improvises a lyrical dance solo – to which music, I can't be sure (maybe to something playing in his head?). Students chat animatedly, fighting to break out over the cacophony.

15

Alec's been separated from me by the crowd. He's studying himself in the mirror at the far end of the studio while a couple of boys and a girl stare at him with their mouths open, whispering among themselves. I know what they're speculating about. Not that any of them stand a chance.

I squeeze onto the end of a bench against the wall and try to quell my anxiety. Everyone finds first days horrendous, right?

But looking around, no one else seems that bothered. Are *any* of them first-years, like me? I'm blatantly the only person not talking or singing or stretching ostentatiously. I watch a group of girls laughing hysterically as four boys do an unrehearsed cod version of the *pas de quatre* from *Swan Lake*.

And then, something strange happens.

A sharp intake of breath. A scrabbling sound as people hastily get off the floor. The air in the studio changes; a cold breeze seems to rush in, and a hush falls over the crowd. A hundred girls breathe in and get thinner, while all the boys simultaneously grow taller. Glossy smiles appear on faces, hands are rearranged neatly in laps, bags hidden behind legs. A couple of boys sprint to get a chair; another *jetés* over to hold the door. I can't see what's going on through the crowd of students, but I can sense something.

Slowly the crowd parts, and I see her.

She's tall, with once jet-black hair now silver at the front, its high hairline betraying years of being scraped into a bun. Her patent heels echo across the studio floor in an elegant ten-to-two position, legs barely bending. She's dressed expensively but

16

conservatively in trousers and a crisp white shirt with the collar turned up, a string of pearls adorning her slim neck, a pair of spectacles hanging from a chain below them. How old is she? Sixty?

I stand up hurriedly with everyone else as she walks slowly to the centre of the studio. She studies each student she passes, returning their desperate smiles with cold scrutiny, instinctively knowing their worst fears and their darkest secrets.

She waves away the chair that has been so delicately set for her. It's removed immediately, a boy snatching it and melting into the crowd like part of a well-rehearsed scene change. Cecile Duke's dark eyes pierce the crowd, a violent shock against her pale skin and red lips, which twitch as she waits for quiet, even though the silence is palpable.

'Good morning, students,' she says. Her vowels are clear, her consonants clipped, and her voice, though perfectly audible, gives the impression of never having to be raised. I feel chilly, but I don't know why because it's a warm September day and I'm still wearing my coat.

'Good morning, Miss Duke,' chants the crowd, not quite in unison.

'I trust you are all ready to begin your classes,' she says. It sounds like a warning. 'Assessments will take place before we break for Christmas. However, it will be worth noting that you are being watched *each and every day* from the moment you step through the doors until you leave at night, so do not think that if you rest upon your laurels for a second it will not be noted. We see *everything*.'

Her last words resonate around the room, devoured by three hundred pairs of avid ears.

'You have the *best* teachers here. The *best* facilities. So I fully expect the best from you at all times . . .' Her eyes scan the room and fall on something that makes them narrow. 'Lauren Rose, *come here.*'

The crowd's attention turns to a girl three rows back, who looks shocked to be singled out. Trembling, she shuffles to the front of the studio, her fellow students moving aside, grateful not to be her.

'Y-yes, Miss Duke?' she whispers.

'Go home,' says Cecile Duke quietly.

'I'm sorry, Miss Duke?'

'I said, *go home.*'

'I-I don't understand, Miss Duke,' Lauren Rose stammers.

Even I, a complete novice at all this, can see she'd be better off scramming and asking questions later.

'Every day you spend at this centre of excellence is a privilege.' She's speaking in a soft voice, but there's danger behind it. 'Every class you attend, every correction you are given, every opportunity you receive to follow your dream of performing is an honour. I have never tolerated complacency from my students, and I do not intend to start now.'

I can feel my heart pounding and she's not even talking to *me.*

'When I wake up in the morning, I ask myself, "What is expected of me today?" And the answer is always this: I am expected to inspire my students; to set a good example; to dress in a way befitting my position at the college; to welcome important guests from the industry who may visit us here – and let me tell you, there are many – and to be a figurehead worthy of the reputation the institution has earned.

'And what is expected of you, Lauren? *You* are expected to work hard; to attend all your classes; to be polite and respectful; and to look your best at all times. I ask you now, are you looking your best?'

There's a small rustling of clothes as necks are craned to scrutinize Lauren Rose. Jeez, guys, give her a break.

But they won't. I know it already and I've only spent five minutes here. They're like a pack of jackals, ready to tear apart anyone who shows even the slightest weakness. One less to compete against.

Admittedly, she's dressed rather scruffily – I guess for a contemporary class: grey joggers with holes in, one dirty once-white legwarmer – and her hair is tied up in the sort of folded-in scraggy ponytail you might have for a bath. She's not wearing any make-up. Personally I don't really see the point of wearing loads of make-up for class, not when you're going to get all sweaty, but right now I'm *so* grateful I applied a full face this morning to hide the lack of sleep.

Lauren Rose hangs her head miserably, cutting a pathetic shape as tears roll off her nose on to her faded burgundy leotard. I wish I could do something. Run over to her and hug her, or take her hand and fly her far away. But I won't, will I? I'll stand here helpless, frozen with cowardice like the rest of them, silently hating myself for it.

Miss Duke's eyes bore into Lauren Rose's miserable face, unrelenting. 'You have no idea what it's like out there after you graduate.' She lets the sentence hang, turning to the rest of us before fixing her gaze back on her victim.

'Here you are protected, cocooned. In a year's time, you will be out there on your own, working two jobs a day to try and make ends meet and spending every spare penny you have to get to class. You're on the dancers course, aren't you?' Lauren nods.

'Tomorrow we have an important choreographer visiting the college. Do you think he'd employ you, looking like that? One day, no doubt, you'll find yourself fighting to be picked out from a roomful of girls by that very same choreographer. When he throws you out at the first cut, regardless of how well or badly you may think you have danced, you'll ask yourself why. The answer is simple: he already knew you couldn't be bothered. If you can't make the effort, Lauren, then neither can I. Go home and think about whether you really want a career in the arts.'

Cecile Duke casts her dark eyes briefly around the room before sweeping towards the studio exit. Two boys fall over each other trying to open the door for her. Another second and she's gone.

Students brush past Lauren Rose without seeing her – or they pretend they haven't. She's soiled goods now. She stands there, head bowed, shoulders shaking, crying silently over the newly sprung floor.

I'm one of the last to leave the studio. As I pass her – I don't know what makes me do this – I stop and reach for her hand. God knows *I've* felt alone the last fourteen months. Maybe I want her to know she has an ally, albeit a pointless one who didn't have the guts to stand up for her when Miss Duke was present.

She pauses for a second, not exactly looking up, but there's a stillness that wasn't there before. Out of awkwardness, I fidget my gaze, and that's when I see Miss Duke.

She's looking at me through the window from the foyer. *Staring* at me like I'm a ghost or something.

She turns and disappears. A second later I hear her beige heels click-clicking up the stairs.

'Thanks,' says Lauren Rose.

I jump. I'd forgotten what I was doing for a second.

'Don't worry about her,' I say, as if I'm some sort of authority on all things Duke. 'She'll have forgotten about it by tomorrow.'

'Cecile Duke doesn't forget,' she says.

It sounds like a prophecy of doom. I squeeze her hand and leave her to it, wondering what Miss Duke could have possibly found so interesting about me.

CHAPTER 4

Back in the foyer, it's show business as usual, students swerving round each other, and studio doors slamming, as everyone tries to get to class on time. Lauren Rose has been forgotten but Miss Duke's message is loud and clear: play her game or suffer the consequences. I need to get *my* head in the game. Like in *High School Musical*. If I'd ever seen that (like, a hundred times, which I definitely won't admit to while I'm in this place).

Someone crashes into me, knocking me clean over. I quickly un-sprawl myself off the floor, feeling ridiculous (and winded).

'Oh no! I'm sorry. Are you all right? Here.'

The voice belongs to a tall, good-looking white guy with light brown wavy hair. He's carrying a battered leather satchel and a guitar. He holds out his hand to help me up. As I take it, I notice how rough it is. His nails are bitten, and his fingers are square and hard at the ends.

'Thanks.' I smooth my dress down at the back to make sure it hasn't got hitched up somewhere. 'I should have been looking where I was going.'

'No, it's all me. I've got my first lecture over in the other building and I was rushing to get there on time. I missed registration today, but I heard the "speech" was a long one, first day of term and all that. Sorry.'

'It's fine, really. Er . . .' I look down at my hand, which he's still holding.

'Oh God. First I charge you down, then I cling on to you like a limpet. I'm basically horrible.'

I laugh as he lets go, and my face feels strange. I haven't laughed for weeks. As he walks towards the front doors, he turns around again, grinning.

'What's your name?'

'Nettie.'

'I'm Fletch. See you around, Nettie.' He disappears into the crowd.

I watch him go, the last embers of a smile still on my face.

Right. Get to class.

I run up the stairs to the top of the building where my changing room is, find a spot on a bench, and start to get dressed for jazz.

The tall blonde girl who who tripped over my bag in the foyer is there. She catches my eye in the mirror and strides over.

'Just so you know, you shouldn't be talking to second-year boys,' she says loudly.

The chatter subsides as everyone stops to listen.

'Pardon?'

'You were talking to Fletch. He's a second-year. You're a first-year. It's an unwritten rule.'

Fletch? The guy with the guitar?

'I'm not really sure what you're—'

'Just leave him alone, all right?'

The bell rings and she storms out of the changing room. The other girls scatter to their lessons, whispering to each other while I try to get my head around what just happened.

'Don't worry about her,' says a girl who's still hanging in the doorway. She's taller than me, mixed race, with auburn hair and hazel eyes. And so, so beautiful.

23

'Yeah,' I say, trying to smile.

'She's just a second-year diva. Plenty of those around, I'm sure . . .'

'Right,' I say.

'First days are so scary,' she says. 'I had the shits and everything this morning. Still, I might lose a couple of pounds. See you in a bit.' She slips out of the door.

I like her.

Glancing at my timetable, I see I'm in Studio Five with someone called Darren Walker. I scramble out of the changing room and down the stairs, two at a time.

The girl who had the shits this morning is already in the class. She smiles and gestures for me to join her in the back corner.

Darren Walker enters the room, bag slung over his shoulder and coffee in hand. It's not long before a loud beat starts playing and he begins doing what I can only describe as *the* most complicated warm-up *ever*. The students in the front couple of rows (presumably second- and third-years) copy him immediately. The girl next to me catches my eye and we follow suit (the only difference being that I'm two counts behind everyone else).

After sit-ups, press-ups, planks and splits in all directions, he beckons to us to go to the back corner. I ignore my shaking legs and arms – I can't be soft on my first day. He demonstrates a complicated pirouette exercise and the students do it across the room, one by one.

I'm the last one to do it. I start well enough, I think, getting through one side without any major problems. As I begin the second side, however, I clock Miss Duke through the window to the corridor outside, staring at me intently *again*.

24

I lose my footing and fall out of my double turn, the bridge of my nose hitting the barre at the side of the studio. It must be bad because no one laughs. In my confusion, I look back at the studio window, but there's no one there.

Darren rushes over.

'Go and get cleaned up. The office'll give you an ice pack. Find somewhere quiet to sit for the rest of the morning.'

My top lip feels wet. I do as he says, too sore to think about how much I just embarrassed myself.

Miss Paige, the secretary, rolls her eyes at my bloody face as I enter the room and shouts back to her colleague, 'Linda! Can we have an ice pack, please. *Another* first-year injury.'

I take the ice pack and traipse back up to my changing room, hoping I don't end up with a black eye. Not helpful when you're trying to be unobtrusive. The rest of the girls will be back up soon and I can do without being stared at. Where else can I go?

The library, of course. It's right at the top of the building, another flight up from my changing room, and full of books only a third-year doing their dissertation would want to read. I reckon I'll be safe there.

It's a small room, stuffed floor to ceiling with books, papers, programmes, sheet music, scripts . . . I'm meant to be resting, but I can't resist. Double-checking to make sure there's no librarian lurking around, I grab a chair and reach up to the very top shelf, skimming the top of a pile of sheet music with my fingertips.

I tug at the corner of a page too quickly and it pulls out a load of other papers with it, which cascade off the shelf and all over the floor. Seriously, I really need to get it together today. Talk about tragic.

There's too much of it to put back in order, so I just start to sweep piles of it from all around the room into my arms. As I'm picking up the last pages, I notice something yellow sticking out from the bottom of the bookshelf. I grab at it, and pull out a brochure for an old production of *Oklahoma!*, barely held together by its ancient staples. Thinking it must be something an ex-Duke's student performed in, I stick it on top of the pile of sheet music and take it to the table in the middle of the room.

I start trying to sort out the papers but something catches my eye in the programme, which has flopped open on the centre pages.

There she is.

She's smiling up at me. Not the Mum I remember – a younger version, surely no older than twenty, with long black hair going all the way down her back. She always said she couldn't remember much about her career as a dancer. I'd no idea she was in this production.

Thumbing through the programme, I see a section entitled '*Oklahoma!* Cast Discovers Denmark!' which shows them all frolicking across the North Jutland coast, posing beside the statue of Hans Christian Andersen in Copenhagen, and lined up in *arabesque* in front of Rosenborg Castle. I find Mum in another snapshot, her head thrown back in riotous laughter (preceding a snort, I bet), arm in arm with a tall, pale-skinned, dark-haired girl, who is also mid-laugh. The caption underneath reads:

> *Best of friends: Anastasia Delaney-Richardson and*
> *Cecile Duke sharing a joke.*

Cecile Duke.

What?

I drop the programme in shock. They were friends. Best friends, if the programme is to be believed. How could I not have known? Why did she never mention it? She knew I had my heart set on going to Duke's.

The facts are mounting in my mind, like little yellow Post-it Notes, one by one, faster and faster:

1. Friends help each other out.
2. Friends help each other's children out.
3. Friends ignore said child's terrible audition and give them a place at their college regardless.

Oh, God. I'm a fraud. How can I have been so naive? Of *course* there was a reason I got in. That must be why Miss Duke keeps staring at me. She's looking to see if I can dance like Mum. Well, she'll be disappointed.

I don't deserve to be here. I should get my things and go home right now.

That's what I should do.

But . . . does any of it even matter? I mean *really* matter? Who cares if my audition was terrible, if – deep down – I know I'm good enough? It's true my voice hasn't been the same since the audition, but I can sort myself out. Nobody needs to know about Mum's friendship with Cecile Duke.

Nobody except me.

I start rifling through the rest of the papers, searching for more pictures of Mum; a clue, anything that'll help me to understand this thing I've just uncovered.

'Excuse me, is this seat taken?'

Oh, God, it's the cute guitar player. Why does he have to show up right when I'm having a major existential crisis?

'It's Nettie, right? Fletch. We met this morning?'

Sweet that he thinks I won't remember. He's still carrying his rough leather satchel and guitar, this time in a case.

'Yes – sorry, let me shift this.' I hurry back to the table and heap all my stuff into one pile.

'Thanks. Bit of a shock, huh, starting at Duke's?'

'That's an understatement.' I smile. Inwardly I'm rolling up into a ball of cringe. He must think I'm a proper geek, sifting through a load of Duke's memorabilia on my first day.

He smiles back and pushes a strand of hair out of his face, revealing straight, even teeth. I need to stop looking. He'll think I'm staring at his mouth in a sex way.

'I was ready to leave after my first day,' he says, oblivious. 'But here I am, a year later.' He pulls a huge stack of manuscripts out of his satchel, and a few stray papers escape and float under my chair. I go to retrieve them, but he stops me.

'No, you're good. I can reach.' Fletch bends down and fumbles around under my chair. The effort of trying to grab the errant papers wafts them further away and ten seconds later he's still feeling around for them underneath me. His face is really close to my thighs. I know I'm going red. (I blush really easily. It's a curse.)

'Sorry. That was awkward.' He resurfaces and sits back in his seat. 'Nice boots, by the way.'

I briefly look down to check which boots I'm wearing (green, suede, vintage), murmur an embarrassed, 'Thanks,' and go back to sorting the spilt papers. Right now you could fry eggs on my cheeks and they'd be fine to eat.

He sifts through the enormous pile of tatty papers until he finds what he's looking for. Then, after some noisy searching in his satchel for a pencil, he begins working.

I try to continue with what I'm doing but I can't concentrate.

There's a Mum/Miss Duke soup sloshing around my brain. And I'm curious to know what Fletch is writing.

I give it a couple of minutes before sneaking a glance over at his work. It looks like he's jotting down music. While I'm trying to decipher the notation, he looks up.

Busted.

'Can I try something out on you?' he says, totally out of the blue. 'It involves me making a bit of a noise.'

'Uh, yeah, sure.' I hope I sound casual, rather than relieved I haven't been caught nosing.

'I can't get the end of this song right.' He grabs his guitar and spreads the pages along the table so they're all visible. 'I could do with another pair of ears. Do you mind?'

I shrug and nod my head. Then, worried it looked like a no, I shake it vigorously.

'Is that a yes, you don't mind?' His eyes sparkle at me.

'Er, sorry, yes.' *I. Am. Ridiculous.*

'OK. So, it's a rough version, but you'll get the gist. I'm going to play two endings. Here's number one.' He starts to play a few chords. 'I'll come in after the bridge. I won't bore you with the whole lot.'

He plays the first ending, picking out arpeggios with his fingers that tingle among the soft chords. I barely breathe, he's so good.

'Right, remember that,' he says, without giving me time to say anything. 'Here's the other one.'

The second one is different – less resolved, more melancholic. Equally brilliant.

'What do you think?' he says.

'Uh, they're both great.' I'm trying to pull off not-too-impressed and yet incredibly knowledgeable. Not confident

29

I nailed it. 'Really great. But the second one was more . . . intriguing. It's difficult to tell without the words.'

'Good point,' he says. 'You haven't heard the lyrics.'

An overwhelming curiosity creeps over me. 'Maybe if you could tell me what it's about?'

He puts his guitar down on the floor and looks back at me. His eyes are a warm brown, the colour of really strong tea.

'It's about loss,' he says.

'Loss . . .' I feel scared but I don't know why.

'Loss, and a kind of longing, I guess. Hoping that someone will come back but knowing that they never will.' He breaks away, looking back down to his sheet music.

I need to hear this song. I'm not sure why, but I need to.

'It's hard for me to help without hearing the whole thing,' I venture. 'Maybe – would you sing it?'

'Definitely not.' He breaks into a grin again. 'We've just met; it would be unbearably self-indulgent of me.'

'Oh no, I'd love to hear it.'

'Seriously?'

'Absolutely.'

'Well, OK. If you're sure. But feel free to stick a hook around my neck at any time.' He picks up his guitar and looks up again with raised eyebrows to double-check.

I nod, my heart thudding at about one-eighty per minute.

He starts singing, and I have to mask an intake of breath. His voice is *beautiful*. Like, the best voice I've ever heard. It's lyrical, melodic, warm – I mean, proper sweep-you-off-your-feet gorgeous. If it's possible to fall in love with a voice, I have, right now, in the library.

I need to get over his voice and listen to the song.

Omigod.

He's singing about me?

It's *my* song.

My life.

I've always secretly longed for a Roberta Flack moment – hasn't everyone? But now, here it is, and it isn't killing me softly – it's battering me to death. I've heard songs that touched my heart before, but this has crawled into my marrow. It's every 'fine' I replied when someone asked me how I was doing; every woman I chased down the street thinking it was Mum; every scream I ever uttered in my bedroom at night, begging her to come back. It's the memory of her singing me to sleep. It's every morning waking up and forgetting for a split second that she's gone, until the realization hits me with a dull thud. It's waking every morning to that dull thud.

He strums the final chord and looks up. Silent tears are streaming down my face.

'Blimey, was it that bad?'

'Sorry.' I wipe my cheeks and try to pull it together. 'Just . . . emotional.'

'Are you OK?' he says.

'Yes, just about.' I manage a little laugh in an attempt to make myself seem less weird. 'Ugh. Sorry. Embarrassing.'

'No, it's nice to get a reaction – assuming it wasn't my playing that made you cry.'

'No! . . . It's just . . . Oh, never mind. It's silly.'

'Please.' Something about the way he says it makes me continue.

'It's just that, well . . . OK, so my Mum died last year –' (deep breath) – 'and for ages I had these thoughts that I couldn't shake.

31

Like a feeling you can't get rid of, right? It sounds weird, but . . .'
I falter. 'You probably think I'm ridiculous.'

'No, please – I know what you mean. Please – don't stop.'

I swallow.

'Well, she died of cancer. And for months after – like *months* –
I kept imagining that her oncologist called me in for a meeting.
Like, *really* imagined it, for huge chunks of the day. I'd arrive at
his office and he would tell me that Mum hadn't died – she'd
been secretly sent to America to try out a new controversial drug,
and that she was OK – she was cured and coming back home. I
know it doesn't make any sense – it doesn't even make sense to
me now. It sounds like something a four-year-old would make
up. I mean, why *would* she get her oncologist to tell me that she
was fine? She would just come home and tell me herself, right?
And doctor–patient confidentiality wouldn't allow it . . . I've been
through it all. Every scenario. I'd get lost for minutes at a time,
so when I'd finally come back to reality, it was like losing her all
over again . . .'

I should stop now – it sounds even worse when I say it out
loud – but he's looking at me so intensely that I carry on.

'I guess, in a long-winded way, what I'm trying to say is that
for me, your song makes perfect sense.' I know I'm gabbling but
I can't stop now. 'It's hard to make people understand what it's
like to lose someone when you're young, but you've summed it
up pretty perfectly there. I mean, I don't even know if the song's
about that kind of loss, but . . .'

It's the most I've said in months. It feels strange to hear my
own voice.

'It is,' he says. His voice sounds tight. 'My brother was killed
in a motorbike crash four years ago. I guess every song I've written

32

since then is about him, in one way or another.'

He gets it.

He holds my gaze for a moment, clears his throat, and goes back to his writing. I watch him for a while, desperate for him to speak. But he doesn't. Or can't.

So I do instead. 'I – I liked the second ending – the one you played just now when you sang.'

This almost-change-of-subject is enough to get him back. The spark is back in his eyes as he looks up.

'How so?'

'Well, it sounded unfinished. And the lyrics kind of make you think that the person is never going to give up hope, even though it's hopeless. So they know they'll never get a resolution.'

'You're right – the music *is* unresolved. I hadn't even thought of that when I wrote it. I just liked the feel of an imperfect cadence. Right, it's in. Thanks – I need to credit you as co-writer.'

The bell rings.

'What's your next class?' he asks.

'Musical Theatre.' My stomach does an involuntary churn.

'Me too.' He grabs all the sheet music and stuffs them into his satchel. 'I'll walk you there.'

As I pack up my things, it strikes me that I've never opened up about Mum like that before. I follow him down the stairs and out through the front doors, wondering if the moment we just had was as huge for him as it was for me.

CHAPTER 5

I sneak a glance at Fletch as we cross Soho Square. I notice other people do too. Hot guy with a guitar – I bet they're checking to see if he's famous. He totally looks it.

'So . . . Nettie,' he says. We stride beneath the shade of a tree, dodging a group of dappled Hoxton types attempting to eat their lunch without getting it in their beards. 'Is that short for anything?'

'Antoinette.' I pull a face. 'I like Nettie, though. How about you?'

'Just Fletch.'

Fletch. Nettie and Fletch. Netch.

OMG *stop*.

'So, you're on the musical theatre course?' I say.

'Writers and MDs course,' he says. 'Second year. It's all I've ever wanted to do, write music.'

'But your singing . . . Don't you want to sing?'

'I like singing my own stuff. I got away with it last year but they want me to do more performing this year, hence being shoved into MT three times a week.' He smiles ruefully. 'Got hauled into Miss Duke's office yesterday.'

'Was that scary?'

'Nah. She's a pussycat.'

She didn't seem like a pussycat while she was tearing Lauren Rose to shreds. Maybe she's nicer to the boys.

'Well, it's a good thing,' I say. 'People need to hear your voice.'

'How about you?' I can tell by the change of subject that he's not up for a bucketload of compliments. 'You're a dancer, right?'

'Er, no.'

'Singer?'

'Sort of.'

'You're a sort-of singer?'

I smile but say nothing, feeling an unpleasant stab of adrenaline. He'll work it out soon enough.

We arrive at an old music hall venue not far from Soho Square, with a faded red-brick façade and a pair of heavy wooden entrance doors painted in black gloss. One is wedged open, a glimpse into the gloom inside.

'Is this it?' I say.

'Nice, huh?' says Fletch. 'This is where the main college was when Miss Duke took over, before she bought the new building. It was only meant to be a temporary venue, but here we are. I know it's run down now, but I kind of prefer it. Feels more like the theatre.'

We make our way through to the dingy corridor, where we're greeted by a collage of overlapping squares of faded neon, mainly bill posters, all with peeling corners and ripped-out sections revealing myriad posters from decades of gigs underneath. They're mostly advertising evenings with Seventies comedians, discos and punk bands.

'Be up in a minute.' Fletch turns left down a dark corridor and indicates a rickety wooden staircase to my right. 'MT's just up there.'

I try not to make great big *doof-doof* sounds as I climb the stairs to a studio at the top of the building, which looks like it's been stuffed there as an afterthought.

The room's full of Duke's students. I'm sure some of them are new, like me, but they're all chatting animatedly to each other. I find it harder to talk to new people since Mum died. It's the expectation that with every person I meet, at some point I'm going to have to explain things, re-live what happened.

I choose a seat at the back of the small studio. The blonde girl who laid into me in the changing room is over the far side of the room, whispering to a redhead, who gives me a side-eye worthy of Regina George.

Thankfully the teacher arrives almost as soon as I've sat down.

'Hi, kids,' he says. He's older – maybe sixty – white, with a greying mop of hair and a kind, expressive face. He's wearing a Liberty-print shirt and a paisley silk scarf with tassels. 'My name is Michael St. John. That's Mr St. John outside this room, Michael in here. For those of you who don't know, I am head of Music at the college. You'll be seeing me for some of your musical theatre classes, along with Miss Clarkson, Mr Turner and Miss Astor.

'Second-years, welcome back. First-years – so, you got into Duke's? Lucky you. Do you know how many people auditioned to be here today? *Thousands*. What does that mean?' He surveys us, eyes twinkling, enjoying the drama. 'It means you are talented, of course. That goes without saying. But there is something about each and every one of you that is special – something that sets you apart. That's why you're at Duke's.'

Or you got in because of who your mum was, despite being terrible in the audition.

'So, what does this year hold for you in musical theatre?'

It's becoming apparent that he begins every speech with a

question he can then answer himself.

'We work on technique, repertoire, theory and performance quality. As well as your classes, there will be the Duke's Awards after Christmas (a college-wide competition), and the Easter Musical, which I expect all of you to audition for. And, of course, the prestigious Summer Showcase . . .'

He leaves that one suspended, rubbing his thick fringe out of his eyes. I look around. The whole room's hanging off his every syllable.

'Today I want to hear you. I want to see how you work. I want to get to *know* you,' he continues, smiling at us. I warm to him instantly (although to be fair, I'd warm to anyone in a floral-print shirt). 'We've got a few visitors from the Musical Directors and Writers course this year, so do be welcoming. Together you're a wonderful mix of creativity and talent, and I can't wait to see what that brings. Someone give out these dots for me.'

A set of sheet music is thrust into my hands. It's 'For Forever' from *Dear Evan Hansen*, which I already know and love. Even though the whole song's meant to be an elaborate lie, there's something about it that just feels so true to me. I listened to it a lot after Mum died. It helped, a bit.

Michael explains that the key will be modified to suit each person's range. He sits at the piano and starts note-bashing it for us, although I suspect that most people already know it. I sing along with the others; well, at least, I *think* I'm singing along. I'm not sure there's a lot coming out.

'I would now like you each to have a go at the first verse and chorus on your own,' says Michael. 'Who's up first?'

A show of eager hands appears. Before I can even assess how I feel about this, the door opens.

37

'Sorry I'm late, Michael.'

It's Fletch.

'Ah, good – I thought I was going to have to play,' says Michael. 'Have you got your guitar?'

Fletch edges through the doorway to reveal a guitar slung over his shoulder.

'Always,' he says to general tittering – especially from the girls, I notice.

'Great,' says Michael. 'Let's go.'

Fletch walks across the front of the room to sit next to the now vacant piano. He grins at me as he passes; I smile back, flushing (annoyingly).

A boy gets up to sing. He tells Fletch the key he wants and walks calmly to the centre of the room. Fletch tries a few chords on his guitar, raising his eyebrows to the boy, who nods. Fletch starts to play the intro for him. His fingers work quickly, picking out individual notes as well as chords.

The boy sings it well, but all my focus is on Fletch's playing. I notice how his hair flops forwards over his eye as he leans over to check an intricate part. As he pushes it back, the pencil behind his ear is dislodged and falls to the floor, but he ignores it, engrossed in the sound.

Student after student gets up and gives their rendition of the song, Fletch deftly changing key to suit range. I remember that it'll be my turn at some point and my stomach tightens. Maybe they'll forget about me. Maybe we'll run out of time. But Michael looks up from his class list, where he's been writing notes on each performance, and sees me.

As I meet his gaze, my heart starts thumping murderously. I knew this moment was going to come, but I thought I'd have more time to prepare, to get my voice back. I need to run, far away from this room, from Duke's, from everyone. Right now.

'Just Antoinette to go now. Antoinette? Wait – it's Nettie, isn't it? I remember you from the auditions,' he says.

Of course he remembers. I was a disaster. I wait for the obligatory humiliation.

'I knew your mother,' he says. 'She was a wonderful woman. One of the greats.'

I wasn't expecting that. He knew Mum?

I get an involuntary flash of her face, but it's not the face I've been longing to remember for months. It's the other face – the raw-skinned, swollen, plastic-tube-laden face of those last few days, sunken eyes lonely in their wide sockets. I see her sadness as I try to get her to drink orange squash through a straw, and her taking it, not because she wants to but because I'm begging her. I see her despair as she watches me grow numb with disbelief at what's happening, dealing with it minute by minute because that's the longest amount of time I can handle.

The flash is brief, but it's enough to make me forget where I am. 'You knew her?'

He nods, his eyes suddenly brighter. In another world I would have run over and hugged him and cried and quizzed him until the bell rang, but suddenly I can feel everyone's eyes on me, oh-so interested that I might have a connection with this teacher, and I hold back. Still, something unsaid passes between us.

'Shall we hear a bit, Nettie?' he says. Pleasant though his tone is, I know I can't refuse. Not in front of the whole class. And not now he's mentioned Mum.

It's fine. I'll be fine.

But something happens to my body. My pulse goes from

andante to *presto* in two seconds flat and everything starts shaking. I get a huge head rush as I stand up.

The journey from my seat in the back row to the centre of the room feels like a trip to the scaffold. I reach the dreaded spot and take a breath in. Fletch mouths '*F sharp?*' and I nod, afraid that if I speak, I'll cry. He plays the introduction. The class waits. My throat closes up as I open my mouth, every last inch of my body shaking uncontrollably now. I see Michael's encouraging smile, Fletch poised to play, the students leaning in curiously . . .

Nothing.

I mean, *actual* nothing comes out. Not even a squeak. I bombed in the audition and now I'm failing again, this time in front of a roomful of people.

Smiling supportively, Fletch plays the intro again. If I wasn't too busy dying inside I'd be grateful. I'm hoping for something, someone to save me. Michael St. John to be called away? Or Fletch to suddenly forget every bit of musical information he's ever learned? Maybe I could faint. Wilder and wilder get-out clauses flood my brain.

But I've missed the cue again. It's over. I know it, and everyone in the room knows it. I can't even speak. My eyes fill with unwanted tears as I shake my head.

Fletch's smile falters as his eyes take in the situation. Intense embarrassment overcomes me and I furiously blink away the tears. Michael says something to me but the bell for the next class drowns it out. The students gather their things quietly, without the usual clatter and chatter, reverent to my humiliation.

I push past them down the stairs, elbowing bags and shoulders aside, desperate to escape. Michael calls my name but I ignore him as I sprint for the doors and run out into the street.

40

CHAPTER 6

I can finally hear the changing room emptying. I've been hiding in the toilet since before lunch. Holy crap – next class is ballet. I can't cope with disappointing people again right now. I kept up ballet lessons because Mum said if I wanted to come somewhere like Duke's, I'd need at least the basics – but it's never felt right on my body. My short bob refuses to go into a bun, so I stick an Alice band on it and hope that'll do.

The lesson's started, but only just. The teacher's showing the class a *plié* exercise. She has her back to me, but as I creep in the door and start to make my way to a space at the barre, she puts her hand up sharply, indicating for me to stay at the door.

I hover near the doorway and watch while she gets the rest of the class to do the exercise in twos, all the time thinking I'd love to have a *Groundhog Day*, to do today all over again without messing up.

It's been at least three minutes since I got in here. She's making me wait until the whole class has finished so she can trash me in front of an audience. I'm her scapegoat, fine. Let's just get it over with.

As the pianist finishes playing, Millicent Moore strides towards me, tall and imposing, carrying a frightening-looking stick. She's like a ballet teacher from a movie, delicate frame, pale skin, grey hair in a high bun, glasses hanging around her neck and her sternum showing through her leotard.

I start to excuse myself. 'I'm sorry I'm l—'

41

'Name,' she says. Her voice is bright but there's an acidic undertone.

I back away against the barre.

'Er, Nettie.' I cringe.

'There's no Nettie here.' Miss Moore taps the register tartly with the back of her hand. Her mouth wears a friendly smile but her eyes flicker with something else.

'It's Antoinette.' I'm practically in the rosin tray now.

She looks down at the register, finds my name and peers back up at me.

'*Full* name,' she insists. It's a dare. She's now speaking in little above a whisper but the entire class is listening in, mesmerized.

'Antoinette Delaney-Richardson.' I breathe out, closing my eyes for a second. It's over. She knew who I was the second I walked in. But now I've said it out loud.

'Antoinette Delaney-Richardson? *My, my*. We *are* honoured.'

Some of the girls start murmuring to each other. Millicent Moore has arranged her face into an even more alarming smile, letting her words settle over the spellbound room before she turns her attention back to me.

'Let me tell you something, *Antoinette Delaney-Richardson*. At this centre of excellence, we turn up to class on time. I don't care who you are. I'm sure you'll be lording it up around Duke's and dining out on some clapped-out notion of heritage you doubtless have. In my class, however, you are *nothing*.'

I get it, lady. Every teacher here needs a Lauren Rose at the start of term. I'm yours. Are we done?

'Well?' she hisses. She cocks her head towards a corner of the barre, the false smile disappearing as quickly as it came. 'What are you waiting for?'

We're done.

I scuttle to a space next to the nice girl I met this morning, who waits until Millicent Moore has turned her long back before widening her eyes in a *I can't believe that just happened to you* kind of way. I respond with a glum twitch in the corner of my mouth. If I can just hide at the back of the room, work hard and keep my head down, hopefully I'll be left alone and spared any further humiliation.

Nope. Miss Moore has other plans for me. She beckons me to the front of the class after the *port de bras*.

'Antoinette?' she says. 'Stand as you were, please, arms *à la seconde*. Now, class,' she continues. 'You see this flabby bit here?' (at this point she grabs the skin on the underside of my arms and wobbles it violently) 'This is what we want to avoid. Bingo wings. Always support underneath.'

She gets right to the bone. It hurts. I run to the back, my cheeks burning.

Ten minutes later, she strikes again.

'Can you see,' she says, with a dangerous laugh, 'how Antoinette doesn't pull up properly? It's all hanging out, darling.'

'Looks like she's pulling up fine to me,' pipes up a voice.

It's my friend from the changing room.

Miss Moore rounds on her. 'When you've been teaching ballet for decades, you'll be qualified to make judgement,' she snaps. 'How dare you interrupt me in class.'

'I was just saying—'

'Well, don't. If I want a first-year's opinion, I'll ask for it.' She glares at her for several seconds before turning back to me. 'Antoinette the pot-bellied pig. Back to your place, fatty.'

The class laughs.

Several things irritate me about this comment: the first is how she throws around 'fat' as an insult. Then there's the fact that this is a ballet class, not a how-to-be-a-Victoria's-Secret-model seminar. Size has nothing to do with technique. Lastly, there's *literally* nothing of me. Calling me fat doesn't even make sense.

Fortunately, Mum was a firm believer in body confidence and brought me up to have no major issues. But I bet half the class do. And I bet this fuels them. Looking around, most are lapping it up with glee, like they did when Lauren Rose got crucified by Miss Duke this morning.

Miss Moore leaves me alone for the next hour. But about five minutes before the end of the lesson, she strides slowly round to the back of the room behind me while I'm struggling to pick up some steps from the girls in front of me.

'No, Antoinette,' she breathes in my ear. 'You didn't listen, did you? You need to *pull up*. Out of your waist and right up into that pathetic little Alice band of yours.' She takes hold of my hair and pulls it slowly upwards.

'That's it, grow, more, up, up, up.' She pulls harder, forcing my neck to lengthen. 'And we really should think about how effective our hair fastenings are in ballet class, shouldn't we?' She rips the band from my head with her other hand and snaps it in two, still tugging at my hair so hard that my eyes begin to smart.

Don't cry. She wants you to.

The girl who just stood up for me has noticed something's going on. She catches my eye in the mirror and winks, almost imperceptibly. It gives me courage. I steel myself and stare straight ahead, defiant.

This seems to annoy Miss Moore, who pulls until my scalp almost detatches from my skull. Something pings painfully in my neck. I spot her smiling in the mirror. She's actually enjoying it.

It's never going to end. I'm going to be stuck here in searing pain until she pulls every last hair out of my head and there's nothing left to hang on to.

The bell sounds, signalling the end of class. As it rings, she does one final yank, taking a good handful of hair with it. I gasp in pain. Shaking my hair off her hand briskly, Millicent Moore sweeps to the front of the room and is now taking the class through a rushed curtsey.

'And *révérence*. Thank you, class. See you tomorrow. Oh, and Antoinette, please make sure you don't look as if you've been dragged through a hedge next time I see you.'

When I get back out into the corridor I find the girl waiting for me.

'I'm sorry,' she says. 'I think I made it worse for you.'

'Nah. She was on me from the start. Thanks, by the way.'

We start walking up the stairs to the changing room together.

'I can't believe what she was saying to you. Are you alright?'

'Yeah. It's OK.'

'If she said something like that to me I'd be in tears. Omigod, if she thinks *you're* fat there's no hope for me. I'm not going to eat for a week now. What was she doing to you at the end? I couldn't see, but I thought it must be something horrible.'

She gasps when I tell her. 'What an absolute bitch troll! I'd heard she was tricky, but that's horrendous. By the way, I meant to ask you at lunchtime, but I didn't see you – was your nose all right after jazz this morning?'

'Yeah, thanks,' I say.

'Thank God for that,' she says. 'I thought you had a black eye coming, for sure. I'm Kiki, by the way.'

45

'Nettie. I'm not usually this much of a disaster.'

'God, I hope not.'

We round the last staircase and go through to our changing room, which faces a row of little music practice rooms. Kiki hops in the shower while I flop on to a bench and start to get changed.

A pair of legs put themselves in front of my face.

'You're in my place,' says a voice attached to the legs.

I look up. It's the blonde girl I had the run-in with earlier.

'Sorry, I didn't realize.'

'Yeah, well, now you know. So piss off.'

It's not the 'piss off' that riles me. It's the way she waves me aside with her neon purple nails that does it.

'I'm not going to do that.'

'What?'

The other girls in the changing room have gone quiet now; all eyes are on us. We're in a stand-off, like Riff and Bernardo in *West Side Story*, except that she has the whole changing room in her gang and I just have me.

'What did you say?'

'Natasha, leave her alone,' pipes up someone from the other end of the room.

'I will not "leave her alone",' says Natasha, doing a sarcastic baby voice. 'She's a first-year. She needs to learn some respect. I saw her walking to MT with Fletch earlier –' she rounds back on me – 'despite that fact that I warned her not to go near him. He's already involved with someone. So stay away. And if I tell you to get off my seat, you shitting well do it.'

Some of the other girls are trying to give me friendly facial hints to do as I'm told. But after the day I've had, something in my head has pinged. The *fuck-it* button, as Mum used to say.

46

'Sure. But here's the thing – you telling me to move in the way you just did, waving me aside like I'm some sort of twat, makes me feel like staying right here.'

I carry on getting changed, ignoring her, although it's hard with her leotarded crotch right in my face. She stands there for a few seconds, fuming, then calmly walks to the mirror, takes a latte someone's left on the shelf, comes back over to me and pours it into my bag.

'And don't think I'm done with you yet,' she says, stalking out of the changing room.

The room is silent. No one seems brave enough to say anything – either for or against me. Coffee drips off the side of my bag on to my ankles.

I grab my stuff and take it downstairs, spilling coffee all the way, not caring that I'm not even dressed properly. I lock myself in a toilet on the ground floor and start to clear up the worst-hit parts. When I've done the best I can and have finished getting dressed, I put down the lid of the toilet and plonk down on to it.

As crap days go, today's up there with the worst of them. Instead of keeping a low profile like I'd planned, I've made enemies of the college mean girl *and* the Cruella de Vil of the ballet world, not to mention the fact that I've failed at singing – the one thing I thought I could do. And now I'm sitting on the bog, covered in coffee, when I should be going back to the halls and trying to make some friends (not that anyone will touch me now that Natasha or whatever-she's-called has singled me out).

I sit there for what feels like hours. There haven't been any doors slamming or people talking for a while now. Everyone

47

must've gone home. I sling my enormous bag over my shoulder and head out to the foyer.

As I reach the front doors, something stops me.

I look to where the door to the studio theatre hangs open.

It's empty.

Call it instinct, fate, random – or the fact that I'm just not ready to go home yet with so much in my brain – but something draws me in.

It's deserted. The usually large room has been divided into two smaller spaces with a pair of huge folding doors spanning the entire width of the studio. I drop my bag under the barre in a cloud of rosin and sit on the floor, staring at the spot where Miss Duke annihilated Lauren Rose this morning. I picture her doing the same to me, the whole college laughing, and I shiver involuntarily.

I *still* can't sing, after all these months. I don't deserve my place here. But what can I do? Leave?

I can't go home. My grandmother's there, for a start. My old friends are all at uni. After the way I treated them at the end of last term, they probably wouldn't be interested anyway. I'm stuck here, doomed to fail.

I should be crying, really.

But I'm not, for some reason.

For some reason, I close my eyes . . .

. . . and *sing*.

It's quiet at first. But it gets louder. After months of agony and frustration, something finally happens. I sing the first song that comes into my head, which is 'Take Me to the World'. Mum liked it.

The sound grows until I can actually *hear* myself. An imaginary accompaniment swells in my head, and I raise my voice to meet it. I'm doing it. I'm singing.

I close my eyes. Mum's face appears for the first time in months. The image gets stronger with every note and I see her smiling, just like she used to whenever I sang to her. It's all for her now.

Wait—

I'm not alone.

The accompaniment isn't just in my head. It's here, in the room. It's real. I look around, heart quickening. Miraculously I keep singing. The sound is coming from the other half of the room – the side beyond the folding doors. There's a chink in the middle but from where I am, I can only see the back of the piano.

I won't stop singing.

I *can't* stop. Like Moira Shearer in *The Red Shoes*, twirling and *fouetté*-ing until she no longer exists, if I stop maybe I'll stop forever. Maybe I'll never see Mum's face again.

Whoever it is, they're . . . *good*.

The last notes fade into the air. The sudden silence brings me back to earth with a jolt. Shocked, I grab my bag and run out of the studio door, through the foyer and all the way to the tube station. I don't dare stop until I get back to the halls. Only when I reach my tiny room do I let everything that just happened filter through.

Who were they? What were they doing in the studio theatre? And how was it I managed to sing with them?

I try singing again, certain that I must be able to do it, but I hear people laughing down the hall and my throat closes up on cue. So I can do it at college in a huge studio with a random stranger, but not in my own room? That's messed up. I should find out who it was. Maybe they can help.

Wait. This is massive for me. It's the first time I've sung since before the audition. What if finding out ruins it? It was surely the anonymity that stopped me drying up. Because I didn't stop, did I? Even after I knew I wasn't alone.

It can remain a mystery. I don't mind not knowing.

But I know one thing. I have a voice.

CHAPTER 7

My radio alarm wakes me with such violence that I sit up and swing for it all in one go, smashing it off the bedside table on to the floor.

It's eight o'clock. Oh, crap. I'm late.

Still wearing the clothes I apparently fell asleep in yesterday, I hastily pack my bag again ready for another day at Duke's Academy of Torture, before stripping off at lightning speed and jumping in the shower.

I do a half-hearted shampoo-and-rinse, my thoughts still on what happened after college yesterday. Someone threw me a lifeline last night in the studio. Maybe things will be better today. I try a few scales into the (now) warm water.

Someone in the room next door coughs.

My voice fails before I've even finished the first arpeggio.

Why can't I do it? It's like last night never happened. This is so frustrating.

After pegging it all the way from Leicester Square tube to college, my bag banging against my legs all the way, I curse to see the students spilling out into the foyer. We're not allowed into class if we miss registration.

'Blimey, Nettie. Way to get noticed.' Alec's standing by the front doors and has just watched me stumble through the entrance with an amused look on his face. 'You'll have them queuing up for tickets by the end of the week at this rate.'

'I'm late,' I gasp, breathless.

'No, you're not, darling. I answered for you in my best falsetto. Nailed it, by the way.'

'Thanks.' I grab yesterday's water bottle from my bag and down the dregs. 'You didn't have to do that.'

He swivels my string of pearls around so that the clasp is behind my neck. 'Darling girl, for someone with your level of fabulous, I'd step out in front of traffic. But to be honest, it would probably stop for me. I have that effect.'

I can't see what he thinks is so special about me, but I don't argue.

'Listen, doll,' he says, 'let's meet for lunch. The cafe around the corner. The veggie one, not the one where the man with the hairy ears works. I need to fill you in on my date with his Royal Hotness Karl Townsend last night.'

He raises a single, perfectly arched eyebrow as if to illustrate that a LOT went on with his Royal Hotness Karl Townsend last night.

'Howdy, partner,' says a voice from behind me.

It's Fletch. I can tell Alec's disappointed he's already raised one eyebrow, because he lifts the other one as well in a *Who's this?* sort of way as he sidles off into the crowd.

'Er, howdy,' I say.

'You know, like "writing partner"? That's what I was going for,' says Fletch. 'In retrospect a mistake. Remind me NEVER TO SAY THAT AGAIN.'

I laugh.

He hoicks his guitar over his shoulder. 'Do you have MT history now?'

I scan my timetable. 'Er . . . looks like it.' I hope it isn't a repeat of yesterday's lesson.

'Want to walk with me?' he says.

We fall into step.

Fletch looks over to me as we cross the square. 'You OK?'

'Uh, yeah . . . just thinking.'

'About yesterday in MT?'

'Er . . . yeah.'

'You know,' he says, 'Michael St. John probably feels really bad. It was unfair of him, especially on your first lesson, to talk about your mum and then ask you to sing.'

'What do you mean?' I say.

'That's what threw you, isn't it?' he says. We stop to wait for a lorry to reverse around the corner. 'That's what I assumed.'

If it looked like that to Fletch, hopefully that's what everyone else thought – not that I'm a talentless waste of space who can't sing. I might just have another chance to prove myself.

When we arrive at the old theatre, two girls are sharing a cigarette on the steps. One of them is Natasha, who poured coffee all over me in the dressing room yesterday; the other is the friend she was whispering to in MT yesterday; also tall, white, leggy and snarly, but unlike Natasha with her voluminous blonde hair, the friend's hair is dyed a vibrant red. She's also severely fake-tanned. In fact, she's so orange that it's hard to see where the tan ends and the hair starts.

'Hi, Fletch,' says Natasha. She manages to smile with all her teeth, even the bottom ones.

'Hi,' echoes the redhead. She lowers her head and looks up at him through thick fake lashes.

'Ladies.' Fletch edges past them through the doors into the darkness.

As I go to follow him, Natasha puts her bag in front of me.

53

'Excuse me.' I wait for her to move it.

She takes a drag from the near-finished fag and blows it in my face like a stroppy secretary in an Eighties movie, slowly nudging her bag out of the way, all the while staring me as if I've just offered her a toenail sandwich.

'Thanks.' I squeeze past awkwardly.

'*Nice coat*,' she says.

I'm wearing a Sixties yellow Chanel jacket with a black collar that belonged to Mum. She had loads of cool vintage stuff, and when she died I couldn't bear to throw it all away. Some of the older stuff can't be washed and still smells of her. I *know*. It's proper icky, but it makes me feel close to her.

As I pass through the doorway, they both collapse into fits of the giggles. I guess they're pissing themselves about the fact that I don't wear pink velour tracksuits everywhere like them. I'm definitely OK with that, by the way.

Fletch is in the dark hallway waiting for me. 'I thought you were behind me. I've just been talking to myself.'

'Got held up.' Actually, I've been dealing with Rizzo and Marty out there.

'After you.'

'OK, guys and dolls, is everyone here? *Right*.'

Michael St. John claps his hands together like an old ham with a line approaching. 'It's musical theatre history today. No singing, just writing.'

Groans go around the room. He sneaks a glance in my direction.

'Yes, yes. Writing. Remember that? So, kids. Your first task is a research project. I need you to pair up with someone who might be interested in the same topics as you. I'd like you to explore an aspect of twentieth-century musical theatre. Here's the brief. Seryn, gorgeous, would you give these out for me?'

Seryn, a tall, slender Black girl with long caramel-coloured hair, jumps to her feet and hands out some sheets of paper. I fantasize about all the midi skirts I could wear with legs as long as hers. Not to mention the fortune I'd save on alterations.

I look around the studio. Natural partnerships have already formed. I get my notebook out, ready to work alone.

Someone taps my shoulder.

'Do you want to . . . go with me?' Fletch is smiling at me hopefully from the row behind.

'Uh, sure.' I try to ignore the obvious connotations in that question and focus on my voice portraying cool not-botheredness. My cheeks betray me, glaring like brake lights.

If he's noticed, he's pretending he hasn't. 'Great. Any ideas?'

'Well, maybe—' I'm interrupted by a mass of red hair in my face.

'Fletch, shall we go and sit over there?' Mean girl *numero dos* is now standing between us with her back *literally* in my face. I remove a crimson hair from my mouth.

'Hi, Jade,' says Fletch. 'I don't follow, sorry—'

'To plan our project.' She takes his hand.

'I'd love to, but—'

'Great. Come on then.'

She whisks him away like Liz Holt leading Ken Railings on to the dance floor for the first time, without a second glance to me. I sit down on a stage block and watch everyone else talking in twos, heads together, ideas flowing.

Great. The one person I can actually talk to and it turns out he's the college bitch's bitch.

To make myself look less like Nettie-No-Mates, I open my notebook and pretend to look through it, all the time wishing I was somewhere, *anywhere*, but here in this room.

'Sorry about that. Bit of confusion over partnering. Shall we?'

Fletch is back, standing over me in front of the window, the sunlight streaming in behind him. All that's missing is a heavenly '*aaaaaaaaah*' in five-part harmony.

'Nettie?'

Shit. I've been staring at him for about seven seconds (which sounds like not very long, until you sit there and count it).

'Oh, I thought Jade . . .'

'So did she.' He moves to shield my eyes from the sun streaming in behind him. 'I explained that you and I were working together, and she's fine about it.'

She doesn't look fine. She looks like she might eat me.

'So, what are you into?' says Fletch. He sits down next to me.

'Pardon?'

'Oh God, that sounded like *sexually*, didn't it.'

'Kind of.'

Fletch scratches his head. 'I'll rephrase. What aspect of musical theatre shall we research?' he says in a BBC accent. 'There. Got it out.'

I muster enough cool to raise an eyebrow.

'I didn't even notice that one,' he says. 'You're depraved.'

'You said it, not me.' Are we *flirting*?

'OK, you got me. So . . . ideas?'

'I'm a little short on ideas,' I say. (I'm not; I've got loads of

56

ideas, but I'm not sure this is the time to reveal I'm a *total musical theatre geek* to the hot guy with the guitar.) 'What music do you like? Maybe that's where we should start.'

'Good idea. I guess I like everything – music mad, my family. Dad's an old rhythm and blues guitarist; Mum's an opera singer. Danny was into grunge and death metal. Bunch of music nuts.'

'Danny your brother?'

'Danny my brother.'

There's a pause.

'How about you?' he says.

'I grew up with Etta and Billie, Judy, Barbra. Marni Nixon – Mum was obsessed with her. We watched a lot of MGM movies . . . Also, I'm a Sondheim nerd.'

'No way. Me too.'

'And obsessed with anything by Lin-Manuel Miranda or Jason Robert Brown,' I say in a *Who isn't?* voice.

'Me too – but I struggle to play JRB.' He matches me with a *Who doesn't?* tone.

'I think that's quite common.'

'What, playing JRB, or liking those guys?'

I laugh. 'Both, I guess.'

'It'd be great to use them in the study,' says Fletch. 'Only, we need pre-1980 twentieth century.'

'Doesn't narrow it down much,' I say.

'I know what you mean – it's like choosing between all your favourite friends,' he says. 'You mentioned Marni Nixon . . . Remind me who she is?'

'She was the singing voice for loads of famous leading ladies in films. Natalie Wood, Deborah Kerr, Audrey Hepburn—'

'That's right. Don't they call it "ghost singing"? What about something like that? Something like "Ghost Singers and Their Influence on Musical Theatre"?'

'Sounds good to me.' Privately I think the title needs work, but I might say that when I've known him longer than five minutes. 'There were loads of them, I think – lots of scope.'

'I think we could be on to something with this.' He reaches behind his ear. 'Where's my pencil? That's the third one I've lost today.' He rummages in his satchel and pulls out a pack of brand-new pencils and a sharpener. He selects a yellow-and-black HB and snaps it in half.

'What are you doing?'

'Can't get it behind my ear otherwise.' He sharpens both halves and pops one behind his ear. I notice how a stray bit of hair curls around his earlobe. 'Two for the price of one. Good job, really, at the rate I lose them. So, when shall we work on this? Can you give me any of your time? Tomorrow lunchtime?'

Adrenaline, hello.

'Works for me.'

'So, you've fallen over, flunked singing, and now Millicent Moore's on the warpath?'

Alec and I are in Sue's Kitchen, on Old Compton Street, for lunch. It's cheap and dingy, which isn't really Alec's style, but the veggie place is closed, and anyway, it's a popular haunt for West End ensemble members. (Alec deems it acceptable for this reason ONLY.)

'Yep. She basically wants me dead.'

'She's notoriously awful if she doesn't like you.' Alec covers

58

his jacket potato with salt until it looks like it's been snowed on. 'I'd go for dead if I were you. What did you do?'

I pause before biting into my sandwich. 'Well, I was a bit late. And . . .'

'And what?'

'This sounds a bit weird, but I think it was something to do with my mum.'

'Your mum the famous ballerina?'

'Well, er—' I can't seem to form an actual sentence.

'I *knew* it!' says Alec jubilantly, as if my lack of words confirms it. He thumps the table, nearly collapsing it in the process. 'I knew it the second I saw you. You're the image of her.'

'Am I?'

'A hundred per cent. Surely Millicent Moore would love you, being related to someone like that?'

I shrug.

'Let's do a quick-fire round,' says Alec. 'I'll go first. Full name?'

'Nettie Delaney.'

'I said *full*.'

I groan. 'It's embarrassing.'

'Go on,' he coaxes. 'Tell your auntie Alec.'

'Promise you won't laugh.'

'I will absolutely not promise.'

'OK.' This is *so* cringe. I loved Mum with all my heart but she really did pick an awful name for me. 'My name is Antoinette Sylvie Moira Delaney-Richardson, and if you ever tell anyone, you're dead.'

Alec snorts into his latte.

'I said *don't* laugh,' I say.

'Darling, I'm not laughing,' he says, his cobalt eyes wider than

59

I've ever seen them. 'That's a *legit* dance-royalty list. So, we've got Antoinette Sibley, Sylvie Guillem and Moira . . .'

'Shearer,' I say glumly.

'Of course!' He slaps his forehead. '*The Red Shoes*. Damn my eternal soul for not getting that one. Such a pedigree you have.'

'Well, don't get excited. I'm no prima.'

'I know,' says Alec. 'I peeked through the window yesterday when you were in ballet. OK, let's move on. Style: vintage eclectic – I *love*. Music . . .' He swipes my phone and starts looking through my playlists. 'Hmm . . . lots of old stuff. Musical theatre – that's good to know. Er, *jazz*? Nothing clubby, I notice. We'll soon fix that. I'm going to need to educate you before you go out with me.'

I grab my phone back. 'What about you, then?'

'Nettie, darling, I thought you'd never ask. My name is Alec Guillaume Jean-Baptiste Van Damm—'

'Ooh, do you speak French?'

'Only when I think it might help me pull.'

'Where did you grow up?'

'A mixture of Chelsea, Sussex and France.' He pronounces 'France' the French way.

'How very rah,' I say. 'France must have been nice.'

'Are you kidding?' he says. 'Unless you're in Paris, there's cock all going on. And we weren't in Paris.'

'So, how did you start dancing?' I'm beginning to feel like Graham Norton with all the questions (except a lot less funny and without the snazzy suit).

'I used to put on my mum's wedding dress and pretend I was in *Giselle*.' Alec mimes a mini *attitude* while *bourrée*-ing under the table. 'I begged and begged her to send me to ballet class.

60

Finally she let me go when I was seven.'

'And you liked it.'

'Darling, it was as if I had been born all over again and sent straight to live in heaven. You know some things are meant to be? Well, my body and dance are meant for each other.'

'Like Tony and Maria?'

'I was thinking more Angel and Collins, actually.'

I take a forkful of my cake.

'Watch out,' says Alec. 'If Miss Duke sees you eating that, she'll have you in the office quicker than you can say "Atkins".'

I nearly choke on a poppy seed. 'Miss Duke doesn't let us eat?'

'Not the girls. And definitely not cake,' he says, leaning over to bite into his own slice. 'Marmite on cucumber, maybe.'

'Well, Miss Duke can do one,' I say. 'I'll eat what I like.'

'Ooh, feisty.'

'To be honest, after the humiliation Millicent Moore subjected me to yesterday, I don't care. I probably won't be here that long, anyway.'

Alec sits up. 'What do you mean? You're leaving?'

My cake suddenly doesn't taste as good. I swallow it with difficulty. 'If I don't, they'll kick me out anyway. I'm pretty rubbish at dance, I've only got drama a couple of times a week, and as far as singing goes . . .'

'What? Don't tell me – you're tone deaf?'

'No. I – I've lost my voice.'

'Your voice sounds fine to me.'

'I know. I just haven't been able to sing for the last few months,' I say. 'It's complicated.'

'Why not?'

61

'I don't know. It's kind of to do with Mum.' My eyes well up uncontrollably without warning.

Alec looks horror-stricken. 'Oh, Nettie, I'm so sorry. I shouldn't keep mentioning her.'

I smile to cajole them into stopping. 'It's fine.'

'I'm sorry,' says Alec. 'We only met, like, yesterday, so I won't pry.'

'Really, it's OK.' I fill him in on the audition and the fact that I still can't get a note out. Alec listens intently.

'It doesn't make sense,' he says slowly, shaking his head. 'Miss Duke wouldn't take you if she thought you were rubbish.'

'Maybe she took me on because of Mum.' Voicing my worst fears doesn't make me feel any better.

'No. I know I joked about it before, on the first day – but that's not her style.' Alec frowns. 'And you haven't sung at all since the audition? Not even on your own?'

I pause. Should I tell him about last night?

'No.' I'm not sure he would get it.

'Nettie, this is a tricky one. But I'm sure you're not here just because of who your mum was.'

'Well, it doesn't change the fact that I'm on borrowed time.'

'OK,' he says. 'Well, let me just say that your fierce classical pedigree aside (although I've seen you dance, and you really don't live up to it), I think you're fabulous. I sense great things for you. Plus, I'm heady with your eclectic vintage style.'

'Patronizing much?'

'A little. Let's head back.'

'OK.'

'Nettie,' says Alec, the most serious I've seen him. 'I think we should be besties.'

'Wow, I'm honoured.' Hard to make this sound sarcastic when I can think of nothing better.

'I know, right. So, what do you say?'

I think I've just found a reason to stay on at Duke's.

CHAPTER 8

My second afternoon at Duke's is less awful. I manage to survive an hour and a half with Millicent Moore, who today resorts to subtle jibes rather than full-on physical abuse. I can take jibes. God knows I've got used to them over the last year living with Auntie.

After ballet is hip-hop. Lucky for me that since Natasha and Jade are both second-years, I'm in little danger of meeting them in any dance class. It's just in MT and the changing room that I have to suffer them. Fortunately they haven't been in the changing room all day.

I'm hoping to be invisible in hip hop and all my other classes until I work out what the hell to do about my voice.

After class, Kiki catches up with me on my way to the changing room.

'You looked great in there,' she says breathlessly, stripping her soaked purple leotard down to the waist, revealing an even wetter blue sports bra and a washboard stomach. 'Blimey, I'm sweating in places I didn't know was possible. I think my eyeballs are sweating.'

I laugh. 'Me too. That was hard.'

'Yeah. Nice to just be able to get on with it, though, without someone breathing down your neck all the time,' she says.

'Yep.'

'Miss Moore's really got it in for you. I watched you do that pirouette in ballet earlier. Your foot was nowhere near your ankle. It looked perfect to me.'

'You don't have to do this.'

'Seriously. It's all her. There's something not right about that one.' She widens her already-wide hazel eyes and shakes her head. 'Hey, I meant to ask, where are you living? In halls?'

I nod. I'm kind of too knackered to speak much.

'Me too. Fancy a drink in my room tonight? I'll ask that boy Alec too, if you like. He said you'd met. We were partnered together in ballet *pas de deux* class this morning. He's *so* good. Have you seen him dance?'

'Not yet.'

'Well, you wait. He's amaze. I would say let's hang out in the common room but not if Natasha Bridgewell decides to take over again. You know. Dancer. Second year. Tall, leggy, hangs out with Jade Upton . . . apparently threw a coffee over you yesterday?'

'Ah, yes,' I say. 'My new BFF.'

I shower quickly, dry my hair, and while I wait for Kiki (who's got extensions to deal with), my mind wanders to Fletch. I want to watch him play guitar again, hear his voice.

By the time Kiki finishes faffing about with her make-up, we're the last ones to leave. I notice how different a place it is without any students in it. Empty, like a warehouse. Like its lifeblood has been drained.

'Oh, crap!' says Kiki suddenly, as we round the bottom of the stairs. 'I left my heated rollers in the other building.'

'You brought heated rollers to college?' I didn't even bring hairpins.

'Well, you heard Miss Duke yesterday. Got to look our best at all times. I'll run ahead in case they lock it. Meet you at the tube.'

'OK,' I say, and I watch her pelt off towards the music hall. I'm about to follow her out of the front doors when I hear someone tinkering on a piano in the studio theatre. Without thinking, I turn and head in there.

There's someone the other side of the folding doors again. The playing pauses as I close the door. Whoever it is has heard me come in. I hardly dare breathe. It sounds like they're not breathing either. Is it the same person?

I *know* it is.

It feels awkward, like neither of us knows what to do next. Maybe I should write off yesterday as a coincidence; a wonderful, life-saving coincidence, which came when I needed it most.

Then I hear music. It's an intro to something.

It's from *Spring Awakening* . . . It's 'Mama Who Bore Me'.

It would have to be about mothers, wouldn't it? I take a breath in, with absolutely no idea if I'll even be able to sing anything. What if there's someone else there, ready to sing on the other side of the doors? What if I've interrupted a rehearsal?

The notes pour out before I even realize what's happening. I'm doing it. Yesterday wasn't a fluke. I *can* sing.

The room turns eerily tense as the song ends. The air seems to have gone wavy like it does on a hot day. I pick up my bag, hands shaking with the thrill, and quietly walk out of the studio. I hover for a second in the empty foyer. Then I make my way to the entrance, push through the narrow front doors, and walk silently to the tube station.

'What do you mean, you don't know who it is?' Kiki pours us a second vodka and Coke. We're sitting on her bed listening to *Dreamgirls*, eating olives and pitta bread. It's all I've had time to

66

eat since lunch and I'm drunk already.

'Just that. I don't.'

'So, both days you've been here at Duke's, a random stranger has started playing a tune you both just *happen* to know, you sing along to the end and then run off without seeing who it is?'

'Well, the first time, it was me who started. But basically, yeah.'

'Don't you want to know?' says Kiki. 'I'd have to peek.'

'But if I peek, I might not be able to sing. This is the first time I've sung for months. I can't seem to do it with anyone watching.'

'Ooh, I know. Next time, I can come with you and hide out. Then I'll know who it is, but you don't have to.'

'I'm not going to do it again,' I say quickly. 'It's getting weird.'

'But you said you were having problems singing,' argues Kiki. 'If this is the only way you can sing, I say go for it.'

There's a knock at the door.

'Jesus, loud much?' shouts Kiki, jumping up to answer it.

'We heard this was where the best people hang out,' says the unmistakeably smooth voice of Alec. 'We brought wine.'

'It's a rather nice Chablis, actually,' says another voice behind him. It sounds posh, a bit like Alec's but without the extra sweetener.

The two emerge from behind the thin door.

'Hi, beauts,' says Alec. 'Mind if we join you? This is Leon.'

Leon smiles amiably. He's shortish, Black, handsome, with neatly groomed hair and the coolest red glasses I've ever seen. His clothes look expensive, like Alec's, but wouldn't look out of place at a Camden gig, as opposed to Alec's well-honed Harvard preppy vibe.

'Anyone who brings wine is always welcome at my door.' Kiki

fumbles around for two cups. 'Hang on. I'll rinse mine and you can have it, Leon. I'll go and get my toothpaste mug. I'm Kiki, by the way.'

'Charmed,' says Leon, like someone from a Forties film. His gaze shifts to me. 'And you must be . . .'

I throw a look at Alec. 'Yeah. Nettie.' Of course he's told Leon who I am.

'*Nice room*,' says Alec, insincerely.

Kiki's room is titchy even by halls standards – a single bed squashed up against the wall, a sink, a tiny wardrobe and chest of drawers, and a postage stamp's worth of floor space. She's done the best she can with fairy lights and posters of dancers – mostly Misty Copeland, but also Koharu Sugawara, Ellen Kim and a random Cynthia Rhodes in the top right-hand corner. She's mounted a load of inspirational quotes in between them, like the kind you scroll through on Instagram and roll your eyes at (unless you're a performer, in which case you live your life by them). Her maroon curtains, which she's drawn to stop the sun dazzling everyone and making the room like a sauna, are casting a pinkish glow around the small space.

'Good music, though,' says Leon. He starts humming along to Jennifer Holliday.

'I can't wait until next year when we can move out of halls,' says Kiki. 'I think I got the worst room. What's yours like, Nettie?'

I'm totally not going to tell her this, but mine's twice the size and has its own ensuite, rather than having to share with about four other rooms.

'Erm . . . Maybe not as bad as this.' I avoid her eyes.

Alec has now sprawled his long body across Kiki's tiny bed, his legs draping over the edge like an expensive denim throw.

He's examining a quote directly above his head that reads:

Anything can happen if you let it.

'*Gorgeous* song,' he says, tracing the words with his index finger. 'Stiles and Drewe, 2004. *Mary Poppins*, original West End production,'

'Actually, I think you'll find they opened in Bristol,' says Leon. He opens the expensive wine and pours everyone half a mugful like a sommelier. 'My parents took me as a birthday present when I was still at prep school.'

Kiki, who's rinsing out her toothbrush mug in preparation for Leon's wine, nudges me. 'Prep school,' she says.

I'm not sure whether I'm supposed to be impressed or amused by this piece of information, so I make a non-committal grunt into the wine Leon's just handed me.

'So,' says Alec, ignoring Kiki's dig. 'Is this –' he indicates the four of us with a sweep of his finger – 'going to be *a thing*?'

'What do you mean, "a thing"?' said Kiki.

'A *friend* thing. Nettie, we've already established that you're fabulous and come from ballet royalty. Kiki, I don't know you well yet, but I do know you've got a triple *en dedans* to die for. And Leon, being the only two benders at boarding school seems to have cemented a lifelong friendship, even though I'm convinced you only followed me here to Duke's to gaze at my gorgeous tight arse and wonder if I'll ever share it with you –' cue Leon snorting wine – 'but all things considered, I'm happy you're here hanging on to my coattails.'

'I got into Duke's *before* Alec did,' says Leon to Kiki and me, turning his back on Alec.

'A technicality,' says Alec.

'Wait, you went to school together?' I say.

'Yes.' Leon briefly touches Alec's head, which has flopped off the end of the bed. 'Seven years at St. Augustine's. Can't get rid of you, can I?'

Alec smiles gratefully at his friend and rolls over on to his stomach. 'Much as I despise him, he was probably my saving grace at school. Weren't you, treacle?'

'Are you . . . together?' ventures Kiki.

Leon jumps back quicker than Dick Van Dyke over a chimney pot. 'God, no! I do have some taste, you know.'

'You've begged me for it every night since I met you.' Apparently Alec enjoys winding Leon up.

'In your dreams.'

Kiki and I look at each other, unsure what to make of this.

'Believe it or not,' says Alec lazily, 'I wasn't always this fabulous-slash-comfortable in my own skin. The first few years at school were hellish for me.'

'Did the other boys bully you?' says Kiki. We all know she means 'for being gay'.

'If by "bully" you mean they jerked off in my face.'

'What do you mean?' Is he serious?

'*What*?' Kiki looks like she can't quite believe it, either.

'Well, one of them did, while three of them held me down.' He says it quite casually, as if it's as normal as tying your shoelaces. I don't think he's joking.

'That's . . . awful.' I glance at Leon, but he's watching Alec intently.

'Why?' Kiki looks horrified.

Alec shrugs. 'Dunno. Power . . . Fear . . . Hate.' There's an

70

almost imperceptible change in his tone on the last word. Almost.

'It's sexual assault,' I say.

No one replies.

'Are you . . . OK?' asks Kiki.

'Darling, I'm *so* OK, I can barely remember it,' says Alec, snapping back to form, although I'm not sure I believe him.

'Did they do stuff to you as well?' Kiki says to Leon.

'My father was a 'friend' of the school—'

'A 'friend'?' says Kiki.

'It means he gave them shit loads of money,' says Alec. 'Helped fund new buildings and stuff. They wouldn't have dared. Also—'

Leon finishes his sentence for him. 'I wasn't out at school.'

'So what happened?' says Kiki, still horrified. 'Did you tell the teachers?'

Alec and Leon exchange a glance.

'Not exactly . . .' says Leon.

'I punched one of the boys. Put him in hospital,' says Alec.

I look at him, surprised.

'What, a queer boy can't hit someone?' he says. 'Anyway, it was all fine, in the end.'

'Fine?'

'Leon got me out of it.'

'How?'

'Well, the father of the boy Alec punched was about to sue Alec's family *and* the school,' says Leon. 'So my father had a little word about *why* Alec felt the need to hit this man's kid. The boy's father soon withdrew the complaint.'

'And that was the end of it?' says Kiki, enthralled.

'Yes.' Leon sets his glass down on Kiki's desk. 'Ironically, the threat of being associated with any sort of "gayness" was enough

71

to silence them, not the fact that their child committed a brutal assault. The school were only too happy to brush the whole incident under the carpet. Funny how people's brains work. Especially when money's at stake.'

No one speaks for a moment.

'That's horrendous,' I say.

'We don't need 'em,' says Alec.

'Or want them, particularly,' adds Leon.

The look they share is loaded with unsaid words, unspoken memories. I feel like I'm intruding on something.

Alec sits up. 'So,' he says briskly. 'Freshers' Ball. Let's make a plan.'

Apparently that's the end of that conversation.

'What's the Freshers' Ball?' I say.

'Oh, Nettie, really? It's the social event of the Duke's calendar. It's a ball to welcome the first-years, but *everyone* is there. Ex-students as well. Only the ones who've done well though; the out-of-work ones keep their distance—'

'Get barred, you mean,' says Leon.

'Why?' I say.

'Oh, isn't she delicious?' says Alec.

'Nettie,' says Leon, in the patient manner of one who is about to explain to a small child why they shouldn't draw on the walls. 'Would you come back to Duke's for a visit unless you had something to show off about?'

'I – what?'

'Oh, treasure. Think about how Miss Duke would treat someone who, let's say, had worked in a call centre for ten months after they had graduated. Do you think she would welcome them back with open arms? Or do you think she would ignore them and pretend they had never trained here?'

'Blimey, she's not that evil, is she?' says Kiki.

'You saw her with Lauren Rose,' says Leon. 'And apparently that was tame.'

'Why would Miss Duke be at the Freshers' Ball anyway?' says Kiki.

'All the staff turn up for the first hour,' says Leon. I've no idea how he knows this after only two days at the place. 'The third-years put on a concert for them. Miss Duke sits there like the queen for a bit and waves and smiles and tells us all how we're at the best establishment and we're lucky to be there, blah blah blah – then she goes home and leaves us to get pissed.'

'She's a strange one, isn't she?' says Kiki. 'That thing with Lauren yesterday, humiliating her like that. Why doesn't she let us just get on with it? It's our training.'

'Not in her eyes,' says Alec. 'It's her reputation on the line. She *owns* our training, our social lives, our everything. For the three years we're here, right up until we walk out of that door on our graduation day, we have Cecile Duke stamped on our arse in indelible ink, and we can't wash it off until we leave. Some people never get rid of it. Even though *she* could end it for any of us any second she likes. One toe out of line . . .'

'She's an enigma,' says Leon. 'No one really knows her.'

There's a pause in the conversation.

'My mum knew her,' I say quietly.

The others stare at me.

'What – how?' splutters Alec.

'They worked together. About thirty years ago in Denmark. They were really young.'

'What was she like? What did your mum say about her?'

73

'Nothing. She never mentioned her. I was in the library yesterday and I found a picture of them together in an old programme.'

'What was it? A ballet?' presses Alec.

'It was a production of *Oklahoma!* at the Tivoli Concert Hall.' It's weird talking about Mum's life before I was born. It's like it happened to someone I don't know.

'Did you keep it?' says Leon.

'No.' I should've kept it. I can't stop thinking about that picture. The way her head's thrown back in laughter, the carefree look on her youthful face – she looks like someone I don't know. Why didn't she tell me they knew each other? She never mentioned Michael St. John, either.

'She must have said *something*,' says Kiki.

'Nothing,' I repeat.

'Didn't you ever ask her?' says Alec.

'She just . . . She never wanted to talk about her life as a dancer.' I can tell Alec's gagging to ask me more but sees my face and thinks better of it.

'Does Cecile Duke know who you are?' says Kiki.

'Kiki,' says Leon, 'maybe it's something Nettie doesn't feel comfortable discussing. She has only just met us, after all.'

'Oh, er, right,' says Kiki. 'Sorry, Nettie – I didn't think.'

'No, it's fine,' I say. 'I don't know if she knows me. I guess so, by name.'

'I'd love it if my mum was bezzie mates with Cecile Duke,' says Alec. 'I'd be swanning around college like a fucking duchess.' He crosses his legs theatrically like Cyd Charisse. 'Right, everyone. Get your timetables out. I want to see if we've got any classes together.'

I produce mine from my bag, as does Kiki.

74

'Where's yours?' says Alec to Leon.

'All up here, my pretty,' says Leon, tapping his temple.

Alec rolls his eyes as he takes (snatches) my timetable. 'Nothing Monday. Nothing Tuesday . . . Oh, look. On Fridays we've got jazz *pas de deux* together. Shall we be partners? I can make literally *anyone* look good.'

'Er, OK,' I said.

'*Er, OK?* Darling, you should be on your knees praising the Lord that he sent me to you. I'm God's gift to partner work. Ah, Kiki, you're in that class too. Damn. I've already pledged myself to Nettie.'

'Seriously. Go with Kiki. I'm fine,' I say.

'No. I'll teach you. Baby-and-Johnny style. Except we probs won't shag due to my extreme queerness. You'll be a star by the time I've finished with you, though.'

'I'll go with you, Kiki,' says Leon. 'We'll be fierce.'

'How come we're only together for some classes, Nettie?' says Kiki, peering over Alec's shoulder.

'I dunno – are you doing musical theatre?'

'No, thank God. Dancers course.'

'That'll be it,' says Alec.

'What?' Kiki even looks beautiful when she's got her nose all wrinkled up in confusion.

'The dancers don't have to sing, but the singers and actors have to dance,' says Alec. 'That's just how it is. Cecile Duke wants everyone to have a grounding in ballet, jazz and tap. Except the writers. They get to pick and choose their classes.'

Fletch is on the writers course. I can't see him in a ballet class, somehow. It doesn't suit his rock star image. Not that he's trying to cultivate an image. He just . . . *oozes* it. The way his hair just

75

falls *almost* over his left eye, and the fact that his battered leather jacket has a worn bit on one side where he's slung his guitar strap over his shoulder so many times. The voice. The way he can write beautiful songs that make my heart hurt.

I've been dreaming. The conversation has lulled. Alec's looking at me slyly.

'What?' I say.

'Nothing.'

'*What?*'

'Literally nothing,' he says. 'So, what's "special voice coaching"? Looks like you've got that tomorrow morning. CD . . . Who's that— *Oh*.'

Leon and Kiki look at each other in horror as an expression of delighted realization sweeps over Alec's face.

'What are you . . .' I begin.

Alec's fingering the paper with a new reverence. He looks up at me slowly. 'Oh, Nettie . . .'

'Omigod, WHAT?'

Kiki snatches the paper from him and hands it to me gently, pointing to the following day's classes.

'CD is Cecile Duke,' she says. 'You've got Cecile Duke for singing tomorrow.'

CHAPTER 9

Giraffe tall, Miss Duke's looking down at me from a great height. She raises a gigantic quizzical eyebrow and demands to know why I'm not singing. Every time I try to explain myself, a squeak comes out instead of words. The squeak gets fainter and fainter until it sounds like I'm squeaking from inside a glass jar. The room and Miss Duke get bigger and bigger. I look down at my hands and realize they're paws. I've become an actual mouse. A pitiful, squeaking mouse.

I wake up with a start, covered in sweat. I feel like Sophie in *Mamma Mia!* after her terrifying attack from a load of neon scuba divers. I'm so thankful it wasn't real that I actually hug my pillow.

I reach for my make-up bag. *War paint*, Mum called it. She very rarely left the house without a full face. She said it was habit from a lifetime onstage. Maybe she and Miss Duke used to swap tips. I imagine them backstage together, getting ready in front of illuminated dressing-room mirrors, laughing like they were in the picture. I'm angry that Mum never told me, and I don't want to be angry with her. It hurts.

Flicking through the clothes in my wardrobe doesn't leave me feeling very inspired. It needs to be an outfit that will both meet with Miss Duke's approval and at the same time not be too noticeable. I try on about seventeen different combinations, eventually going for what I hope is elegant but conservative: a dark green pencil dress and heels.

I'm early for college. So early that I'm the surely only person in the building. I dump my stuff in the changing room and head back down to the foyer, worrying about what Miss Duke's going to do with us. Maybe my throat will unfreeze today. Maybe I'll be fine now.

My stomach lurches as if to answer, *I'm not so sure.*

I sit down under a picture of the 1986 cast of *Cats* and a signed ten-by-eight of an RSC actor. The door to the studio theatre's open on the opposite side of the foyer. Michael St. John is in there, setting up several pages of sheet music in a long line on the piano. He sits down and starts running through the song. It's 'Unworthy of Your Love' by Sondheim. He plays it beautifully. I hum it in my head, wishing I could sing along.

Michael spots me and waves me over. I get up and go into the studio, quietly panicking that he might ask me to sing.

'You're early, poppet.'

'Busy day . . . Wanted to prepare myself.'

'Very wise.' He folds the music into a neat pile. 'I'm without a pianist today, so I thought I'd better get some prep in myself.'

I hand him the top sheet, which has fluttered under the barre. 'Why do you use a pianist? You play so beautifully.'

'Thank you, Nettie. I try to avoid playing for class – I find it lowers my status. If they can't see my face over the top of the piano, people switch off. Trust me, I spent enough years watching MDs struggle in rehearsal.'

Fletch appears from behind the far door with his guitar, which he puts down beside the piano.

'Hi, Nettie,' he says. 'Still on for later?'

I do a too-big thumbs-up and instantly regret it.

'You'll have to excuse us, Nettie,' says Michael. 'We've got an early-morning piano lesson.'

'I didn't know you played piano,' I say to Fletch. Is there no end to this boy's talents?

'I don't,' he says. 'Yet.'

'That's the attitude,' says Michael. 'You'll get there.'

I say goodbye to them and go up to the empty changing room, thinking things over. Could it be *Michael* I've been singing with? Surely he'd just tell me it was him. But then, I guess he wouldn't know it was me.

At least I can rule out Fletch if he's only learning to play. That would have been awkward.

Registration's a brief affair (Why do things always go quickly when you're wanting time to drag?) with Alec, Leon and Kiki all offering me silent pats and hugs of reassurance. Their acts of kindness seem more like parting gestures to me, but I appreciate them. I make my way to Studio Five upstairs, the dread growing with every step. Miss Duke is going to expel me on the spot before the hour is up.

Everyone else is already there. Horrifyingly, they're dressed in tracksuits and dancewear. I look completely out of place. But there's no time to go and revise my outfit because the door sweeps open, and in strides Cecile Duke.

Everyone stands up and smiles artificially. Again, bags are kicked behind legs, stomachs sucked in. Phones are quickly turned off and hidden in pockets.

'Good morning, girls.'

'Good morning, Miss Duke.'

'Leah, go and find out where our accompanist is,' she says. 'I want Peter or Stephen. And come straight back.'

Leah all but curtseys before speeding out of the room. Miss Duke says nothing; she silently scrutinizes us all one by one, up and down. I feel a trickle of sweat roll down my back and fall into my knickers, but I don't dare attend to it because right now one move could destroy everything for me.

Leah returns, panting, dragging an old man with her, whom I presume is our pianist.

'Sorry, Miss Duke. Wasn't on my timetable,' he says.

'Ah, then thank you for accommodating us, Stephen,' says Miss Duke. I notice the inequality in how they address each other. He sounds a bit scared of her.

'Here are the dots.' She hands him a batch of sheet music. I can't make out the title from where I'm standing.

She turns her attention back to us.

'Before we start, class –' (her tone is ice; shivers travel up the sweat tracks on my spine) – 'I would like to know why a group of my best third-year students have to be taught how to dress for class by an inexperienced first-year.' She gestures in my direction without looking at me. 'Did I *not* make it clear on the first day that I expect you all to be perfectly groomed at *all* times?'

'Yes, Miss Duke,' echoes a hallowed mutter.

'Shall we go and—' starts one eager beaver.

Oh God, be quiet, girl. Quit while you're ahead.

'I haven't got time to wait for you all to go off and sort yourselves out now,' snaps Miss Duke. 'But from here on in, I expect you to be dressed smartly in this class, as if you mean to be taken seriously. Unless, of course, you don't mean to be taken seriously – in which case, you are very welcome to leave now.'

She waits for a good twenty seconds before continuing. I mean, *twenty*. It feels like minutes. Obviously no one leaves.

'I assume you all know why you are here? No?' She sighs theatrically. 'You are here, girls, because we think you are a cut above the rest. You have potential to go all the way. And next year, when you leave, you could be the stars of tomorrow. We just need to hone you. That's what this class is for. To be honest, I'm quite looking forward to getting my hands dirty. We shall learn a song of *my* choosing every week –' (here she emphasizes the word 'my' as if we're all about to argue for our own song choices; as *if*) – 'and you will perform it one by one, while I critique your performance. Each and every one of you can learn from the others' mistakes. So get used to being torn apart in front of your peers. Here, there are no barriers. This class is not for the faint-hearted.'

My heart instantly begins to feel faint.

It must be a mistake. They're all third-years. Surely I'm not meant to be here – especially as no one has ever heard me sing. Should I say something? Maybe she'll dismiss me . . .

Or maybe she'll annihilate me.

'Alice, hand out sheet music. Let's begin learning this song.'

The song in question is one I don't know. Looking around, it seems that no one else is familiar with it either. I've stayed too long to leave now. I'm just going to have to stick it out.

'We will sing it twice through with Stephen,' says Miss Duke. 'You may have the dots. By then, you should know it perfectly. No excuses for not knowing it after that.'

We learn the song, united in fear. I can feel *some* sound coming out, although it's small and strained. Any second now she'll realize I can't sing and it'll all be over. I should have left when I had the chance.

'Rochelle, would you start, please?'

Rochelle obliges, bumbling her way through the first verse and chorus. It's clear that she's got a great voice, but she's straining at the high notes with nerves.

(How not to get the best out of people. Massively raise the stakes and then stress them out to the point of exhaustion.)

Rochelle finishes, somewhat diminishingly. She tucks her hair behind her ear as the music ends.

'Rochelle.' Miss Duke strides around from the other side of the piano. 'I'll ignore the fact that you limped through the song. I'll even ignore the fact that some of the high notes sounded like five squirrels dragging their claws down a blackboard. But did you see, girls? She finished the song, fiddled with her hair and looked at the floor. An apology, if ever I saw one. Never apologize for your performance, girls. NEVER. Whatever happens, however wrong you may think it has gone, never apologize. Let your audience be their own judge of what they have just seen and heard. Believe me, if it's bad, you won't need to tell them.'

Rochelle looks as if she's going to spew. I can't tell if she's upset at the criticism or relieved it's over. She scuttles back to her place.

Other girls have their turn. One by one, they fail in some way or another; one by one, their performance gets ripped apart.

'I've heard better pitching from pre-schoolers.'

'TOO MUCH RIFFING! Where's the *tune*?'

'To be honest, I can't remember a single thing about this one. I was too busy being distracted by that unattractive tuft of hair falling over one side of your face. Quite unsightly.'

The moment's here. Cecile Duke turns to me.

'Antoinette.'

'Yes, Miss Duke.' My left knee's out of control, trembling comedy-style. Except that this is in no way funny.

'You're up.'

The same old dread creeps over me as the intro starts. I can't do it. I'm going to fail, in front of everyone, in a spectacular fashion. I'm going to die on my arse.

The intro finishes and I try – I *try* – but nothing comes out. I mouth the first few words in little more than a whisper.

'Enough,' barks Miss Duke over the music.

I stop. She moves close to me, piercing me with her dark eyes. I meet her gaze, shaking, feeling every bit like Lauren Rose on the first day. I wonder if she can hear my heart pounding.

'You're under the weather,' she says. 'You have no voice today. And yet you were prepared to put yourself on the line.'

She turns to the group. 'Never explain, never complain. Antoinette has demonstrated just that. I commend you, Antoinette. Despite your inexperience, you have proved that I was right to put you in this class. Girls, you are dismissed. And may I suggest we all turn up with a similar attitude next week.'

It's not until everyone has left that I let myself collapse. *Both* my knees are trembling now, as are my hands and, weirdly, my left cheek. I sit down where I am in the middle of the room and hug my knees. What just happened? I take a few deep breaths, trying not to feel overwhelmed.

Suddenly Miss Paige, the college head secretary, pops her head around the door. 'Antoinette?'

'Er, hello, Miss Paige.' I get up awkwardly.

'Miss Duke has requested that you go upstairs immediately and see Miss Andrews.'

'Sorry, but who is Miss Andrews?'

'Vocal coach. Studio Nine, third floor. Opposite the top changing room.'

'But I've got ballet now.' Unfortunately for me.

'Miss Duke says that this overrides your timetable. Any teachers whose classes are affected have been notified.'

She doesn't wait for me to agree or disagree but thrusts a new timetable into my lap and leaves the room. I hear her heels clipping down the stairs to the office. Confused, I pick up my stuff and trudge up to the top floor.

I reach Studio Nine and pause outside. There's no sound coming from inside the room. Tentatively, I knock.

'Yeah,' says a voice.

I enter. The owner of the voice is a beautiful woman of about forty. She has warm brown skin, glossy black hair and brown eyes. She's sitting at a piano but looks like she'd be tall. Her clothes are all neutral tones and long lines – how I always imagine I'll dress when I'm older (in a parallel world where I'm not short and obsessed with vintage flower prints).

'Er, Miss Duke sent me to see you?' I say.

'Hi. Yes. She just came upstairs to ask me. A rare visit. Must be important. What's your name?'

'Nettie.'

'Good to meet you, Nettie. I'm Steph. I'm the advanced vocal coach here at Duke's. What's the problem with your voice?'

I pause.

'Take your time.' She sits back from the piano and clasps her hands.

I feel like I'm in therapy. I open my mouth and close it again, quite a lot like Dory.

'It's fine if you don't want to talk. I can wait. But we need to get to the root of the problem.'

'I . . . I don't *have* one,' I say.

'A problem?' she says. 'Miss Duke said—'

'No. A voice. I don't have a voice.'

She takes a moment to measure what I've just said.

'OK,' she says finally. 'No voice. We can rule out laryngitis, because speaking-wise you're fine. So there's another problem with it.'

For a second, I consider lying. The truth makes me look a bit, I don't know – attention-seeking? But something about the way she's sitting there so calmly, without judgement, gives me courage.

'It's just when I sing, lately, nothing comes out. My heart starts beating at, like, two hundred a minute and it's like I can't get any air into my lungs. And all that comes out is a whisper.'

'Has it always been like that?'

'No! Only since . . .' I falter.

Steph leans forwards, resting her arms on the piano. 'So there was a trigger.'

'I guess.'

'Tell me, if you can. Everything you say to me stays within these four walls.'

She comes around the piano while I try to explain in five minutes what's been happening over the last year and a half – Mum's illness, her death, the audition, the voicemail . . . It's not easy. But I get it out, mostly.

'Nettie. Thank you for sharing that with me. You've been through such a lot. That can't have been easy. It seems that the shock of what happened to you at the audition has triggered a physical response, which now surfaces every time you try to sing. A bit like stage fright.'

'But I've never had stage fright,' I say. 'I used to sing all the time in front of people.'

85

'The brain is a complex thing. Think about professional athletes. They have a team of psychotherapists working alongside their coaches to get the absolute best out of them. And in my opinion, singing is at least fifty per cent psychological.'

'It just feels so weak,' I say. '*I'm* weak.'

'You're not weak. You're *bereaved*.'

The word makes tears spring up to my eyes. I blink them back.

'Believe me when I say I can help you through this,' says Steph. 'It's going to take a lot of hard work, and I'm going to ask things of you that you might think are odd. But I *can* help you. All I ask is that you trust me.'

I nod.

'Great,' she says. 'So, just to clarify, it's *all* singing that has been affected, not just public singing?'

I hesitate. 'Well, occasionally I can get the sound out on my own.'

'That's a start. I'm going to ask you to sing a note for me. Just a G above middle C. But first I'm going to leave the room.'

'Sing a G?'

'Yes.'

'When you're out of the room?'

'Exactly. It's virtually soundproof, so no fibbing. The trust thing has to go both ways if we're going to fix this. Here's the note.' She plays a G and promptly leaves the room.

I stand up and step behind the piano. It feels safer there. I sing the note but it's quiet.

'Now sing me an A,' says Steph, opening the door a tiny bit and speaking through the crack.

I don't know whether she heard me or if she's just assuming I sang the G, but I sing the A obediently, although now my hands

86

are shaking and the note is barely audible. Steph comes back into the room.

'Great. That's all for today,' she says. 'Well done.'

'I didn't do anything.'

'Yes, you did. You trusted me, and that's something we can build on. I'll see you again in two days' time at eleven.'

'I've got ballet then.' I open my bag to look for my timetable.

'From now on, you'll have to miss ballet. This is more important. Is that OK?'

Not seeing Millicent Moore four times a week? How will I cope?

'Uh, sure, it's fine.'

'Great. We're going to be good together, Nettie. We're going to mend you.'

He's not coming. Obviously. He's probably cosying up with some hot third-year and has forgotten all about meeting me.

I'm sitting at a little table outside Cafe Boheme feeling awkward. It's in plain view of every student who decides to go down Old Compton Street (i.e. the whole college). It's ten past one and so far, no sign of Fletch. I put my headphones on and carry on listening to 'Taylor, the Latte Boy'. I've already ordered a coffee (probably what made me think of 'Taylor'). It looks like I'm going to have to neck it on my own and scram.

'Sorry! Michael had me playing for third-year MT.'

Fletch has just finished a sprint down Frith Street, guitar case slapping against his back as he comes to a halt next to my table.

'That's OK. I literally just got here.'

'Black Americano? Sorry about the wait,' says a waiter, appearing from nowhere.

Awks. I'll ignore that.

'Thanks. What would you like, Fletch?'

I like saying his name.

'I'll have a latte, please,' says Fletch. (I immediately picture him in a Starbucks uniform, serving Kristin Chenoweth.)

He turns a chair round and straddles it. His thighs are thick and rugby-ish. I see the waiter clock them too as he walks back into the restaurant.

'Do you mind it? Playing for classes all the time, I mean.'

'Not at all. It isn't that often, actually. And it's only guitar, so I can do it with my eyes closed.' He takes his guitar off over his head. I hope he didn't notice me looking at the little bit of stomach he revealed as his T-shirt rode up. 'I need to improve at piano, especially if I want to write my own musicals or be an MD. When I got into Duke's, it was on the provision that I studied piano. Let's just say I'm not exactly Liberace.'

'Do you play piano for classes as well?' I say.

'No, I don't think Michael's ready to let loose my piano skills on the college yet. Not sure I am, either. Anyway, tell me how your day's going.'

'Better than yesterday, but really odd,' I say.

'What happened?'

'Well, I had a singing class with Miss Duke—' I begin.

'Wow. She never singles out first-years. You must be good.'

'That's just it. I'm not. Ever since my audition, I can't sing.'

'What do you mean, you can't sing?'

I fiddle with my jacket button. 'If I tell you, promise not to think I'm weird.'

'Weird can be good, as far as I'm concerned, so don't worry about that.'

88

I take a breath and tell him everything. The audition, the class with Miss Duke, my visit to see Steph Andrews. He listens without interrupting, nodding occasionally, until I tail off.

'And you haven't been able to sing since. At all?'

'Well . . .' Should I tell him? He might be able to shed some light. He knows all the musos.

Then again, it does make it sound as if I'm making the whole thing up. *I* can't even understand how I can sing in one random place but not anywhere else, so there's little hope anyone else will.

'A tiny bit. Not much, though. Steph says it's triggered some sort of stage fright.'

'Grief does funny things to you,' he says. 'I didn't touch my guitar for a year after Danny's accident. Even the thought of playing made me feel sick.'

'What changed?'

'I was halfway through my A levels,' he says. 'It was two years after Danny's accident. I was going through some old school stuff when I found a photo in a pocket of an old backpack. It was of me and Danny jamming in our garden – a hilarious photo that our friend had taken, and I'd kept it to show people because we were both pulling this really silly face in it. He'd written on the back "The Aye-Ayes forever".'

'What's that?'

'Oh, that was the name of our band.' Fletch stirs sugar into his coffee, which has just arrived (a lot quicker than mine, I notice). 'The Aye-Ayes. It was just me and him – I was on guitar and vocals, and he was on drums.'

'A bit like the White Stripes?'

He laughs. 'I guess. Something about the photo made me realize I couldn't stop playing, not when music had meant so much to Danny. So I got my guitar out of the attic and started practising again. I got a job in a local record store and spent all summer working and gigging in between shifts. When I went back to school for my final year, I carried on gigging, still not sure if I should make a go of my writing. I made the decision to audition really late. I think I scraped into Duke's on the very last round.'

'Do you still miss him?'

'All the time. It's been four years, but I'm always thinking about him.'

'I thought it was meant to get easier.'

'It gets quieter.'

Fletch takes my hand. His palm is smooth and warm.

'You'll be fine,' he says. 'You just need to find your reason to sing again.' He releases my hand and grabs the pencil from behind his ear. 'Do you have any paper? I've left my notebook at college.'

I hesitate. I've only got my own little notebook that I use to write letters to Mum – silly, I know, seeing as she'll never read them. But he might think I'm weird. There's also a few lyrics in there that I *definitely* wouldn't want him to see.

'Er, sure.' I produce the book, taking care to open it to a blank double page for him first.

'Right.' He scribbles down a title at the top of the page. His handwriting's a bit unruly, like his hair. 'The project beckons. I find it hard to get on with work when I'm with you.'

I'm finding it hard to get on with anything when I'm still thinking about your hand on mine. Is what I *don't* say.

'Nettie?'

'Right. Yes. Marni Nixon. Go.'

We work for a while, researching different names and planning

90

how to link them up in our project. The cars steer around pedestrians who've spilt out on to the road. My chair gets knocked several times by passers-by.

'This is no good,' says Fletch. 'It's too busy here.' He pulls my chair towards him to get it off a bit of uneven pavement. My thigh bumps his.

'You want to go and work in the library?' I say.

'They've got second-year MT degree course happening in there. We could probably squeeze in the corner?'

With Natasha Bridgewell watching my every move? No thanks. 'Er . . . what about the canteen?'

'Too loud,' he says. 'What are you doing after college?'

'Nothing.'

'Great. Meet me in the square at five. But not in that.'

I look down at my green dress. 'Okaaay . . .'

'No – I just meant wear something warm. I thought we could go for a ride.'

'A ride?'

'On my motorbike. I've got a place I want to show you.'

My last class finishes early, at four, and I pelt it to the tube and get back to the halls in a record fifteen minutes. I grab some jeans and biker boots (not real ones, but they'll do), a long-sleeved body, and my vintage purple leather jacket that I got from Haynes Lane Market and love the bones of. I quickly do the front of my hair in two French braids to avoid helmet annihilation and bung some red lipstick on. That'll have to do.

I don't see him at first. Then I spot him on the other side of Soho Square, straddling a motorbike. He just got one hundred per cent hotter.

He lifts his helmet up so that it's resting on his forehead. 'Hey, Nettie. Ready?'

'Yup.'

'Been on one of these things before?'

'Nope.'

'You're gonna love it.'

He hands me a spare helmet, which I put on. It feels tight. He reaches round behind my neck and does up the straps at the front. I can feel the heat from his face, it's so close to mine. Or maybe it's my face that's hot.

'It's fiddly at first,' he says. 'Hold on, and don't lean too much. Let me do that.'

I nod and swing my leg over the bike.

It's smart . . . I think it's a Triumph. It looks kind of vintage. I sit behind him and look around for a handle.

He turns around. 'You have to hold on to me,' he says through his helmet, which he's now pulled back down. I'm glad he can't see my face through the visor on mine. I put my hands on his sides. He moves them further forward so that they're wrapped around him, and as he pulls out of the square, I get a rush that's got nothing to do with acceleration.

We ride past college. I look up, kind of wishing Alec could see me right now. He'd take the piss, but it'd be worth it to see his face.

I do see two other faces at the window.

It's Natasha Bridgewell and her friend Jade Upton, with matching expressions of hatred on their faces. I can't help thinking of Velma and Amber Von Tussle in *Hairspray*.

They're going to be vile tomorrow. Oh well – I'm on a Triumph holding on to a gorgeous musician. I'll take the trade-off.

We ride up Charing Cross Road, on to Tottenham Court Road, take a left and head up past Regent's Park. It's a warm late-September afternoon, before the evenings have started to take on a chill. It feels so free to be out riding through town, weaving in and out of traffic, smelling the end of the summer on the breeze. I feel happier than I've felt for months.

Fletch stops in Camden, parking the bike on Parkway near a Japanese restaurant. He takes his helmet off and shakes his hair (while I imagine it in slow motion). I take mine off, patting the French braids to see if they've survived. I think they have.

'This place is so cool,' says Fletch. 'You're going to love it.'

I'm going to love the Japanese restaurant?

No. He takes me to a cafe next door, the windows filled with posters of bands and solo artists. Inside, bistro tables are dotted all the way to the back of the bar, where a stage area is set up in front of red curtains.

'What would you like?'

'A green tea, please.'

Fletch goes to order while I sit down. The stage is all ready to go; it looks like they have someone playing live later.

'Do you like it?' He puts two green teas down on the table. 'They have some great acts playing. Sometimes it gets a bit folky, but the music's really diverse. Jazz, roots, blues, sometimes a bit of bluegrass.'

'It's really cool.'

'It's one of my favourite places in the world. I thought we could work here. Is that OK with you?'

Work here, to live music, in a secret location where no one can find us?

'Definitely.'

I float into college the next morning, all Eliza Doolittle after the ball. Last night was *a*-mazing. We stayed in the bar for hours, got to watch two amazing singers, talked, ate, laughed . . . I mean, technically we were working on our project, but it *really* felt like a date. A date with no kissing.

The bubble bursts as soon as I get up to the changing room and find the Von Tussles waiting for me.

'I saw you last night,' says Jade, without so much as a 'hi'. She's backcombing her hair in the mirror. I don't know why – it's already big enough to house seventeen squirrels. 'Getting on the back of Fletch's bike.'

'Did you?' I busy myself getting things out of my bag for my first class. 'Well done.'

'He's taken me out loads on it,' she snaps.

'Good for you.'

She gets out a large can of hairspray and sprays it so that as much as possible goes in my face. 'Where did he take you?'

'Sorry, is there a reason for this interrogation?' I say. 'It's just that I've got a busy day. So unless you've got something specific you want to say—'

'Just stay away from him,' says Natasha from behind her. 'Jade and Fletch were a thing way before you showed up.'

'You had a thing?' I say. 'What, you were together?'

Jade glances at Natasha. 'We—'

'Just keep out of his way,' says Natasha. 'Unless you want your life here to be miserable.'

'What are you going to do? Throw coffee over me every day?'

'We'll do more than that.'

94

'I lost my mum to cancer last year,' I say. 'I doubt there's much you could do that'd be worse than that. But be my guest trying.'

And . . . *mic drop*.

I don't usually do that, but it's one way to win an argument. Even Jade and Natasha can't better it. Jade stares at me, stupefied, Natasha fuming behind her. I stuff my bag in my locker and head out.

CHAPTER 10

'I could get you in with Miss Bond three times a week. You'll only be able to have Miss Moore once a fortnight now, what with your extra singing lessons with Miss Andrews. That'll have to do.'

I've just tactfully explained to Miss Paige in the office (without mentioning what's *actually* happening) that now I'm seeing Steph three times a week in place of Miss Moore's lesson and I only get her twice a week, it might be better if I have ballet at a different time (more importantly, with a different teacher). It was Alec's idea, of course.

'That's great! I mean, it's a shame I won't be having Miss Moore much anymore, but thanks for sorting it out for me.' I all but skip out of the office.

Alec's waiting for me at the end of the corridor, leaning up against the doorframe with an elegant loucheness that echoes how he dances. He raises a seductive solitary eyebrow, and I do the tiniest of nods. He grabs my hand and runs us out into Soho Square, occasionally twirling me or lifting me up, the people in the street dodging us as we pass them, used to this kind of behaviour from the performing-arts students next door. We eventually land on a piece of grass on the north side, me on top of him, both hysterical with mirth.

'So you got out of it?' he says.

'Yep. No more Millicent Moore for me. Well, only once

every two weeks, and I can totally deal with that. Got Miss Bond instead.'

'So maybe now you can enjoy yourself and talk Freshers' Ball with me.'

'Sure. What's the plan?'

'So, tomorrow morning, I come over to yours and do your nails and take you for a spray tan.' Alec rolls me off him and props himself up on his elbow.

'Whoa, hang on – spray tan?' I say, alarmed. 'Have you seen me?'

'Yes, Nettie, darling. You're basically reflective.'

'I like being reflective. It's my thing.'

'OK, fine. So you come and wait for me while I have a spray tan. Then we'll get lunch somewhere fabulous (*not* Sue's Kitchen; my treat), go back to halls, open a bottle of fizz and make ourselves beautiful. By the way, what are you wearing?'

I pick a bug off his jeans. 'Just . . . an old dress. It's nice.'

'It'd better be more than "nice" if you're expecting to be Alec Van Damm's arm candy.'

'Don't worry. I won't let you down.'

I'm awoken on Saturday morning by the sound of Alec and Leon singing 'Wake Up, Little Nettie' (in perfect thirds, obvs) outside my door. I let them in, bleary-eyed, and put the kettle on.

'Right. What colour's your frock?' says Leon. He roots through an enormous bag of nail polishes and apparatus Alec's brought with them.

'It's here. You can have a look.' I open my wardrobe door for him.

Alec and Leon both gawp at my dress. It's pale yellow

97

duchess satin with a lace-covered bodice.

'But, darling, it's . . . Dior,' says Leon in wonder, checking out the label.

'It's a hand-me-down.' My voice breaks a little. Mum threatened to come back and haunt me if I didn't wear all her clothes. A lifetime's work, she always said, her wardrobe. I don't usually tell people; they'd probably think I was a freak or something. But then, they probably never had too-hip-for-their-own-good vintage-loving mums.

The boys don't seem to notice. They're too busy fingering the bodice.

'Look at this lacework,' says Leon. 'Ten points for fabulousness. You'll make quite the entrance.'

'Yes, well, hands off; she's mine,' says Alec, slapping Leon's wrist.

'Ooh, harder.'

Alec obliges.

'I think we need the Chanel Opulence,' says Alec. 'My God, Nettie, what are these abominations?' He brandishes my own hand at me.

'Ugh, I know. Beautify them, please, nail-maiden.'

Alec produces a bag of cotton wool pads out of his enormous make-up box and sets to work. 'I'm so happy I get to use this,' he says.

'You can always wear it yourself.'

'Yeah, that'd go down really well with Cecile Duke.' He soaks a piece of cotton wool with acetone and applies it to my thumb. 'I can imagine it now. "Alec, take that filth off your face. You look *completely unemployable.*"'

I laugh. 'I bet you'd look hot.'

'Actually, I don't think *this* needs it.' He circles his beautiful face with his other hand.

There's a knock at the door. Leon jumps up to answer it.

'Hi, guys! Jesus – is this your room? You said it wasn't much better than mine!' Kiki bursts through the door, clearly not impressed. '*And* you've got your own bathroom. And what's behind this door – a kitchenette? Omigod, she's got a kitchenette. Did you know about this, Alec?'

'It's only a sink and a fridge,' I say, sparing Alec. 'I just lucked out, I guess.'

'You just lucked out even more, babe. I'm moving in with you. Don't worry, I don't snore. Cute dress. Where's it from?'

'It's Dior,' says Leon, as if he's announcing a minor royal.

'Nice,' says Kiki, absently. 'Mine's ASOS.'

Alec and Leon exchange a look.

'Don't be snobby,' I say.

'You're the one with the Dior dress, darling.'

'I'm the one with the dead mum.' Gotta stop doing that. Leon looks horrified.

'Is that what you meant by "hand-me-down"?' he says.

I nod.

'Oh, poppet, I'm sorry for being so insensitive.' He reaches over and hugs me.

'It's OK; I'm fine.' Today, anyway.

Alec is now filing my nails with unapologetic vigour.

'So,' says Kiki. She opens the other wardrobe door and sucks her stomach in as she turns sideways to observe. 'Who's going to hook up with who tonight?'

'Karl Townsend, obviously,' says Alec. 'He's desperate for me. I've kept him waiting and now he's gagging for it.'

'You definitely didn't keep him waiting,' says Leon. 'That didn't happen.'

'I let him wank me off in the first week –' Alec dodges as Leon throws a pillow at him – 'but that doesn't count. Hey, if I don't nab him, someone else will. Head boy; already promised a job with Matthew Bourne when he graduates; handsome as hell.'

'What happened to good old-fashioned fun?' says Leon. 'Can't you enjoy yourself without hooking up with someone?'

'Not really,' says Alec. 'There's no thrill without a hook-up. Or at least the potential of one.'

'What about you, Nettie?' says Kiki. 'Got your eye on anyone?'

Argh! Face going red.

'I'll be mainly staying out of Jade Upton and Natasha Bridgewell's way,' I say, trying to cover for myself.

'Why? What happened?' says Leon.

'They're not exactly Nettie's new BFFs, are they, Nettie?' says Alec, who knows everything except the bit about me liking Fletch, although I think he's got an idea.

'They hate me, for some reason.'

The reason being Fletch. *Did* Jade have a thing with him last year? She didn't exactly admit it when I asked her outright in the changing room, but she didn't deny it either.

After several rounds of tea and much buffing and undercoating, the boys are happy that my nails are up to a high enough standard (Kiki's already got a full set of acrylics), and we all set off for the tube. Alec, as an incarnation of Richie Rich, likes to share the wealth with anyone he cares about; he insists on buying us lunch, and then pays for treatments for all of us at a swanky beauty parlour in Kensington ('I've been coming here for years, treasures').

While Alec and Leon are having massages, Kiki and I sit and

drink some fancy water infused with all sorts of fruit.

'Did you ever find out who the mystery piano player was?' says Kiki. 'Ugh, this stuff needs some sugar in it. It tastes like really weak lemon squash.'

'No,' I say. 'I thought it might be Michael St. John, but I'm not so sure now.'

'Omigod, I forgot to tell you!' Kiki almost spills her water in excitement. 'I overheard a really weird conversation between Miss Duke and Michael St. John yesterday. They were talking about you, I'm sure they were.'

'About me?'

'Well, how many other people have a mother who knew Miss Duke and also are brilliant singers?' she says. 'That's what they were talking about. Miss Duke said she hoped your lessons with Steph Andrews were helping to bring out your exceptional vocal talents, and Michael St. John was saying that he wasn't going to push you to sing in class when you clearly weren't ready, after all you'd had to deal with when your mum . . . you know.'

I've noticed people don't like to use the word 'died' in front of me. Like hearing it is going to make what happened somehow worse.

'They haven't heard me sing, though,' I say. 'I might be awful, for all they know.'

'Well, you're not awful, are you?'

'To be honest, I don't even know any more,' I say.

Kiki adjusts her robe, which is threatening to flop open, and curls her feet underneath her on the sofa. 'Maybe it *is* Michael St. John who's been playing the piano,' she says, retying the belt. 'It makes perfect sense, Nettie. That's how he knows you can sing! We should find out.'

'Maybe,' I say, but to tell the truth, I'm not keen on the idea. Why mess with the only thing going well for me at Duke's?

We all amble back to the halls, looking in shop windows on the way. When we finally arrive back, Alec turns to us all seriously.

'Right, you lot. You've got an hour and a half to spruce yourselves and be back here looking gorgeous. Laters.'

He bounds off to his room. I climb the stairs to my corridor, searching around in my bag for my keys.

'Hello, you.'

It's Fletch, looking particularly sexy in a Jimmy Hendrix T-shirt and battered jeans.

'Oh, hi!' Could I sound any more eager? No. No, I couldn't. 'What are you doing here?'

'Dropping off an oboe for someone. This your room?'

'Yes.'

'I was on the next floor. It was grim. Couldn't wait to get a flat. What are you doing?'

'Just getting ready for tonight,' I say. 'Are you going?' Until now, I've avoided asking him about the Freshers' Ball. I mean, I kind of get the vibe that he likes me. But sometimes when we're working on our project, I see him staring off into the distance and I'm pretty sure it's not me he's thinking about. Maybe I'm reading into something that's not there.

'Yeah, I'm on the stick for the third-year show. But I'll see you after?'

'Uh, yeah.'

There's a stray curl over one of his eyes. I imagine wrapping my fingers around it.

'OK, cool,' he says. 'Maybe we can hang out?'

102

'Sure.' My heart is hammering. He's not taking anyone else.

'Great.' He tucks the curl behind his ear. 'See you later.'

'See you later.' My hand's trembling as I put the key in the door. Fletch wants to hang out with me at the ball. Hang. Out. With. Me. At. An. Actual. Ball.

I'm already humming 'Nothing Short of Wonderful' as I close the door.

CHAPTER 11

Duke's at night is a different place. Glowing with fairy lights, it looks other-worldly, seductive. Passers-by, usually oblivious to the vast pale building, stare in, necks craning to see what's going on.

'They think it's a premiere or something,' says Leon. 'So many attractive people glammed up and all in one place.'

'I thought it was *my* job to be arrogant,' says Alec.

'I'm not saying it to be arrogant. It's true. Look around.'

'Omigod, it *is* true,' says Kiki. 'Where are all the *ugly* talented people?'

'I can't believe we're having this conversation,' I say.

'Seriously,' says Kiki. 'He's right. I knew it was hard for poor people to get a place, because I basically am one, but I didn't realize it was the same for ugly people. Do they just not go to college?'

'They probably do,' says Alec. 'They just don't get to go to Duke's. Apart from the odd character actor, that is. And even they've got a certain appeal about them.'

'That isn't true,' I say.

'Fine, Nettie, darling. Find me a minger on Monday and I'll eat my words.'

'I am *not* going to do that.'

'Can't, you mean.'

A roaming waiter hands us champagne in chilled flutes as we

104

edge our way further into the foyer.

'*Darlings*.' Michael St. John appears from the crowd. He's wearing a single-breasted black DJ, which would be entirely unremarkable if it weren't for the fuschia-pink paisley bow tie and cummerbund he's teamed with it. 'Nettie, you look divine. Alec, Leon. And who are you, beautiful? Our paths haven't crossed yet, have they?'

'Hi. I'm Kiki Steadman. I'm on the dancers' course.'

'Pleasure,' says Michael. He pulls her in for an air kiss. 'I think I get you for a class next term. I hope I can convert you to the wonderful world of musical theatre.'

Kiki pulls an I'm-not-holding-out-any-hope smile. 'Can't sing,' she says. 'You wait till you hear me. I'm proper shocking.'

Michael laughs and turns to me. 'Nettie, I hear you're working with Miss Andrews this term. Good news. I think she'll be great for you. Oh, look! There's India Lovejoy. Must dash. Love to you all, my dears.'

He starts waving at an incredibly suntanned middle-aged woman in a red dress who's just coming in the door, presumably a casting director or someone equally important because she's flanked by two young assistants carrying her things. She zhooshes up her pouffy blonde-grey bob and waves him over.

'And that,' says Alec, 'is how to work a crowd.'

Leon shushes him. 'Never mind that. Nettie – you're singing with Steph Andrews?'

'Uh, yeah.'

'She's meant to be amazing.'

'She's a legend,' says Kiki. 'You're gonna learn loads.'

I probably would, if I'd actually been able to sing anything for her. I take a too-big sip of my champagne.

105

'They're going in.' Alec gestures towards the stream of people heading through the doors to the studio theatre. We follow the herd.

The studio theatre has also been transformed. Raised seating has been set up in one half of the studio, the other half having been turned into a working stage, complete with proscenium arch and wings, just by letting down a few curtains and switching on some stage lights I'd never even noticed before. Seating and stands for a small band has been set downstage right. We take our seats, making sure we don't step on anyone's gown. (Most of the girls have gone full-on red carpet, and there's a lot of tulle floating around.)

Although I don't know all their faces yet, the audience seems to be made up of Duke's kids and lots of showbiz people. I don't know who any of them are, but they all have that 'industry' look about them.

When everyone's seated and relatively quiet, the house lights dim. A figure in a tuxedo steps out from the wings and walks centre stage, to general applause. I feel a whoosh in my stomach as I recognize the figure as Fletch. He smiles and nods to the audience, before beckoning to some musicians by the door, who join him stage right and sit down with their instruments, ready to play. It's a bit of a squeeze. Fletch stands up and starts conducting them. A handful of third-years emerge from the wings in their ball gowns and dinner jackets, singing a medley from *Carousel*.

They smile their way through several classics, Fletch's mini-orchestra accompanying them from the corner. I can't take my eyes off him, how the tension in his biceps shows through the jacket as he leads them through 'A Real Nice Clambake'. The energy in his eyes as he shifts tempo. The way his hair bounces when he gets to a fast section.

After two choruses of 'June is Bustin' Out All Over', I become aware of Alec's gaze on me and hastily turn my attention back to what's happening on the stage. I think he might be on to me.

The concert finishes to enthusiastic applause. Miss Duke rises from her seat in the front row like Elizabeth the First and steps on to the stage area. Someone hands her a microphone, which she accepts, beaming, and takes her place in front of the performers. While the applause continues, she looks over the crowd with affection. She's the leading lady in this show, make no mistake.

'I didn't know she had smiling in her repertoire,' murmurs Alec into my ear. I stifle a giggle.

It's true. This Cecile Duke is a different person. I see a glimmer of it when she talks to the pianist in the singing class I have with her, but it's always quickly suppressed when she addresses the class. Tonight, she's radiant. Warmth oozes from every pore as she stands there, resplendent in a black fishtail gown with long sleeves and a glittering net train, looking at us as if we're her oldest friends, a fondness in her eyes I couldn't have imagined existed.

'Ladies and gentlemen, students, *friends*,' she says, her already-clear voice amplified perfectly by the microphone. 'I want to thank you all for being here to share tonight with us. Many thanks to our third-year MT students for putting together so beautiful a piece in such a short space of time –' (Alec told me they'd been rehearsing all term, so *that's* a lie) – 'and to our wonderful Fletch, for his musical direction.'

Cue more applause and a few wolf whistles as a grinning Fletch stands up and nods to the crowd.

'And to our industry friends, I thank you wholeheartedly for taking the time out of your incredibly busy schedules to come and support us at Duke's Academy of Performing Arts. I know our students are excited to meet you.

'This year, we welcome another group of talented individuals into our fold. First-years, congratulations for making the grade. The faculty and I are looking forward to seeing you realize your full potential.

'So enjoy tonight, meet new people, make connections. Have fun.'

She hands her microphone to one of the third-years behind her and quite deliberately strikes up a conversation with a man in the front row. A few people follow suit, and within seconds the entire room is filled with the sound of overeager chatter, as hopeful students fight to get noticed.

The crowd begins to move, in small groups, towards the foyer again, and into the studios on the ground floor. As we make our way into the foyer, music has already started playing. More waiters are roaming around with champagne and canapés. They're all male and without exception have ripped bodies and magazine-cover faces.

'Is this . . . bad taste?' I say.

'It's *hot*,' says Alec. 'I recognize that one from Abercrombie. Wonder if any of them are queer . . .' He disappears into the crowd.

'Tart.' Leon watches him go. 'Come on – let's get a drink.'

He leads Kiki and me through to Studio Four, now less dance studio and more disco joint. Silver streamers have been hung from the high ceiling and coloured lights installed. There's even a glitter ball hanging in the centre of the room. Actually, with all the mirrors, it looks like *three* glitter balls. A glitzy champagne bar has sprung up and a chocolate fountain bubbles smoothly in the corner. I bet a million pounds no one approaches it until Miss Duke has left the building.

'Here's to surviving our first month.' Kiki scoops up three glasses of Veuve and hands them out. 'Well done. We're all still here.'

But for how long? I fiddle with my champagne flute. I'm trying to enjoy myself, but I've got a feeling like the bottom of my stomach has fallen out. What did Miss Duke say? 'Realize your full potential.' I'm not realizing any potential, am I?

I *have* to get something out this week. Even just one line of a song. Just one note. I have to.

I down my drink and reach for another as a waiter passes by, accidentally brushing his well-toned set of abs in the process. He looks at me like I've just groped him.

'Watch out – Nettie's on one,' says Leon. He mock-steers Kiki out of the way.

'It's been a tough few weeks,' I say, hiccupping the word 'few'.

'No, you let it all out, girl,' says Kiki. 'Hey, isn't that the guy who MD'd the show? The hot one? He's smiling – do you know him?'

I choke. 'Uh, yeah, he's in my MT class.' Casual.

'He's coming over,' she says.

I turn away from her and Leon and do a quiet panic burp. Better now than all over Fletch.

'Hi,' says Fletch.

'Hiya,' I say. Omigod. Who says 'hiya' these days? Literally who?

I manage to recover enough to introduce him to Leon and Kiki, who thankfully are very interested in him (funny how hot people are always interesting). As they bombard him with a flurry of questions, I relax a bit.

I shouldn't stare at him. It's just his face is so stare-worthy. And then there's his voice. And his amazing musical talent. And his motorbike.

'. . . he actually turned around and asked which side of his ball bag it was meant to go,' says Leon.

Kiki's in stitches. 'That's hilarious. Who was it?'

'Some poor creature who'd apparently never seen a jock before and had it on back to front. I didn't get his name. I was too busy trying not to stare at his half-protruding knob.'

'Hi, kids.' Alec's returned from the prowl. 'Who's this?' He knows exactly who it is.

'I'm Fletch. Second year. Writers and MDs course.'

'Alec Van Damm,' purrs Alec, putting his hand out for Fletch to kiss.

Fletch obliges charmingly.

'Well, I do declare.' Alec fans himself coquettishly. 'Someone pass me the smelling salts.'

Fletch smiles. I wonder if he's gay. That would suck. How can I find out? I can't *ask* him.

'So, Fletch,' says Alec. 'You'll be in Nettie's MT class – am I right?'

'Yes – actually, we're partnering up for our research project.' He takes a sip of his beer.

'Nettie didn't tell me she had such a handsome friend.' Alec's in full-on Alec mode.

'Maybe she doesn't think I'm handsome.'

Unavoidable Automatic Cheek-Reddening Happening Right Now.

'Not possible.' Alec holds his gaze seductively, ponderously. 'OK. I think we're all dying to know, aren't we, kids—'

'Alec—' I start. I know what's coming.

'. . . if you like the boys.'

'Alec, that's rude,' says Kiki, horrified.

'Only if you're uptight.'

'It's fine,' says Fletch. 'And Alec, I do like the boys, but not romantically. I'm straight.'

'Could've put money on it,' says Alec. He sighs theatrically. 'Well, you can make up for it by getting me a drink. They're serving vodka martinis at the bar in Studio Five.'

'Five martinis coming up,' says Fletch. 'Nettie, could you give me a hand?'

'Sure.' I clock a surreptitious knowing glance from Alec, and deliberately tread on his toe as I pass him to stop him saying anything else excruciating.

Studio Five's got a different vibe. Ella Fitzgerald's grown-up tones echo over the sound system, as if Miss Duke's put her on as a reminder of decorum and class. (Apparently, last year someone was sick all over the Steinway in Studio Six. You can only imagine what happened to *their* college career.) The usual strip lighting has been completely covered in thousands of fairy lights to look like the night sky. Coupled with the bistro tables and chairs set up in cosy arrangements around the floor, they make the studio feel like something out of *The Band Wagon*.

I follow Fletch to the bar, which is three-deep already. Why do I feel self-conscious? I've stood at a bar with him at least three times before. Throw in a bit of atmospheric lighting and the fact that we're at a ball together and I'm a mess. OK, find something to say.

111

'Uh . . . Great conducting earlier.' Poor effort, Nettie.

'I made a few mistakes,' he says. 'I'm much happier on guitar.'

'It didn't show.'

'Well, thank you. Anyway, *wow*. You look beautiful, Nettie. You're stunning in that dress.'

Heart. Thudding. Uncontrollably. He can probably see it.

'Thanks. It was Mum's.' I hope he doesn't think that's weird.

'I've still got Danny's old leather jacket.' OK, so he's weird, too. That's a relief. 'It smells of him. Well, it doesn't really any more, but I still kind of imagine it does. Mum and Dad wanted to bury Danny in it, but I wouldn't let them. We had a massive fight about it. I wear it when I'm writing at home – it makes me feel like he's still here, like he's looking over my shoulder. Makes me want to write better . . . Sorry, by the way.'

'What for?'

'For talking about Danny every time you mention your mum. I'm going to stop doing that.'

'Please don't,' I say. 'It's nice to talk to someone who understands.'

We take the drinks back to Studio Four, but there's no sign of the others.

'They must've got sick of waiting,' I say. 'Do you want to leave them with me?'

'I'd rather stay with you, if that's OK. Unless you're trying to get rid of me?' He puts the three drinks he's carrying down on a nearby table and takes off his jacket.

I try not to think about sliding my hand between his shirt buttons. 'I just meant if you had something better to do.'

'Than talk to the most interesting person in the building? No thanks.'

112

He must like me. Surely he likes me.

'Do you want to go back next door?' he says. 'I preferred the music.'

'Sure.'

We leave the others' drinks and head back next door. Fletch steers us over towards a table in the corner of the room.

We talk for hours.

At one point, I see Alec's face appear at the window on to the outside corridor, but just as I'm about to mouth something like '*Sorry*' and '*I'll get more drinks*', he starts doing a mad interpretive dance, which I read as *Don't stop on my account; he's completely hot* and *We'll talk about this on the phone later.*

'Can I ask you something?' says Fletch.

'Uh, sure.'

'Feel free to say no.'

There's literally nothing he could ask me right now that I would say no to.

'It's just that, I know we haven't known each other long but . . . would you consider writing and performing a song with me? I really feel like it's going to work.'

I hear an imaginary jukebox whirring down to a halt.

'You haven't even heard me sing . . . What if I'm rubbish?'

'You're not,' he says. 'You're so musical, you can't be. And you said yourself the vocal problems were getting better. After you helped me with the end of my song on our first day, it got me thinking – I need a writing partner. One who really *gets* me. You and I have the same musical tastes, same sense of humour – it's a no-brainer for me. Will you do it? I want us to perform it at the Duke's Awards in February.'

'What are the Duke's Awards?' I say cautiously. I *did* tell him my voice was getting better but only because I was fed up saying 'no improvement' every time he asked.

'Big college competition in February. Agents' first look; casting directors get invited as well. The whole college watches.'

No. No, no, *no*.

'I, uh . . .'

'I know it's a bit of a commitment, and you'll have to put up with spending loads of time with me, but I think we can make something beautiful.'

Huge puddles appear as large parts of me melt on to the floor. 'I'd love to.'

'Great! I was nervous about asking you. You sure?'

I'm *not* sure, but I can't resist the offer of more time with him. 'Definitely.'

Something white catches my eye. It floats down and tickles my ear. I put my hand up but can't find anything.

'That's weird. A feather just landed on you,' says Fletch.

'A feather?'

'Yeah, like a tiny white one. Shall I get it off?'

'Uh, sure, thanks.'

He leans in and gently brushes my hair. I can feel his breath on my cheek. He pauses there for a moment, and I hear him breathe in as he lets his cheek rest on mine. I close my eyes.

'Fletch?'

It's the unmistakeable bark of Natasha Bridgewell.

'Hi, Natasha. All OK?' says Fletch, completely unruffled.

'Miss Duke asked me to come and find you. She wants to see you downstairs.'

'What about?'

'Don't know. She just said to send you down immediately.'

Fletch turns back to me. 'Excuse me.'

'Sure,' I say. 'See you later.'

He leaves, but Natasha doesn't go with him. Instead she stands in front of me.

'So, enjoying yourself at Duke's?'

I smile. She tries again.

'I'm *loving* your dress. Where's it from?'

'It's vintage,' I say, standing up. 'Dior, if you really must know.'

She looks me up and down like I've just told her it's from Poundland. 'Nice. Oh, here comes Jade.'

Jade Upland is sprinting over with two red wines in her hand. 'Hi guys – oh, whoops!'

She literally *throws* both of them at me. I gasp, from the shock of being covered in liquid and also from the realization at what's just happened.

'Omigod – I'm so sorry! I tripped! All over your dress. Was it expensive?'

'It's *Dior*,' says Natasha.

'Dior?' Jade whistles. 'You'd better go home and take it off, before it stains forever.' She smiles at me nastily.

'You did that on purpose.'

'No, darling,' says Natasha. 'The coffee was on purpose. This was an accident.'

I'm stunned. All I can think about is Mum. As I try to brush the wine off my dress that hasn't sunk in yet, I'm vaguely aware of Ella Fitzgerald lilting her way through 'But Not for Me'.

A snort of laughter from Jade brings me back to reality and I turn towards the studio door, tears falling out of my eyes. Jade calls after me.

'I'll let Fletch know you've gone.'

CHAPTER 12

'Nettie. Nettie, darling, it's me. Can I come in?'

It's Alec. I get out of bed and plod to the door.

'Nettie, what happened? You were there one minute, and then when I came back, you'd gone.'

With a lurch, I remember the dress. I pick it up off the back of the chair and show Alec the stain. In a panic last night, remembering something about white wine being good for red wine stains, I threw an entire bottle of Echo Falls all over it. The effect is . . . pink.

'Oh my God. You weren't even drinking red wine.'

'Jade Upton threw it over me. Two massive glasses.'

'And you just ran off into the night, like Cinderella?'

Admittedly it seems dramatic now, in the hard October morning light, but yes. That is what I did.

'I panicked,' I say. 'It was Mum's.'

'Of course.' He turns me round and starts walking me towards the bathroom. 'You need to get rid of these panda eyes and get dressed, and I'll google a dry-cleaner who's open on Sundays. Let's get the kettle on.'

I stop to open a pack of wipes for my face.

'Nettie, darling, that's not going to cut it. You look like Trixie Mattel after fourteen gins and a spin class. Plus you stink of booze. Pop yourself in the shower, love.'

I have a thirty-second shower, throw some clothes on and blast my hair.

'Low maintenance,' says Alec approvingly. He watches me smooth my fringe down while downing the tea he's made me. 'Are you going to put some make-up on?'

'Should I?'

'Of course.'

'Sexist.'

'Not possible. *I* wear it.'

'You said you didn't like wearing it because it spoils *this*.' I trace an emphatic circle around his face.

'Well, don't tell Leon, but I never go anywhere without my Touche Éclat.'

We're in St Martin's Lane, in a little coffee house just by the Noël Coward Theatre. I've dragged Alec in there because it's after twelve, I haven't had caffeine yet, and I feel a bit shaky. I've got a strong black Americano in my hand and Alec is sipping a macchiato. The dress has been delivered to the dry-cleaners, with the promise of it returning pristine. Alec dealt with it, giving them the whole sorry tale and, of course, ending up with a huge discount. Turns out, my life's a sob story. Still, if it gets the dress clean.

'So, what did you get up to at the party?' I say.

Alec gives me a well-honed pout-smile, like a drag queen saying 'new shoes'.

'Oh, I got right up to Karl Townsend. He was loving his life last night with me on the dance floor.'

'Did you kiss?'

'Darling, we shagged each other's brains out. I'm surprised you didn't hear us. We were still at it at five this morning.'

'You don't look bad, considering.'

117

'It's called a post-coital glow.'

'Glad someone got some action last night.'

'You know that Jade Upton's had a thing for Fletch for over a year now?' says Alec, completely out of the blue.

'Er, really?' I say, trying to sound uninterested. It comes out like someone trying to sound uninterested.

'Come on, Nettie. It's me you're talking to. I knew on the first day when I watched you talking to him on the stairs.'

'Are you literally always watching me? And how could you possibly know? *I* didn't know then.'

'Some things are just written in the air. I'm good at spotting love at first sight.'

I do what is meant to be a disbelieving guffaw, but it sounds more like I'm choking on my coffee.

'It's fine. We're just friends.'

'For *now*.'

'If Jade wants him so much that she's going to make my life hell, then she's welcome to him,' I say. 'I'd rather not have the hassle.'

'You don't mean that,' he says, ready to fight me as always, 'I can see how much you like him.'

'OK, fine. I do like him. But at the moment, I've got bigger stuff going on,' I say.

'Like what?'

'Er, like the fact that since I got here, I haven't been able to sing a single note out of my face. Like the fact that Miss Duke has got me going to remedial lessons with Steph Andrews and I've only sung one note for her. The fact that Millicent Moore is determined to, like, 'get' me or something. Like . . .' I trail off.

'Like what?'

'Like, I miss my mum. I can't get it together. I don't know what the hell is wrong with me.'

'Just give yourself some time, Nettie.'

'That's what I'm afraid of. I don't have time.'

'Nettie! Wait.'

Fletch catches up with me as I come out of a particularly dynamic jazz class.

Yay. Bright red beetroot face with a sweaty top lip and a soaking wet fringe.

'What happened to you at the Freshers' Ball?' he says. 'I came back upstairs and you'd vanished.'

'Didn't Jade tell you?'

He looks blank.

'No, of course she didn't,' I continue. 'After you went to see Miss Duke, she threw red wine all over Mum's dress, and I had to go home and try to get it out.'

'She threw it on you?' Fletch looks incredulous.

'Well, according to her, she tripped and "spilt" it, but it's not the first run-in I've had with her.'

'I'm sure she wouldn't do something like that on purpose,' says Fletch.

I begin to feel irritated.

'Well, of course you wouldn't see the bad side of her, because she's always nice to you.'

'I'm not sure what you mean.'

'Oh, never mind. It's done now,' I say. 'Did you have a nice evening?'

'I spent most of it looking for you.'

I look at him disbelievingly.

'Maybe if I had your number, I could call you next time, instead of wandering around college like a lost puppy,' he says, handing his phone to me for me to type in my number. 'I can't believe we've been working on that project for three weeks and we haven't got each other's numbers.'

Instant mood lift. 'You've got my Snapchat.'

'You're never on Snapchat.'

'OK, fine.' I start putting in my number.

'I'm going to call you right now, so that you've got mine,' he says, watching me type.

'Just text me.'

'No way,' he says. 'You might have given me a fake number.'

I roll my eyes and hand him back his phone. He rings me.

'See? Ringing.' I show him the display on my phone.

'Answer it.'

I give him a *Really?* look, but answer it anyway. 'Hello?'

'Hi,' he says, looking at me and grinning.

'Are we done?'

'I was just calling to see if you'd like to have coffee with me after college.'

'Oh, wait – the line's breaking up . . . I'd . . . l . . . ha . . . becau—' I hang up.

'Very funny. So was that a yes?'

'Remember when you promised we could write and sing a song together?'

I swallow my vodka and Coke and take a breath. Coffee has turned into drinks, and the room's a bit spinny.

'I remember.'

'Tomorrow lunchtime work for you?'

120

'Sorry.' I pretend to look in my phone's calendar. 'I promised Alec I'd help him with something.'

'OK, the next day then.' He moves his chair next to me to see.

'Sorry.' I put my phone face down on the table and stare at it.

'Next week?' He waves his hand to get me to look him in the face.

'It's just—'

'Nettie, what's wrong? Have I done something to annoy you?'

Oh God, those eyes.

'No. No, of course you haven't.' I shift in my chair.

'Then what is it?'

'I just . . . I'm still finding it hard to sing at the moment.' He looks surprised. 'Look, I'm trying to sort it. God knows if I don't, I'll get kicked out of Duke's. I promise I'll sing. Just give me some time, OK?'

He looks at me for a few seconds, then nods. 'Sure. But when you do sing, I want to be the first person to hear you.'

One day at the beginning of November, something weird happens. I go to the studio theatre after college hours, and the mystery pianist is there. They're playing the intro to 'Everlasting' from *Tuck Everlasting*.

Tentatively, I join in, and manage to sing the entire thing without my voice faltering. It's reassuring. I was beginning to doubt I could still do it. I leave quickly, but halfway to the tube I realize I've forgotten my phone, so I double back.

When I reach the studio, the dividing doors have been pulled back to reveal the other half of the room, where Jade Upton is sitting at the piano, a book of sheet music in her hand. I stop dead.

'What are *you* doing here?' she says, emphasizing the word 'you' like it's something she trod in.

'I, er . . .' What *am* I doing here? Oh, yes. 'I forgot my phone.'

'Well pick it up and get lost,' she says. 'I'm trying to practise.' She looks at me suspiciously as if about to say something else, but seems to think better of it.

'Right.' I grab my phone off the floor. As I go to leave the room, something occurs to me. 'What are you practising?'

'None of your business,' she says.

I wasn't really expecting a useful answer, but it does give me time to catch a glimpse of the book she's using. It's *The Best of Miller and Tysen*.

I leave Duke's as quickly as I can and speed across Soho Square, ignoring the crisp auburn leaves blustering about my face, focusing instead on how quickly I can google the songwriters, already filled with dread at what I'm going to find. Hands shaking, I type in their names.

> Miller and Tysen are an American musical theatre songwriting team consisting of composer Chris Miller and lyricist Nathan Tysen. They started collaborating in 1999 at New York University's Graduate Musical Theatre Writing Program. Together they have written the scores to *Fugitive Songs*, *The Burnt Part Boys*, *The Mysteries of Harris Burdick* and *Tuck Everlasting*.'

Tuck Everlasting.

Shit.

Jade.

*

'Jade Upton's your mystery piano player?' says Kiki in disbelief.

We're huddled in the halls kitchen corner together while Kiki makes a Pot Noodle.

'That's just . . . so many levels of wrong. I thought we'd decided it was Michael St. John?'

'She had the sheet music for the song I'd just sung,' I say quietly, looking around to make sure no one's listening. A second-year called Seb has got Neil Patrick Harris belting out 'Angry Inch' over the speaker and is doing a complex and fairly sexually charged *pas de deux* with Alec, much to everyone else's delight. 'It's got to be her.'

'OK – but three things,' says Kiki. 'One, I very much doubt she can play the piano. For a start, she doesn't look like she can. Two, if she could play as well as you say this person does, she'd be living her life boasting about it every five minutes.'

'What does a person who can play the piano look like?' I say.

'Not like Jade Upton.' She stirs a sachet of something brown into the Pot Noodle. 'And three, she's like the most self-centred person ever. There's no way she'd be into any sort of collaboration, least of all with another female – you know, her *competition*. She's a second-year on the MT course. She's never giving another Duke's girl the chance to practise. I still think it's Michael St. John.'

That does make sense, I guess. But I can't shake the look she gave me when I went back to get my phone. If anything, it's put me off going.

The next few weeks pass without too much happening. Millicent Moore keeps the abuse to a minimum, and fortunately only delivers it in a whisper when no one else is listening, which saves me a lot of embarrassment. I keep out of Jade Upton's way, and she leaves me alone.

I haven't been back to the studio theatre to sing since I discovered her at the piano. I know it's probably not her, but it makes me feel weird.

Miss Duke still never *quite* gets to my turn when she teaches the advanced singing class, and Michael never seems interested in picking me to sing alone in MT. After Kiki told me what the two of them said about me, I guess they're just giving me a break, but it still feels like I'm sitting on a ticking time bomb. I manage to get a couple of notes out with Steph, nothing more. It's frustrating because Fletch keeps asking me when we can start writing together and I have to keep putting him off.

Then a brilliant thing happens. I get laryngitis.

It's so bad that I can't speak. The doctor forbids me to sing and signs me out of all vocal lessons. I'm only allowed to watch and take notes. I hope it lasts until I sort my head out.

I go up to Steph's room to tell her I can't do her sessions for a while.

'Actually, Nettie,' she says, 'I wasn't going to do singing with you today.'

'What were you going to do?' I croak-whisper.

'I was going to ask you to tell me about your mum.'

'What about her?'

'Tell me one memory you have of her. Can you still do that with no voice?'

'Er, sure,' I say. 'Like what?'

'Anything you like.'

'Um . . .' It's hard to think of something when you're put on the spot.

'Tell me what her favourite thing to do was,' says Steph.

That's easy.

'She loved going shopping. Mainly in charity and vintage shops. We used to go to Brick Lane a lot. We were the same size, so we used to get a load of stuff and try it on together. Mum had a knack for spotting a neglected designer jacket and getting it for a bargain. She loved anything vintage. Our house was full of stuff she'd picked up, like old gramophones, and lamps made from weird things like petrol cans, and toys from the Fifties – stuff that was completely useless and of no value any more, but that she thought would look cool.'

'What happened to all that stuff?' says Steph gently.

'Most of it's in boxes at my grandmother's house,' I say.

'I'm sorry – are you OK talking about this?'

'Yes – it's nice to talk about her. I don't get to much. When she died, she wanted me to stay with my grandmother. I had to clear out our house so that it could be let out. The money from that pays for my college hall fees with a bit left over to live on.'

'Who sorted all that out for you?'

'I did it all. There was no one else to help me.'

'And your grandmother . . .'

'Hates me. Mum didn't speak to her for nearly twenty years, although they seemed to reconcile in the days before she died. I don't know what was said, but the upshot of it was that I had to go and live with her. It's the only way I could've come to Duke's. But it's kind of torture living so close to my old house and knowing I can't go there. I try not to think about it too often because it hurts so much. I miss it.'

There's a pause while I think about Mum pottering in the

kitchen, dancing to records while she made dinner. Steph watches me.

'Are you having counselling, Nettie? There are groups you can go to; people you can see—'

'I went to one session, but it wasn't for me.'

'I just think you need to talk about this with someone.' She folds her hands on her lap. She's wearing a black jersey maxi-skirt and khaki jumper.

'I'm not going to counselling.' I pick a flake of lipstick off my top lip. I didn't get time to reapply after hip hop.

'It might be helpful.'

'I'm not going.'

'Well, listen,' says Steph. 'I think you've got a lot of stuff to let out before you can release your voice. I'd like you to tell me one thing about your mum before we start every session. Just a memory. Good or bad, it doesn't matter. Just something. Then at least you're talking. Would you be up for that?'

'OK.' I guess I don't mind talking to Steph.

With my new ready-made get-out-of-jail-card laryngitis, I decide to ask Fletch when we can start writing the song. I broach the subject after MT one afternoon.

'You want to start now, when you've got no voice? I've been asking you for ages.'

'Well, I can still write lyrics,' I say in an enforced whisper. 'And hopefully my voice will come back before the Duke's Awards.' I mean that. Maybe my voice *will* just come back when the laryngitis clears up. It'll all be like a bad dream and I can start again from scratch.

*

'Do you like that?'

'Yeah, but it needs to go up more. Sort of . . . swirl upwards.'

We're working in the library after college. It's just us there. (Why *would* anyone else be in the library after hours?)

'*Swirl* – is that a technical term?' He grins at me.

'Yeah – haven't you heard of it?' I throw my pen at him. 'Call yourself a musician.'

He plays it again but this time it's different. Swirlier. 'Is that better?' He looks up from his guitar.

'Yes!' I don't even bother hiding my amazement. 'Totally. How do you do that?'

'Do what?'

'Just – just *know* what I mean.'

'Maybe you're a good communicator.'

I roll my eyes. '*Swirl?*'

'OK – you're not.' He thinks for a moment. 'Maybe . . . we're just good together.'

'Yeah.'

Neither of us speaks for a few seconds.

'You know, I'd love to hear what it sounds like with both of us singing,' he says. He notes the latest changes on his paper.

'As soon as it's back, you'll be the first to hear it.'

Despite my non-voice, we finish the song in a little under a week. Fletch is keen to write more. What I really should be concentrating on, I know, is getting my voice better. The thought of spending more time with him is just too much to resist.

The laryngitis starts to improve after a fortnight. I try to hide it, but it's kind of impossible.

'Do you want to have a go at singing this together?' says Fletch one afternoon, after a particularly noisy explosion of laughter from me.

'I don't think my voice is quite there yet,' I say, panicking.

'OK. Tomorrow. And I'm not letting you off.'

Halfway through an exercise, I randomly burst into tears.

'Nettie, what's wrong?' Steph stops playing. It's not been a good lesson so far.

'I'm sorry, Steph, I hate myself for crying, it's just that . . . having laryngitis was a relief. I had an excuse for not being able to do it. Now I just *can't* do it.'

'Nettie. Nettie. It's OK. Just breathe.' She waits for me to calm down. 'OK . . . Tell me a song your mum used to like.'

'I won't be able to sing it, if that's what you're hoping.'

'Don't get ahead of yourself. Didn't you say she played you a lot of Sondheim when you were a kid? Were there any particular songs of his that she liked?'

'She loved 'Being Alive' from *Company*.' I can't bring myself to mention 'No One Is Alone'. It's too raw.

'Great song. I've got it here somewhere.' She begins searching through the shelves and shelves of sheet music. 'Ah, here it is. Right, I'll play – you speak.'

'You want me to *speak* it?'

'Yup.'

'OK, fine.' I take a breath and begin. My brain seems to know it's a song because it makes my voice suddenly very quiet.

'Perfect. Continue,' says Steph, as I speak the lyrics over the music.

'Now close your eyes,' she says.

I shut them tight.

'Great – now sing!' shrieks Steph. She starts hammering the piano like it's just admitted it's been cheating on her. Pencils fly off it at an alarming rate.

My whole body starts shaking and my throat constricts. It's pitiful. My voice is barely a whisper, no louder than when I had laryngitis. I shake my head at Steph and shrug, but she points at me ferociously and screams, 'Don't you dare stop! I don't care how terrible it is!'

I finish singing (let's call it that, but it was really more of a whimper). I crumple into a chair.

'Nettie,' says Steph softly, closing the lid of the piano. 'It's a start.'

'I can't—'

'I'm not expecting miracles. I just needed you to commit. And you did.'

'I don't normally sound like that,' I say for the umpteenth time this term.

'We'll get there,' she says. She's still kind, even when I must really be frustrating her. 'Baby steps. That was huge for you. Well done, Nettie. We're done for today. Keep practising whenever you can be alone. The sound's still coming out when you're on your own, isn't it?'

I nod, despite not having been to the studio for weeks. *Thanks, Jade.*

'Great. Then it's just a matter of time. We've just got to unlock whatever it is that's stopping you. I'm not giving up on you, Nettie.'

I meet Fletch in the library after college.

'Ready?' he says. He starts getting out stacks of our notes.

'Actually . . . can we just ride somewhere?' I can't write songs today.

He nods and grabs his jacket.

Ten minutes later, we're pulling out of the square. We ride the same way as usual, towards Green Note, our cafe in Camden, and I think he must be taking me there, but then he bears left at the top of Regent's Park and rides along past the zoo.

He stops in Primrose Hill, on the edge of the park.

'Shall we just sit and look at the view?' he says.

It's exactly what I want to do. I love that he knows that.

We sit on the grass for about half an hour or so, watching the sun set over central London. All the usual suspects are there – the Shard, the London Eye, Centre Point – but to me they look novel because they're all the wrong way around, with the Eye on the right of the picture.

'Best view of London,' says Fletch.

I look up at him. 'Nope.'

'You know a better one?'

'*Way* better.'

'Come on, then.' He gets up and reaches for his helmet. 'Where are we going?'

'Saarf London, naturally.'

'Cool. Where?'

In my opinion, the best view of London is that sneaky glimpse you get just beyond the top of my old road in Crystal Palace. You're walking along past Crystal Nails minding your own business and suddenly the land falls away and you can see all the way to the Shard. But it's a poky viewpoint, and not everyone gets it. So I take him to Greenwich.

We ride down past Russell Square, across Waterloo Bridge,

130

down the Old Kent Road (actually quite fun when you're on a bike and can beat the traffic), through New Cross, and up the hill to Blackheath. Fletch parks right outside the Royal Observatory, and we climb over the little barrier separating the car park from the grass.

'Wow.'

'Ever been here before?' I say.

'No. OK, you win.'

We sit at the top of the hill and look out over Greenwich and the city.

'Mum used to bring me up here with my friends on Sundays,' I say. 'We used to roll down the hill.'

'Do you still see your friends?'

'I haven't seen them since my Duke's audition. It feels like too much time has passed now to get in contact. I guess it might be weird. They're all at uni, anyway.' I pull a piece of grass out of the ground and shred it with my fingers.

I think Fletch senses it's a sore point. 'Wanna roll down the hill?'

It's almost dark. There's probably about twelve minutes of fading light.

'Go on, then.'

It's a colder experience at the end of October in the early evening than during August at midday, but the ground's dry, and our bike-proof clothes offer some protection.

'Aaaaaagh!' I hear Fletch yell from behind my head as we gather speed, and I see land, sky, land, sky, quicker and quicker until my head nearly explodes. I roll to a stop near the bottom, giddy and laughing, and see Fletch a little further up the hill, having come to an early halt.

'I can't believe how fast you went.' He's out of breath.

'I've done that roll a hundred times,' I say. 'Well practised.'

'I'm going to plead lack of hills in my childhood for being so rubbish,' says Fletch. 'That was fun.'

We climb back up the hill and lie down next to each other, our heads propped up against our bike helmets.

'Mum loved this view,' I say.

He holds my little finger in his. I put my head on his shoulder and he doesn't move away.

After the sun has finally set, Fletch takes me back to the halls and I invite him into the common room. Alec and Leon are in there, among others, and they beckon us over.

'Where've you been?' says Alec.

'Greenwich,' I say.

'Have fun?'

'We – we rolled down the hill.' I catch Fletch's eye and we both start laughing.

'Like that, is it?' says Alec.

I give him an imploring look that I hope Fletch doesn't see. Alec ignores it.

'Seriously, you guys are like *always* together these days,' he says. 'Have I missed something?'

'We're writing together,' I say quickly, looking at Fletch.

Alec comes between us and slings an arm around both our shoulders. 'Well, that sounds divine. I'll be first in line for your debut album.'

'Omigod, me too,' says Kiki. '*The Songs of Nettie and Fletch.*' She does a your-name-in-lights hand movement.

'*The Songs of . . . Netch,*' says Alec. The two of them burst into peals of laughter.

'*Alec*,' I say, kicking his shin with my heel, my face scarlet with embarrassment. I swear he's got some sort of scary access to my brain sometimes.

Fletch laughs. 'I like *Netch*. It's got a ring to it.'

I'm glad Alec is still between us because the heat coming off my face is solar.

'Have you eaten?' Leon comes to the rescue. He's always mopping up after Alec.

'No – we forgot,' I say gratefully.

'Will you be joining us, Fletch?' says Alec in a Mae West voice. He takes his arm away from my shoulder, fingers his own chest and looks up at Fletch through his eyelashes. 'We're getting pizza, you know.'

'I've got to meet my flatmate, actually.'

'Well, bring her along,' says Alec.

'Well, I—'

'Alec, it's fine if Fletch has plans,' I say. Inside I'm praying he'll stay.

'I could message him. He's only round the corner,' says Fletch quickly.

'Ooh, *him*?' says Alec. 'Even better.'

Fletch disappears down the hall (while I beg Alec not to embarrass me further), returning a few minutes later with a tall, incredibly good-looking second-year boy.

'Have you guys met Luca?' says Fletch. 'He's on the writers course with me.'

'Only briefly.' Alec smiles dreamily at Luca like a teenager from the 1950s meeting the high school heart throb. 'Hieeee, Luca. Lovely to meet you.' He cocks his head to one side and extends his hand, which Luca takes, laughing.

'Hi, Alec. Good to see you again.'

'This is Leon, Kiki and Nettie,' says Fletch. His eyes flicker back to Luca as he says my name, too quickly for anyone to notice. But *I* notice.

'Hi, guys. Nettie, I'm going to be joining a few first- and second-year MT sessions after Christmas. You're in that class, aren't you?'

'Yes,' I say.

Alec groans. 'MT gets all the hotties these days,' he says.

'Aren't you and Fletch working together on your MT history project, Nettie?' says Luca, clearly trying to steer the conversation somewhere else. 'What are you studying again?'

'Ghost singers.'

'Good topic,' he says.

'Don't you think it's ironic that Debbie Reynolds had one for *Singin' in the Rain* when she was playing the part of an actress dubbing for someone else?' says Leon.

'I hadn't actually thought about that before,' says Luca.

'Of course you hadn't,' says Kiki. 'Because you're not a massive geek.'

'Until you get him started on Bernstein,' says Fletch. 'I thought *I* was a music nerd until I met Luca.'

'Are you writing anything at the moment, Luca?' says Kiki.

'I'm working on a revue – a collection of songs all linked by a common theme. Some of the third-year MTs are going to perform it next year, hopefully.'

'Wow. We'll definitely come, won't we, Nettie?' says Kiki. 'OK, who wants tea?'

She takes orders and drags me over to the kitchen corner, which is fast becoming our place for secret chats.

'So?' she says, her eyebrows practically in her hairline.

'So *what*?' I say.

'Luca?'

'Oh. He's cute, I guess?'

'Babe, that goes without saying.' She empties the fur out of the tatty common room kettle and refills it. 'I meant do you think he could be the piano player?'

'No, he couldn't be.'

'Nettie, think about it!' She grabs my cheeks and pulls my face close to hers. 'He's on the writers course, so he plays instruments. He's a musical theatre geek – Fletch said so.'

'With logic like that, it could be half the college,' I say. 'This place is full of musos. Anyway, I've still got a suspicion it's Jade.'

Kiki lets go of my face and starts fishing in the cupboard for tea bags. 'But Luca's so hot,' she says, ignoring my comment. 'All that silky black hair and those massive arms.'

'What's that got to do with anything?' I hand her a chipped mug with a faded *Grease* logo on it that looks about as old as me.

'It just makes this so much better!' She scrapes a bit of dried soup off the rim and pops a teabag in. 'Nettie, don't you want to find out for sure?'

I think for a second. 'No. I could've looked through the doors any time, and I didn't. Anyway, I've only been back once since I saw Jade in there.'

Thankfully, I was still able to sing, but it was all I could do not to conjure up images of Jade, sitting at the piano on the other side of the dividing doors, oblivious that she was playing for her worst enemy. (Logic tells me it's not her, but I still feel weird about it.)

'You really think it's Jade?'

135

'I don't know. I think I'm done with it all now anyway.'

We make the drinks and take them back to the boys. Alec has found an old acoustic from somewhere and is making Fletch play Christmas songs in A Minor on a classical guitar while he improvises Flamenco. Luca's bashing out intricate rhythms on the guitar case, and the entire common room is clapping in time and cheering. I smile, glad that Fletch gets on with my friends. Then I remember he's not actually my boyfriend and my heart gets a bit lower in my chest.

On the last day of term, I come in for registration, and Alec points out my name on the board in the foyer.

'Cecile Duke wants to see you at ten.' He puts a hand through his well-groomed hair.

'Omigod. What about?' My heart starts hammering violently.

'Either something very good or something very bad. Best hope it's the first one.'

At ten o'clock I climb the stairs to Miss Duke's office, feeling like I'm about to hear the verdict in the trial of my life.

Theatre paraphernalia lines the walls. I spot Elaine Paige, arms raised, smiling at me in her white ball gown as I pass an old poster for *Evita*. Is she willing me on or laughing at my fate? As I reach the door, the secretary pops her head out of the adjoining office.

'Antoinette? Miss Duke's been delayed by a few minutes. She's asked that you wait in her office for her.'

I nod and push the door open.

Cecile Duke's office is everything I could have imagined, and would have imagined, if I hadn't been too busy worrying about what she was going to say to me. It's like the star dressing room, complete with ensuite bathroom, lounge area and grand piano, as well as an ornate oak desk. The walls, like the stairs and landing, are almost completely covered with theatre and film posters, adorned with messages such as, 'To Miss Duke, Thank you for everything. I wouldn't be here without you', and 'Miss Duke, you have been an inspiration to me'. It's a room filled with joy and success, not the fear and dread I'm currently feeling. There's a paperweight on the desk that catches my eye. It's a little glass dome with two ballerinas inside. I pick it up. It feels cool in my hand and somehow calming.

The door opens abruptly. I hastily put the paperweight back, but it's all too obvious what I've been doing.

'Good morning, Miss Duke,' I say, my crimson face incriminating me further. Great. I'm now going to be bollocked for being light-fingered as well as whatever else I'm in here for.

But nothing can prepare me for what Cecile Duke says next.

'Your mother gave me that.'

What?

'My mother?' I look down at it again.

'On our opening night of *Oklahoma!* – our first job together.' She walks around the huge oak desk and sits down. 'So strange that you were drawn to it.'

'In Copenhagen?'

'Yes.' She seems surprised.

'I'm sorry—'

She holds up a hand to silence me. 'You knew we were friends?'

'Only recently. I . . . I found an old photo of you together.'

'I didn't think she would've told you. We were as close as you can be, until Ana . . . well, life gets busy as you get older. I had Duke's, and she had you. Now, I imagine you know why you are here.'

137

'I—'

'Let's not pretend it's going well for you at Duke's.' She leans forwards and clasps her hands on the desk. 'I've had reports from your singing and musical theatre teachers that you haven't sung a note since you arrived. I know there's a vocal issue, and I know you're working with Miss Andrews to resolve it. But I need to see progress – quickly. I've got a list, as long as Ute Lemper's legs, waiting for someone to drop out.'

'I know. I'm –' I want to concentrate on what she's saying but all I can think about is Mum.

'Need I remind you that you are in a very privileged position?'

'No. I'm sorry, Miss Duke.'

'Don't be sorry. Just get it together.'

'Yes, Miss Duke,' is all I say, when what I really want to do is ask her a million questions about Mum. But her manner prevents me.

'That will be all.'

'Thank you, Miss Duke.'

I close the door softly behind me. I *know* she was holding something back. What was it she said? *We were as close as you can be, until Ana . . .* Until Ana *what*? Miss Duke never finished her sentence. Did they fall out? It would explain why Mum never mentioned her. I guess I'll never know now. I round the stairs slowly, my brain overflowing with questions.

The questions will have to wait. That meeting with Miss Duke was a warning. I have to sort myself out. There's too much at stake now.

CHAPTER 13

I delay going home for Christmas as long as I can. Kiki went straight back to Southend, and Alec flew to France for Christmas yesterday. Leon's still around for an extra couple of days. We mostly stay in the halls, or mooch around town – Leon's idea of shopping is way different to mine, as I realize when I watch him buy a pair of sunglasses in Harvey Nics that cost three hundred pounds. (He looks amazing in them, but for that price I'd be wanting them to belt out 'I Dreamed a Dream' to me while dancing the Mistoffelees solo.) He begrudgingly lets me drag him into a couple of charity shops, but it's not the same as when Alec comes because Leon won't try on any of the sparkly stuff with me.

'What are you doing for Christmas?' I'm tucking into a huge bowl of pasta Leon's made. We're sitting in an otherwise empty common room.

'Going home tomorrow,' he says. 'Mum's working right up until Christmas Eve, so I'll be alone until then. Dad's home from Germany for a week, then off again somewhere. We don't see that much of him.'

'At least you get Christmas with him.'

'Yeah.' He stares into his pasta.

'Don't you get on?'

'We do . . .' He lifts up his glasses and rubs the bridge of his nose. 'It's just that I have to pretend to be straight for a week.'

'He doesn't know you're gay?'

'Mum didn't even know until this year,' says Leon. 'She made me promise I wouldn't tell Dad.'

'Why?'

'I just don't think he'd take it well. My parents aren't very liberal about things like that. Dad would disown me if he found out I was gay.' He looks miserable.

'But your mum knows?' I say. 'And she's OK with it?'

'Yes – as long as she doesn't have to talk about it or acknowledge it in any way,' says Leon matter-of-factly.

'And you're OK with *that*?' I say.

'No, not really. I'm living a double life.'

'That sucks, Leon.'

'I know – it's vile. If you can't be yourself to your family, what's the point of anything? But what can I do? Estrange myself?'

'I don't know,' I say. 'That's a heavy secret to be carrying around.'

'It feels lighter when I'm here,' says Leon. 'Being able to have a fresh start at Duke's was a relief after years of hiding who I was. When I saw what Alec went through at school, there was no way I could come out there. I only told Alec two years ago, you know – just to have *someone* who knew. But I felt like a fraud, especially after Alec was so honest about his sexuality. It takes a lot of guts just to say, "To hell with it. This is me."'

'Your dad helped Alec, though.'

'He didn't know Alec was gay.'

I go round the table and hug him from behind his chair. He reaches up and puts his hand on my arm. I guess it's not just me who isn't looking forward to Christmas.

*

140

They're closing the halls today for the holidays. I guess I'd better pack. Alec Snapchats me a picture of a snow-covered chateau with the message '*So, so bored.*' I send him one of me doing a duckface in the kitchen.

The common room's quiet. I can hear the echo of a vacuum cleaner from the upstairs corridor. In the absence of an audience, I try singing a couple of notes. They come out, albeit quietly. This gives me courage to attempt the start of a song. It's not bad. Not *really* bad, anyway.

When it's there, it's good – it just keeps cutting in and out. It might be the laryngitis. My speaking voice still does that when it's tired. But still, this could be the start of something. Maybe next term I'll get my voice back.

I can't believe it's Christmas Eve tomorrow and I'm only just going home. It's sad that I'd rather stay in empty, grotty halls than be anywhere near my grandmother, but there you go. I collect my suitcase from my room and head down to the tube. Maybe I could stop off in Covent Garden on my way. Anything to shorten the stay at home.

My phone pings as I walked down past the Barbican. I stand up my case for a second to look. It's Fletch.

Fletch:
Back in town today. You around?

Yes. *Yessssssssss.*

I'm just leaving the halls. Where shall I meet you?

Chappell's in fifteen?

> Give me half an hour. I'll be
> the one with the suitcase.

?

> Going home later ☹

??

> Long story.

I've got all day.

He has all day. Yay, yay, yay. I inwardly skip all the way to the tube. I'd be doing *actual* skipping if it weren't for the heavy suitcase I'm dragging.

I get to Chappell's to see Fletch in the entrance looking at a white grand piano. He grins up at me and pretends to walk into the glass door.

'I'm sorry – I was looking for someone cool?'

'Merry Christmas to you, too.' He kisses me on the cheek. It tickles. I've never seen him with stubble before – he looks older. 'I've been downstairs geeking out over all the guitars I can't afford.'

'Got time to look on this level?' I say.

'Definitely. I'd happily spend all day in here. I love this place.'

I love it, too. Vast portions of my early teens were spent in here, rifling through the books with Mum, looking for the score

142

of a new Off-Broadway musical we'd recently discovered, or some difficult-to-get-hold-of vocal selection. We'd start in Chappell's and then head down to Dress Circle on Seven Dials to buy the CD (Mum didn't trust iTunes). The last time I came here was with her. I close my eyes and inhale, remembering how much she loved it.

I don't buy a lot of sheet-music books these days. I just download it like everyone else. But there's something about just being *in* here, surrounded by all the millions of dots dancing around all the thousands of pages, that I adore. It feels more musical somehow.

It kind of makes me forget about Fletch as I rummage through the shop. Ah, amazing – an Adam Gwon songbook . . . And – what's this? A Joe Iconis selection? These are going to be great. (When I can sing again, obvs.)

I'm flicking through a Sara Bareilles piece when I feel him behind me. Actually, I think I *smell* him first – not in a creepy way, just in a leather, clean washing and deodorant way. His hand lightly touches my waist.

Omigod, he's going to make a move on me, right here in the sheet-music department of Chappell's. This is, like, the most romantic thing ever.

Oh, wait.

It's less of a move; more of a manoeuvre. He's trying to squeeze through the aisle without touching the old man on the other side who's looking at *Lloyd Webber Greats*. Not that the old man looks as if he'd mind being touched by Fletch at all; on the contrary – he's been checking him out since we came in here.

'Sara Bareilles?' Fletch has disentangled himself from Mr *Lloyd Webber Greats* and is now standing next to me, reading over

143

my shoulder. I fight the urge to lean my head back on his chest. 'The *Waitress* writer?'

'Yes – you need to get into this. Pre-*Waitress*.' I hand him the other book. 'And this. Some great stuff here.'

'Looks tricky to play. Might be good to practise, though.'

'Do you practise a lot?'

'As much as I can,' he says. 'It's kind of essential if I want to MD. Are you buying it?'

'Yep.'

'Let me go halves with you.'

'Why?'

'Then I won't feel so bad about nicking it.'

We pay for the books and leave. It's one of those first cold days in London that makes everyone look like they're breathing out cigarette smoke. I shiver.

'You cold? Here.' He offers me his elbow. I take it, and he pulls me close to him.

We walk around Soho and Covent Garden for the next hour or so, taking it in turns to pull my suitcase, looking in shop windows and occasionally going in. Mostly we just talk. I don't ask Fletch what time his train is. I don't want to remind him.

'How are you on skates?' he says out of the blue. We've stopped to look at the enormous Christmas tree in the piazza.

'Roller skates?'

'Ice skates.'

'Er, I'm OK.' I'm not OK; I'm dreadful.

'They've got ice skating at Somerset House. Wanna go?'

'Sure.' Is this turning into a date?

It feels like one ten minutes later as Fletch takes my hand and whooshes me around the rink. I'd expect Alec to be amazing at something like this. But Fletch? No way. He's actually *really* good. He reminds me of Gene Kelly roller-skating through Manhattan in *It's Always Fair Weather*. If I didn't know him better, I'd half expect him to break out a casual tap dance.

I'm terrible on skates, so I don't discourage the help. Also, I like the feeling of his hand in mine.

'Wow, you're good,' I say, as he steers me round a corner, neatly avoiding two kids and a grandad.

'You sound surprised.'

'I am, a bit.'

'Don't laugh,' he says, 'but Danny and I were on the local street-hockey team for a while.'

I snort. 'That's hilarious.'

'Actually, we were cool.'

'*Were* you?'

'*So* cool.'

An hour whizzes past. I mean, like, I blink and it's over. He'll be catching his train back home soon, which means *two weeks* without seeing him. I doubt he'll come into town again.

As we come out of Somerset House, I'm fully expecting this to be goodbye. But he doesn't go; instead, he starts walking over Waterloo Bridge with me.

'Doesn't your train go from King's Cross?' I say.

'Yes.'

'Well, that's in the other direction.'

'I know. I'd just prefer to hang out with you a bit longer, if that's OK.'

'OK.'

We stroll along the South Bank, Fletch pulling my case for me, and head all the way up to Borough. We stop for a moment to watch a busker. Fletch puts his arm around my shoulders. Which you'd *think* would be enjoyable, but is actually exhausting because now I can't breathe. (I don't dare, in case it reminds him that he's got his arm on me and he pulls it away.)

What is *with* me? I've *never* been like this with a guy.

Maybe I've just never felt like this about anyone.

We keep walking and eventually stop at a bar covered completely with fairy lights and a full-on window display with a sign reading: 'Mulled-Cider Happy Hour'.

We go inside and find a little booth, my suitcase sealing up the end. It feels cosy, intimate. I notice it's dark outside. We've been walking for two hours.

Four drinks later, our fingers are almost touching on the table. I can feel the heat from his hand.

'OK. Truth or dare,' he says.

'Truth.'

We've been playing this game for about fifteen minutes. So far, Fletch has licked the bar and let me put my lipstick on him (hot); and I've let Fletch put an ice cube down my back (fairly sexual) and asked a famous actor for his phone number (success times two: got the phone number and hopefully made Fletch jealous).

'Do you have a crush on anyone at Duke's?' he says.

I pause. 'Yes.' I probably shouldn't have said that but I'm feeling light-headed. My foot touches his under the table. He doesn't move it away.

'Who?'

'That wasn't the question. You drink.'

'Dammit.' He drains his mulled cider.

'OK, my turn,' I say. 'Do you?'

146

'I might have wanted a dare.'

'OK,' I say. 'I dare you to take all your clothes off right here.'

'You got me,' he says, laughing. 'I'll take truth. Although I just want you to know that I've got nothing to be ashamed of physically. But, you know, the winter and . . . well, the police . . .'

I laugh. 'So *do* you have a crush on anyone?'

Omigod, we're like a pair of thirteen-year-olds.

His middle finger touches mine.

I should just kiss him.

'I—' He falters.

We're so close I can feel the warmth from his face as well now. He wants to kiss me, I know he does. What's stopping him?

He leans in to me. Our lips are nearly touching now. What am I waiting for? I should just go for it. I'm ninety-eight per cent sure he'd kiss me back . . .

'Do you think it's possible to be into two people at the same time?' says Fletch, moving back suddenly.

Erm, *whatttt*?

'Pardon?'

'Do you think it's possible to have feelings for two people at once?'

'*Do* you have feelings for two people?' I say, moving my hand away slowly.

'No. I don't think so. Probably not,' he says. He picks up his cup again and drinks the last drop. He already finished it a minute ago; it's like he just needs something to do.

Probably not? What does that even mean?

I don't say that, but I can tell he knows I'm thinking it.

'I can't really explain it,' he says heavily. 'I just mean . . . Not being able to get someone out of your head? Like they just live in

147

there, and you can't get rid of them?'

'You can't stop thinking about someone? *Two* people?'

'Kind of. It's weird.'

The sick feeling in my stomach is only half down to the cider. I'm naive. Of *course* he doesn't like me. Or if he does, then he likes someone else more. It makes sense – he's never made a move, and most of the time we've spent together has been writing . . . Maybe *that's* it. He just sees me as a writing partner. I've obviously mistaken it for something else. Thank God he said it before I let him know how I felt. But the moment we had, just then – our lips were literally millimetres away . . . He *must* have felt something.

'That *is* weird.' I feign detective-level curiosity, not wanting him to see the obviously written-all-over-my-face devastation. 'Who—'

'I'll tell you what we need,' he says. 'We need a change of scene. Let's go across the road to that bar over there. It looks like they've got live music.'

'Actually, I should really think about going.'

'Come on. Please.'

'I need to go, Fletch.' I stand up and move my suitcase aside to give myself room to get out.

'Nettie.' He stands up too.

'What?'

'At least let me walk you to the station.'

'No, you'll miss your train.' Breezy, breezy.

He holds on to my face and looks straight into my eyes. We both know he's messed this up. It's just easier if neither of us says it.

He kisses my forehead and lets me go.

148

My head's racing as I walk to the tube. All the way home, I try to figure out what's going on, but it's difficult after a lot of alcohol. I've got that sicky achy feeling that comes just before a hangover, and my heart seems to weigh more than normal, which I don't think is anything to do with being drunk.

I can't get it straight in my head. He *nearly* kisses me at the pub, just before telling me he can't stop thinking about someone else.

Did he nearly kiss me? Maybe I imagined it. Maybe I just projected what I wanted to happen on to him.

No, it definitely happened.

I feel confused. I can't even phone Alec because it's so late. I get my phone out, thinking I'll message him, when something pops up from Fletch on Instagram.

Best day ever.

There's a picture of the ice rink. He must've taken it before we got on. I hit like and put my phone down. We had such a good time today. He was *definitely* flirting with me in the pub. But what did he mean about having feelings for two people at once? Jade Upton flashes across my mind. Please, not her. Anyone but her. She did hint that they were together last year. And she tried to get me away from him at the Freshers' Ball.

It might not be Jade. He's never mentioned her in that way. Maybe he's got a girlfriend back home. Oh God, what if he *does* have a girlfriend, and *I'm* the girl he's got feelings for . . . What if *I'm* the other woman?

I should just stay away from him.

I *will* stay away.

Whoever this other girl is, she can have him. I'm not doing this any more.

It's just going to be hard now.

Now that I'm completely and hopelessly in love with him.

I try to open the front door quietly, but for some reason I can't get the key in until the third attempt. It opens more suddenly than I'm expecting, making me fall into the hallway in a sort of jazz-split position.

Shit. Shit, shit, shit. I bet she wakes up. OK. If I can just get to my room—

'Did you have a good term, Antoinette?'

I peer through the kitchen door. My grandmother is sitting at the table, sipping tea from a bone-china teacup and doing the crossword. She's wearing her dressing gown and slippers, but her hair and make-up are immaculate.

'Er, not bad,' I say, uncertainly. I'm waiting for a big bollocking about staying out until the day before Christmas Eve.

'There's tea in the pot,' she says coolly. She doesn't look at me.

'I'll probably just go to bed, if that's OK,' I say warily.

'Just make sure you're up by eleven tomorrow. I'm hosting lunch for the ladies from the tennis club.'

That's fine by me. I can move back into Mum's house when I graduate. We just have to tolerate each other until then, and only in the holidays. Then we'll be rid of each other forever.

I slump off upstairs and throw myself on to my bed. It's two whole weeks until I'll see Fletch again, and that's almost too much to bear. I'm so tired, but everything's jumbled up in my brain and I can't sleep.

I want my mum.

CHAPTER 14

Alec:
Happy Boxing Day, gorgeous.

You too. How's France?

Ennuyeuse. How's 'Auntie'? ;)

Hardly seen her. Apart from
Christmas Day. That was fun.

???

She invited a load of friends round for lunch.

She didn't cook it

She hired caterers

I like her style.

I only said that in case you think she's some
benevolent granny who bakes for people. She
was nice to me while her friends were here and I
had to pretend to be the doting granddaughter.
She barely spoke to me after they left.

Jokes, Nettie. What's her problem?

I think she's still sulking about me going to the Duke's audition without her. She was looking forward to swanning around college with everyone looking at her and telling her she was wonderful. All the teachers would have recognized her.

She's still angry?

Your audition was like seven months ago

I KNOW

My poor darling girl

I might come back early

PLEASE come back early!

I'm losing it

OK, I'll see what I can do.

What I don't tell Alec is that by eight o'clock on Christmas evening I was curled up on the sofa, sobbing in front of *It's a Wonderful Life*. (Mum and I used to watch it every Christmas. Now I watch it alone.) Auntie stayed upstairs. I've no idea what she was doing up there; I don't care.

I fell asleep with the TV on and a tissue stuck to my nose.

*

Auntie goes out early on Boxing Day, leaving quietly before I wake up. I stay at home and listen to a playlist of angry songs I've put together to help me get over Fletch. Stuff that'll make me hate him.

'I Don't Remember Christmas' from *Starting Here, Starting Now* comes on. It doesn't make me hate him, though.

It makes me hate Mum.

This is my second Christmas without her, and I've begun to treat it as normal. It's like I've forgotten how things were before. How she'd lift me up when I was little to put the ballerina on the top of the tree, dipping me down into *arabesque* as I hung it; watching her make her terrible Christmas cake that I loved anyway; belting along to 'Christmastown' from *Elf the Musical* at the tops of our voices.

It's been nearly two years since she died. It feels like another lifetime that we were together. How could she leave me like that? Sometimes I miss her so much it stings like a brand-new burn. Even now it's still raw.

I rip the earphones out of my ears and throw them down on the bed. Then I roll on to my front and scream into my pillow.

Auntie's the only family I have; the only person related to Mum as much as I am; my only biological link to her. I want to like her, but God, she's vile. No wonder Mum didn't speak to her for years.

I remember bumping into a woman when I was out with Mum once.

'And this must be Antoinette,' said the woman, in that semi-interested way that strangers do about children of acquaintances.

'Yes; she's eight now,' said Mum. There was a quaver in her voice.

'Short for her age,' remarked the woman.

After we'd gone our separate ways I asked Mum who the lady was.

'That,' said Mum, 'was your grandmother.' She said nothing else until we got home.

In all the time I lived there with Mum, it was the only time we ever saw my grandmother. Her house was on the other side of the park from us – the Sydenham side – but it could have been a different country, for all we saw of her. She phoned Mum once a year on her birthday, and after the incident in the park, she began to send me small presents on mine. But that was it.

I wish I knew what had caused them to be estranged for so many years. I kick myself for not asking more questions.

Like, for example, who my dad is? I did ask her once, but Mum said she didn't know. I bet she did. It was hardly going to be one of those *Mamma Mia* situations where she'd slept with several men in the same week and had no idea which one was the father – although thinking about it, I know so little about her life before me, I guess it could be.

God knows I could do with a dad right now.

I'm in the kitchen with a pain au chocolat and a coffee when my grandmother comes in, dressed in sequins and a gigantic fur wrap. Four days at home and it's beginning to do my head in.

'I'm going out,' she announces. She says it as if it's obviously to somewhere very important/glamorous/interest-piquing.

'Great. Where?' It's easier to let her tell me than spend the next few weeks being ignored because I didn't show enough interest.

'It's a benefit ball at the Waldorf. Don't wait up. I'll get a car home.'

She probably means a cab, but 'car' sounds grander. 'OK. Have fun.'

'Antoinette, should you be eating that?' She points to the pain au chocolat.

'Why shouldn't I be?' I say, instantly riled. After living with her for nearly a year, I know what's coming.

'Well, you do start back at Duke's soon, and I'd hate for you to be left out of any ballet events they might be holding.'

'Two things, Auntie: number one, I'm not at Duke's to do ballet; and number two, I am *not* fat. I'm not even a tiny bit fat. And *even* if I was, who cares? I'm allowed to be. It's rude to tell someone what they can and can't eat.'

'I'm not saying you're fat, darling; I just think you shouldn't go back to Duke's all soft around the middle.'

I can feel the blood in my ears. There's enough of this at college. I don't need it at home as well.

'So, what *are* you saying? That I shouldn't eat?'

'Look, this is getting silly,' she says. 'I only said—'

'You want to pick me to pieces because it makes you feel better about yourself. You spent your life surrounded by people who encouraged you to be relentlessly critical, not only of yourself, but of everyone else around you. What I eat is none of your business. In the seventeen years that I knew her, Mum didn't once comment on how I looked, apart from to tell me that I was beautiful or strong. So I don't see why I should start taking this crap from you.'

My grandmother looks affronted. She draws herself up and turns towards the door. I shout after her as she walks out.

'Oh, that's it, walk out – make your point. Is this what Mum had to put up with for all those years? No wonder she hated you.'

She says nothing, but pauses at my last words before opening the door and slamming it shut behind her.

That's it. I'm not staying here. I bung a load of stuff into my case, forming a vague plan to head into town. I've no idea what I'll do when I get there because the halls are closed over the holidays and I can't afford to stay in a hotel. I don't care; I have to get away from that woman. Jesus, no wonder Mum grabbed the chance to go to Duke's aged sixteen.

My phone rings just as I step on to the train.

'Nettie, *ma cherie*.' It's Alec.

'I might lose you in a minute.'

'OK,' he says. 'I'm back, treasure. You busy?'

'You wouldn't believe how busy I'm not.'

'Great. Meet me on Floral Street in forty-five.'

'OK, but I've got my suitca—' The line goes fuzzy.

'What?' he shouts. 'You're breaking up.'

'I said, I've—'

The line's dead. What did he say? Floral Street? Is that the one behind Long Acre?

The lifts at Covent Garden are out of order. Well, there's one working, but the queue reaches down the platform. I should've just walked from Charing Cross. There's no way I can drag my case up the (193, according to the sign) steps to get out. I do a one-eighty to go back to Leicester Square, accidentally tripping up a commuter. She scowls and tuts at me.

'Nettie!' Michael St. John's jogging down the platform, waving frenetically and wearing a fur hat and a full-length Cossack coat.

'Hi! Happy Christmas.'

'And to you, darling girl. Need a hand with that?'

'I was going to go back to Leicester Square.'

'No, come on. I'm strong, for an old man.'

We start the climb fairly cheerfully, but after about eighty steps it starts to get hard.

'Look, here's a little nook,' says Michael, panting. He takes off his hat and dabs his face with it. 'I'm going to have to stop for a minute.'

'Thanks for helping,' I say. 'You really shouldn't have.'

'I *really* shouldn't,' he says. 'Someone pass me a stent.' He takes a few gulps of air. 'So, good holiday? What's the plan for today?'

'I'm meeting Alec.'

'With that?' He points to my suitcase.

'Been away.' Please don't ask where.

He doesn't. He picks up my suitcase again and we start lugging it up the remaining stairs.

'I meant to say, Nettie . . . Fletch told me you'd written a song together and are hoping to enter it for the Duke's Awards.'

'Uh, yes – hopefully.'

'I know there've been some issues –' he's still panting – 'but I'm really looking forward to hearing you sing.'

I smile, but it's a veneer-thin smile. 'I hope that'll be soon.'

'Yes, me too. And, Nettie,' he says, 'if you ever need a friendly ear, you know where my office is.'

After trudging up and down Floral Street twice, I eventually find Alec waiting outside the Royal Opera House stage door (where else?), complete with a gigantic tartan scarf and a wistful look in his eyes like he's on a shoot for *Bazaar* or something.

'Darling, how are you? You look gorgeous. You're so thin.'

I'm conscious of how much weight I've lost, so his comment irritates me. My ribs are protruding. 'Is that how we measure gorgeous now?'

'Oh, Nettie. Of course it is. That vintage parka is just hanging off you. Didn't your grandmother feed you over Christmas?'

'No. She tends not to.'

'Good way to get skinny every holiday.'

'I'd prefer to be fed.'

He realizes he's touched a nerve. 'Oh, Nettie, you know I'm just joshing. Come on, let's go to the flat.'

'What flat?'

'My mum keeps it for when she's in London,' he says. 'But she rarely is. So you can stay there with me, if you like. Will your grandmother mind?'

'I honestly don't care,' I say. 'Where is it?'

'Here, actually.' He gestures to a building just down the road. We've meandered across Long Acre without my even noticing.

I gaze up at a recently converted penthouse above a huge shop. 'Omigod, you're so posh.'

'One of my many charms.'

Inside, it's stunning. The living area and kitchen are open plan and decorated in tasteful shades of grey and white, the only splashes of colour coming from several large modern paintings on the walls. Lavish curtains adorn the huge windows. I can see right into Pineapple Dance Studios.

'Wow, you can see them dancing.' I lean on the windowsill and peer through the studio windows across the road.

'I know. I get free class right from the comfort of my own living room,' says Alec. 'They hold a lot of the big auditions in that studio. It's marvellous to watch people's faces when they get cut.'

'Alec, that's mean. You won't be saying that—'

'When it happens to me one day?' he interrupts. 'Nettie, we both know it won't.'

I mean, he's right – it probably won't, but his cockiness is still unbelievable.

'So, why don't you live here?' I say. Sometimes it's best to change the subject with Alec. 'While you're at college, I mean?'

'Believe me, darling, it's not for want of trying. Mum wanted me to stay in student halls for my first year. Some crap about "getting to know new chums", or something equally wanky. I'll be here next year, if I can convince her to give it up.'

The thought of something existing that Alec wants but can't have is vaguely appealing.

I'm grateful to have somewhere to live for the rest of the holidays. We mainly stay in, watch telly and eat: all the things I couldn't do at home. It's good to have a change of scene. It makes me miss Mum less. It's not that I don't *want* to think about her; it's just that sometimes it's good not to have the constant ache in my stomach, and being with Auntie is an ever-present reminder of what I've lost.

'Chill out. They're not going to serve you for ages.'

'Watch.'

It's New Year's Eve. I don't know how, but Alec has convinced me to go out. We're in G-A-Y, along with half the gay population of London, or at least the ones brave enough to face the crowds. I've no idea what it looks like in the daytime, but tonight it's a ceiling of purple lights and a throbbing carpet of sweaty bodies.

I play along, half knowing he's taking the piss. But Alec does something extraordinary. He stands up tall and starts to radiate . . . *gorgeousness*. I suddenly notice the blueness of his eyes, the sharpness of his cheekbones, the subtle muscle tone under his T-shirt.

I've heard people on documentaries say that Marylin Monroe could go from anonymous bystander on the street to Hollywood goddess without even changing her hair. She would simply *glow*. Well, here's Alec, doing the same thing. The people in front of us seem to be aware of something happening behind them and turn around. They part to stare at him, and Alec steps through the gap. I feel like I'm watching it in soft-focus slo-mo. It repeats three times until Alec's at the front of the queue. It's like magic. Or Moses, or something.

'What can I get you?' A barman appears out of nowhere.

'Hi, gorgeous,' says Alec. He throws me a subtle wink. 'Can I have four apple sours and two double vodka and Diet Cokes, please. And your number.'

The guy giggles hysterically and writes his number on a beer mat, before serving Alec his drinks and moving on to the next customer without charging Alec a penny, who smugly hands me the sours and steers my arse with his free hand to a corner of the club.

'Alec—' I say.

'Bollock me in a minute.' He puts the drinks down on a ledge. 'Let's do these first. Down in one.'

'In one?'

'Yes, come on. On eight.'

'What?'

'It's a Duke's thing – *five, six, seven . . . eight!*'

160

The sours seem to go straight from the back of my throat to my brain. My head feels warmer, softer. But not soft enough not to say anything about what just happened.

'You're not going to call that guy.'

'Of course not.' He hands me another shot.

'Alec, that was—'

'What? Mean?'

'That poor boy,' I say. 'You totally used him to get a free drink.'

'Don't tell me you've never done that,' he says.

'I've never done that.'

'Well, you should. You've got a good face for it. Oh, Nettie, don't be cross with me,' he says, stroking my cheek and turning it into a hair adjustment. 'He knows I'm not going to call him. I mean, look at *me* –' (I snort, but it's unconvincing even to me) – 'and look at *him*. Unfortunately, that's the currency here. Anyway, it's not about the shag. It's about the *potential* of a shag. I've probably done him a favour.'

'How, exactly?' I fold my arms.

'Imagine you're a sweet but fairly average-looking barman. Then imagine the hottest guy in the club walks up to you and asks you for your number. How are you going to feel? Great, right? Fabulous, even. On top of the world. So, you work your shift, and then when you knock off, you're still feeling great. *So* great, in fact, that you manage to pull someone else who's possibly also a bit out of your league. Listen – what's the sexiest thing in the world?'

'Talent?' I say, immediately thinking of Fletch.

'Confidence,' says Alec. 'Although I agree talent comes in a close second, along with devastating looks and a washboard stomach. So, I get free stuff, he gets a shag with someone else and a huge ego boost. Maybe even meets the love of his life. Everyone's a winner. Including you, who just downed that second tainted shot I hustled. Come on. Let's dance. "Freestyling with Alec" is an experience you won't forget.'

He drags me on to the dance floor, turning the drag into a twirl and a backbend dip. I laugh in spite of myself. He's right – dancing with him *is* unforgettable. I mean, obviously Alec's amazing, but he makes whoever he's with brilliant, too. He grabs me and shouts 'Salsa!' in my ear. I've never done any salsa before, but I have to pick it up quickly because he's flinging me all around the dance floor within seconds.

We've partnered each other before, in jazz *pas de deux* class, but this is all improvised. It's fun.

I'm giddy but I don't care – not even when Alec throws me to another boy, shouting to him, 'It's OK – she's good!' Before I know it, I'm whirling round with partner number two while Alec disappears.

He's a good dancer. And so is partner number three, and four, and five . . .

After a while, I look around for Alec. He's on his way back from the bar, this time with a whole tray of drinks. Panting, I slip out of my current squeeze's grip and trot over to him.

'*You* got these,' says Alec.

'What?'

'I just pointed you out, and they gave them to me. Fierce dancing, Nettie. You're really whipping your head.'

'I'm *so* thirsty.'

'Here.'

I down it, grimacing. 'Blimey. What's that?'

'Malibu and Coke,' says Alec. 'I thought it would be refreshing.'

'I need some water.'

'Jesus, Nettie, you're as bad as Leon. Such a square.'

'Talking of Leon, he told me that his dad doesn't know he's gay.'

Alec sips his drink and looks at me expectantly. 'And?'

'Well, isn't that horrible for him?'

'Yes.' He downs the rest of his drink. 'Come on, drink that. I want to dance.'

'Is that all you've got to say?'

'What else is there to say? Life's not like Duke's, Nettie. It's not all a big melting pot of creativity and acceptance.'

'I know, but—'

'Sometimes it's shit being gay. Let's go.'

Alec's bleak acceptance shocks me. And I feel that maybe there's more he's not telling me. I haven't got time to ask him anything else, though, because he's whizzing me back to the dance floor. There's more booze, and dancing, and booze – I think I even spot Alec snogging someone in the corner at one point. By the time Alec drags me through the corridor and into another room, I'm like a rag doll.

'So what is it with you and Fletch?' Alec plonks me down at a table.

'You've been planning this convo,' I slur, swallowing a burp.

'I wouldn't have to if you weren't so uptight.'

'OK, *okaaay*. I basically love him.' Agh, I can see four Alecs. If I focus on one of them, I might be able to look at him properly.

'He's head over heels for you,' says Alec.

Through my drunken haze, I almost feel a spark of excitement at his words, but the feeling's dulled by several rounds of shots and an immediate sense of gloom.

163

'He's not,' I say. I think I'm slurring.

'The way he looks at you, though—'

'He's in love with someone else.' I leave what I think are a few seconds to let that bombshell settle, but I might have zoned out, because Alec jabs me in the ribs.

'Ow!'

'So?'

I tell him what had happened at the end of term. I think I just about cover the important points, but Alec looks confused.

'Hang on, you're not making sense. So, he took you on a date ALL DAY and then when you were just about to kiss, told you he had the hots for someone else?' says Alec.

I think he's angry. He sounds a bit shouty.

'Kind of. I can't really remember right now. It was something about having feelings for two people at once.'

'Charming that he wanted your opinion on the matter,' says Alec. 'But there's someone else? Who? Who, Nettie? We have to beat her!'

I try to give him a withering stare but my eyes are half closed anyway so it might not be reading.

'I dunno who,' I say. 'Probably Jade Upton. She's been sniffing around him since September, and God knows how long before that, because they're both second-years. They were at Duke's together for a *whole year* last year before we even got here. They've got history.'

Alec snorts. 'She's a talentless twat. There's no way he'd go for her.'

'It *can't* be her personality he likes.' I think I'm leaning on my glass. 'Maybe he just fancies her.'

Alec shrugs. 'If you like pramface.'

164

I'm too pissed to argue. I slump down with my head in my hands, closing my eyes to the blur around me.

'He keeps messaging me –' Alec lifts my head up to hear me better – 'He hasn't said anything about that night; it's like that whole thing didn't happen. He's all, *Our project* this, and *Let's write more songs together* that. But I've definitely stepped back now.'

'There's nothing wrong with a bit of competition,' says Alec.

'For you, maybe. I don't want someone who wants someone else.'

'You should've just shagged early on,' says Alec. 'Cleared the air.'

I ignore this. 'He wants me to sing with him at the Duke's Awards. Our song that we wrote. But I can't.' My voice breaks. I can feel my eyes starting to leak.

'You can't what?'

'SING!' I shout. 'I can't sing. It's like my voice is there, but it won't come out. I'm trapped in my own body. One day Cecile Duke is gonna turn around and tell me to get out. "Get out of my establishhment," she'll say. "You're taking up the place of someone who could actually *get* somewhere at Duke's. You're a wassteofsssspace, Nettie."'

'But she hasn't actually *said* that to you, has she?'

'She might as well've said it.'

'Oh, Nettie, don't cry.'

'I'm NOT CRYING!' I yell. Snot and tears pour down my face in an indistinguishable stream. 'I'm just frustrated. What's wrong with me? Everyone else seems to be able to do it.' On the word 'everyone', I make a sweeping gesture to emphasize my point, which promptly knocks three empty glasses off the table.

165

They smash, causing a 'Wehey!' from the people nearby.

'Come on,' says Alec. 'We need a change of scene.'

'Where are we going?'

'Next door. Karaoke bar.'

'I'm not—'

'Singing,' he says. 'I know. Come on.' He grabs me and pulls me back through the club to the front doors.

Shit.

Fresh air.

Gonna vom.

I throw up violently in the gutter by the corner of Frith Street, in front of several perfectly groomed men sipping coffee outside Bar Italia, who shake their heads and turn away in disgust. Through my dripping hair I can see the people queuing to get into Ronnie Scott's across the road looking over with interest. Then I must have blacked out because I can't remember a thing after that.

CHAPTER 15

I wake up to the sound of the kettle boiling and Alec riffing his way nicely through an Ariana Grande song.

OK. I feel OK. Although sound seems to be hurting my ears.

I open my eyes. I'm on the sofa. The room is swimming sideways at me, drifting from left to right. Or maybe I am; I can't be sure. I close my eyes again but I still seem to be moving. My head feels like someone's dropped *The Complete Works of William Shakespeare* on it and there's a sharp pain in the cheek I'm lying on. Feeling around, I realize my earring has embedded itself in my face.

The effort of removing it makes my stomach lurch. I sit up quickly in dreaded anticipation of what's to come.

'The bucket! I have a bucket!' shrieks Alec, *jeté*-ing over to me like Carlos Acosta and thrusting a basin under my trembling chin. I barf obediently into it while he holds my hair back.

'Good girl. You'll feel better after,' he says soothingly.

I eye him suspiciously mid-spew, but he looks sincere.

'Omigod,' I gasp after the thirteenth retch. 'What have I done to myself?'

'You need carbs.'

'Ugh. You're kidding. I need a shower. If I can walk that far.'

'I'll make you a bacon sarnie while you're in there.'

I shuffle to the bathroom, bucket of spew dangling in my limp hand.

Alec's right; I do feel better after a good ralph. I emerge from the shower ten minutes later, clean, devoid of make-up, but with a rather large octagon-shaped indentation in my right cheek.

'Good look.' Alec's busying himself over a pan of bacon. 'Better than the sight I came into this morning, which was a cross between Sweeney Todd and Bette Davis in *What Ever Happened to Baby Jane?*'

'Such a specific and well-referenced insult from one so young.' I hand him the clean bucket.

'We try.' Alec watches slyly while I gip my way through breakfast.

'What?' I say, paranoid.

'Do you remember last night?' he says.

'I remember humiliating myself outside Bar Italia. Did we come home after that?'

'Not exactly.' Alec reaches for his phone. 'We made a movie.'

'What are you talking about?' This is too much on a hangover.

'Just watch this.'

He scrolls through his phone until he comes to a series of videos. It looks as if I'm in all of them, a blurred thing with black hair and a sequinned dress in various states of motion. I hope I didn't ruin another dress. I got that one from Beyond Retro.

The first video's outside a club.

'*Okayyy. So, apparently we're going to a karaoke bar. Ka-r-a-oke. Alec's going to sing and I'm going to daaance.*'

'I'm so pissed!' I say. 'I don't remember that.'

'I'd have thought you'd remember giving your finest Kate Bush around the lamp post.'

I'm swaying from side to side in what seems to be some sort of interpretive dance, using a lamp post and a bin to steady myself.

Alec narrates from behind the camera.

'*And then we're going to swap, aren't we, Nettie? I'm going to dance, and you're going to sing.*'

'*Except that I doooon't sing.*'

'*Apart from tonight. Tonight you do.*'

I look at Alec suspiciously.

'Ring any bells?' he says.

I shake my head.

The next video is in the bar. It's hard to make out what we're saying because of the background noise, but we seem to be discussing songs. I'm apparently coming round to the idea.

'Are you ready?' says Alec.

I don't know why, but I feel a pang of nerves go through my stomach.

He shows me the next video. It's me again, staggering up on to the little makeshift stage. I grab the mic like Cha Cha after she's just won the Rydell High dance-off and grin at the crowd.

'*Hi, I'm Nettie, and I'm going to sing "Don't Rain on my Parade",*' I announce. The crowd woo and cheer. I don't seem fazed – on the contrary, I put my hands out to hush the crowd as the backing track starts up. Weirdly, it works.

The video stops. Alec flicks quickly through the remaining movies.

'Agh. Phone ran out of memory. So I missed a bit while I deleted loads of selfies, no mean feat when you look as good as I do. Ah, here we are.'

This one comes straight in at the bridge. I *look* a bit strange, swaying around trying to be Barbara Streisand and mistakenly grabbing the mic stand for support (it gives me none), but I sound fine.

Sounds like me.

I watch the rest of the video, waiting for my voice to break or for me to start crying, but neither happens. On my last note, the room erupts. I smile and promptly pass out into the crowd. I hear Alec say '*Fuck!*' as the phone drops into his lap and films the floor for a few seconds while he runs to get me.

'What happened? Did I hurt myself?' I feel my body to see if I'm sore anywhere.

'Fortunately you fell straight at a couple of bears, who caught you and helped me get you home,' says Alec. 'No cab driver would touch you. So we carried you across Charing Cross Road and back down to Seven Dials. Nice guys. They came in for a coffee. Geoff and Jack.'

I rub my cheek. 'I can't believe you got me to sing.'

'Forget that,' he says. 'I can't believe how amazing your voice is, Nettie. What are you playing at? You've *got* to sort this out.'

'I'm trying.'

'Well, try harder. Your public needs you, and I can't afford to buy you nine vodkas every time.'

On our way to the halls the day before term begins, Alec announces he's adding me to his plan.

'What plan?'

'My plan for world dance domination and sexual happiness. I've added an addendum, which states that I will help you find your voice and make the man you love realize he loves you too.'

'I'm an addendum?'

'You're privileged to be in there at all. You're not exactly taking control yourself, are you? I must say, Nettie, you have a pretty shabby attitude towards the matter of your own life.'

'Lucky for you you're so perfect.'

He stops and looks at me. 'Do you honestly think I haven't had my fair share of shit to deal with?'

'You always seem so together.'

'Yeah, well, I've had to be. Look, I know I joke about it, but it wasn't easy, what I went through at boarding school.'

'I'm sorry. I didn't mean . . .' I feel terrible. It must have been horrendous for him.

'I know you didn't,' he says. 'I was illustrating a point. It didn't help that I was dealing with all my own shit while helping Leon through his. I don't know who had it worse. Me, for being out, or him, for being in.'

'I'm sorry,' I say. 'That's tough. For both of you.'

'It *was* tough. So do me a favour and write me a song about it. And fucking well sing it.'

Duke's has ramped up a notch for the new term. The teachers are more demanding, and the classes a lot more difficult. My first commercial lesson renders me unable to walk up and down stairs for three days without clinging to the hand rail for support, and my neck is so stiff I can't turn my head to the left for at least two.

Millicent Moore is apparently annoyed I didn't die over the holidays and takes great pleasure in pointing out my every fault.

'Antoinette, you've got shoulders like Quasimodo,' she says in my first lesson back with her. I've lost so much weight that I think even she realizes calling me fat is ridiculous (or maybe she sees it doesn't bother me). Instead, she's resorted to insulting random body parts. Apparently I've also got 'feet like bananas' and a '*penché* like Superman' (which definitely *isn't* a compliment).

171

I almost admire her creativity. 'Fat' is by far the most effective insult around here, so she's digging deep.

Natasha Bridgewell has decided to join the class and guffaws loudly at every insult. I want to wipe the little smirk off her face, but Kiki catches my eye and shakes her head the tiniest fraction, which stops me. She sticks her foot out as we all pile towards the door after *révérence*, just in time for Natasha to trip over it and go head first into the rosin box, covering herself in sticky white powder. Kiki is clever enough to do it when I'm ahead of of Natasha *and* a bunch of other girls bearing witness so she can't blame me. I mean, she'd definitely try.

'Thanks.'

'Small victories,' says Kiki quietly. 'Let's give it a minute before we get changed, in case she's in the changing room. I'm not sure you should let her see you when she's this angry. Man, how'd you get to be this skinny over Christmas? I could feel my arse jiggling around in the allegro section just then.'

'My grandmother starves me. I'm trying to put some weight on so that my clothes fit me again. But back to you. You *are* joking, right? You know you're gorgeous?'

'*I* can feel the difference, even if you can't see it,' she says seriously. 'I want to be a commercial dancer when I leave Duke's. Have you seen the dancers in music videos these days? They're, like, *tiny*. Also, did you see that video Richard Danes put up on Instagram of open auditions for his new TV show? There were girls dancing in their bra and pants. Their *actual* pants. At an audition. Not even as part of a costume. By *choice*. And let me tell you, no one with even a millimetre of wobble got kept after the first round. It's unachievable.'

'Well, remember you're an amazing artist.' I'm not sure I'm

comfortable with 'unachievable', but it's not worth pointing that out when Kiki's on one.

'Yeah, well, unfortunately for me that also means being perved over and fat-shamed.'

Fletch catches up with me in our new acting-through-song class (I'm relieved to see on my timetable that it's replaced my singing lessons with Cecile Duke). Michael St. John is delivering a lecture on the importance of status. Fletch comes in late, sits behind me and whispers, 'Hi, Nettie,' in my ear while he fumbles about for a pen in his bag.

I turn around and mouth '*Hi*' back, feeling the familiar ache in my stomach that's been there since Christmas. As I turn back to Michael, I notice Natasha Bridgewell watching us. She's still got white powder in her hair from her fall in the rosin tray earlier. She nudges Jade Upton, who's sitting next to her, and whispers. I deliberately don't look as they continue their obviously-about-me conversation. All the same, I can't help feeling that they're up to something.

'. . . and what we find is that whoever has the power in the scene – the upper hand – has the higher status,' says Michael St. John. 'Can you give me any examples where this might be the case?'

I can give you two, from the looks on their faces right now.

The lesson continues but I can't concentrate. I'm surprised when Jade rushes off at the end of the class. I assumed she'd hang around to walk with Fletch. But she runs off giggling inanely with Natasha.

'So, hi.' Fletch is still behind me.

'Hi,' I say, trying to be normal. He leans in and kisses me on

173

the cheek. Considering the last time I saw him we were nearly snogging and then I ran away, it's a bold move. Maybe *he's* trying to be normal. 'How was your New Year?'

'Not as good as yours, I hear,' he says.

Omigod, has Alec shown him the video? 'Alec didn't—'

'Yes – Alec told me. You were wild, apparently. Dancing with anyone and everyone. And were you sick outside Ronnie Scott's?'

'Did he tell you anything else?'

'What else *is* there to tell?' he says. 'So, were you?'

'Yep. Mortified.'

'Wish I'd been there.'

'So, what did you get up to?' I say. It comes out like an interrogation. Why did I even ask? I don't want to know what he's been doing. (Or who he's been doing it with, more to the point.)

'Had my mates round from my old band,' he says. 'We have this tree house that my dad built years ago with Danny. It's enormous – sort of built into the ground but then goes up the tree as well. Bit of a hobby for Dad. Anyway, it's where we always used to have our band rehearsals. It's kind of cool.'

'Sounds awesome.'

There's an awkward pause.

'Should be ready to hand in our project by Friday,' he says, changing the subject. 'I reckon we need one more library session to get it really tight. Is that OK for you?'

'Er, maybe.' I thrust my folder at him under the pretence of getting my timetable out of my bag, but it's really to hide my trembling hands. I can't spend any more time with him. I can't do that to myself.

'Luca and I are helping Seb move into our flat tonight,' says

Fletch. 'So later in the week is better for me. When's good for you?'

'I'm not sure – can I let you know?'

'Sure. Nettie, is everything OK?'

I smile brightly. 'Absolutely.'

Fletch looks at his watch. 'I've got to get to the main building for composition. Which reminds me – shall we start rehearsing our song next week? For the awards? I'd love to hear you sing.'

'I can't, sorry.'

'Is it your voice still?'

'I just – I can't, Fletch.' I'm already walking away.

My hands have only just stopped shaking as I enter Steph's room and she drapes her long slender arm around me for a hug. She's dressed in a long navy-blue knitted dress today, her hair swept up in an enormous bun on the top of her head.

'Good to see you, Nettie,' says Steph. 'Shall we get started? Tell me about your holiday.'

'It was fine – good, thanks.' I'm impatient to get on with the singing. I *have* to crack it this term. Miss Duke needs to see progress. (Also, I can't help thinking that in Fletch's eyes, I'm just the loser who can't do anything.)

'Even the first bit when you ran away from your grandmother's house?'

'How did you—'

'Alec.'

'Why would he do that?' I think aloud, angry that he's broken a confidence.

'Alec wants to help you, Nettie,' she replies simply. 'And now that I've heard you sing, I can understand why.'

'He showed you the video?'

175

'He did. I thought we'd start with some William Finn today. Something up tempo. Sound good?'

'Er, sure.' She's too nice to argue with.

Steph opens the piano lid. 'But first, give me a memory.'

'A memory?'

'Of your mum.'

'Oh, er, OK.' I wrack my brains for something to tell her. 'Like something that happened when I was little?'

'Sure – or something about her. Did you ever see her dance?'

'No. Occasionally she'd mess around, doing *petit allegro* in the kitchen, but she never showed me videos of her dancing. I don't think she had any? I mean, she never talked about her career – she used to say she couldn't remember most of her life as a dancer. She never even told me she knew Miss Duke.'

'So you feel like there's parts of her life you didn't have access to.'

I nod. 'I don't know what she had to hide. What was the big secret?'

Obviously Steph doesn't know, but it's nice of her to listen.

'OK. Leave that one with me. I might be able to help.' She folds the book inside out to break the spine and places it on the stand. 'Let's sing.'

If she was expecting the Nettie she saw on the video, she must be disappointed. Despite my best efforts, I wisp my way through her warm-up exercises, apologizing after every arpeggio. Steph doesn't care; she just pushes on.

'That's great, Nettie.' (It isn't.) 'Let's move on to the song.' She plays the intro. It's 'I'm Breaking Down' from *Falsettos*. Apt.

I try to get it out, but it's only intermittently audible.

'Sorry,' I say mid-verse. 'I want it to come out; it just won't.'

'It's fine. That's why we're here.' Her fingers are paused over the keys. 'Can you close your eyes and take yourself back to the club? Recall how you felt on New Year's Eve? Try that for me.'

'I'm really sorry, but I can't remember any of it.' I wish my brain would come through for me, but I already know it won't. I've spent most of January trying to get back my memory of the evening. 'The last thing I remember is being sick outside the club.'

'And you still managed to sing like that, excessively drunk and presumably with horrendous acid throat-burn. It's hard to sing when you've been sick. I was concerned there might be something biological going on with your voice – something pre-nodular maybe – but having seen the video, I'm convinced the problem is in your brain. We just need to work out how to rewire you, Nettie.'

Alec is keen to discuss the Duke's Awards at every opportunity. He's becoming a bit of a bore about it. He's all, *What music are you using? Shall I wear the mesh top or the vest? Do they know who's guest-judging the finals yet?*

Leon yawns, sprawling himself across the common-room sofa. The four of us are in there after college, all exhausted from the start of term. 'We all know the awards are happening. Just because you're going to win doesn't make it any more thrilling for the rest of us.'

'I'm just saying, maybe it's time you started thinking about what you're going to do. Everyone has to enter in at least one category.'

'I'll probably do a jazz,' says Leon. He pats his hair absent-

177

mindedly. 'But don't expect me to have it choreographed much before the day. It'll be a last-minute wing-it job.'

'What about you, Kiki?'

She does a comedy body lock. 'Commercial, babe.'

'And Nettie's singing.'

'Not at this rate,' I say. 'I had a really crap lesson with Steph again.'

'What *are* you singing?' said Leon. 'I literally can't *wait*. Alec show—'

Alec nudges him sharply in the ribs.

'Alec showed you what?'

'Nothing.' He looks at Alec.

'You showed him?' I say, turning to Alec.

'Nettie, it was amazing! Don't be mad at him,' says Kiki. 'He only wanted us to see how talented you are.'

'You showed both of them? *And* Steph?'

'What's the problem?' says Alec. 'It's not like I showed them a video of you being bad. You're awesome in it.'

'Yes, well, in case you hadn't noticed, I'm struggling to be awesome in real life,' I snap. 'It's bad enough without people's expectations being even higher.'

'Aha, so you admit you're awesome,' says Alec, like a 1930s detective cross-examining a perpetrator.

I huff. He just doesn't get it.

The next day I'm in the changing room after jazz, when Jade breezes in, Natasha on her tail.

'It's *soo* exciting,' Natasha is saying loudly, obviously wanting to pique everyone's curiosity.

'I know. I'm so grateful for the opportunity,' gushes Jade.

178

'What's exciting?' says one of the third-years, taking the bait.

I've noticed over the last few weeks that the other girls don't seem keen on Jade and Natasha, either, but they sensibly keep them close enough not to be in the firing range.

'Jade's been singled out,' says Natasha, with more than a touch of smarm, 'to audition for the lead in the college musical at Easter. It's by invitation only – just a *select few*. Michael St. John wants her to go and sing now for him and Miss Duke.'

There are murmurings of *Well done* and *Nice one*, but I can tell they're insincere. A couple of the third-years look pissed off. I guess they would be, when a second-year's been asked to audition and they haven't.

'Plus, guess who's up for the male lead?' says Jade excitedly, like Patty Simcox announcing she's up for student council at Rydell High.

No one replies.

'Fletch!' Natasha gasps, barely able to contain herself. 'He's auditioning with Jade later. It's like fate!'

My heart sinks.

Kiki's emerged from the shower now and is heading over to Jade and Natasha.

'That's brilliant news, Jade.' She smiles warmly. Only an expert (me) could tell she's faking. 'I'm sure you'll get the part. Reminds me, actually – how are the plans for the Upton Wing going? Hasn't your dad commissioned two new drama studios? That's going to be *so* fantastic for Duke's.'

The dressing room is quiet now. Everyone is watching the exchange, unsure of which way it'll go. Jade looks at Kiki for a second, apparently making up her mind. But she's obviously determined to let nothing spoil her good mood because she giggles and turns to the mirror to do her hair.

'They start knocking through into next door in September.' She's got her back to Kiki but makes eye contact with her reflection. 'Just a couple of things to get through planning first.'

The changing room becomes full of questions and comments about the new wing. Jade's clearly *loving* the attention.

'I mean, Dad told me not to say anything until it was announced, but . . .'

They're all over her, clamouring for information. Kiki grabs my arm and we slip out into the corridor.

I check there's no one around. 'Do you think it's true, what Natasha said about Jade and Fletch?'

Kiki nods. 'Like, almost a hundred per cent. Fletch is amazing; Jade's bought her way in. If Miss Duke and Michael are seeing them for a special audition, you can guarantee they'll give them the leads.'

'How did you know about that?' I say. 'The thing about Jade's dad, I mean.'

'Overheard it in the office this morning,' says Kiki. 'Nice to have a rich dad to buy your career for you.'

That helps, but not much.

'Does everyone at Duke's have a rich dad?' I say.

'There are about sixty funded places across the different degree courses, and five "personal scholarships" handed out by Miss Duke every year. So, when you think there are a hundred and seventy kids in our year, it's made up of predominantly fee-paying rich kids. Not to say they're not talented – it's just a bit shit for everyone else who can't afford to come. I reckon there's a load of talent out there that just doesn't get the opportunity. So in answer to your question about rich dads, pretty much. Apart from you and me, babe.'

'Actually, I don't know who my dad is,' I say. 'For all I know, he could be Daddy Warbucks.'

CHAPTER 16

'Nettie, wait.' Luca's sprinting down the front staircase after me as I make my way through the foyer with Kiki. We stop and wait for him.

'You're in a hurry,' I say, smiling.

'Just wanted to catch up. Haven't really seen you this term. Hi, Kiki.'

To tell the truth, I've been avoiding Luca. He's too close to Fletch.

'Hi, Luca,' says Kiki. 'How are you?'

'Good, thanks.' He turns to me. 'Fletch said he's been trying to get together with you to write.'

'Yeah – just so busy,' I say. Fletch has messaged me three times this week to ask if I could meet him to write. I've made an excuse every time.

'I know the feeling,' he says. 'I was moving Seb in last week. That boy has a *lot* of shoes. My composition assignments have doubled, and I'm joining MT part time from next week. So much to do.'

I'd forgotten about that. 'Ah, it'll be nice to see more of you.'

Kiki doesn't exactly give me a look, but I can sort of feel that she wants to.

Luca smiles. 'Hey, do you want to get a coffee with me – maybe after class one day?'

Kiki's definitely giving me a look now.

'Uh, sure,' I say.

'OK, great. See you later.' He goes back through the crowded foyer, head and shoulders above everyone else.

'Bye.'

'Bye, love you,' echoes Kiki from behind me, smirking.

I drag her out of the front doors.

'Omigod, did you just agree to go on a date with Luca Viscusi?' she says, as soon as we're outside on Frith Street.

'No! It's just coffee.'

'Are you joking? It's like I wasn't even there – he's so into you.' She laughs at my bewildered face.

'We'll never get time to meet up anyway,' I say. 'We're both so busy this term. And even if we do, I'll probably just spend the whole time trying not to ask him about Fletch.'

'Might be a good distraction,' says Kiki. 'I wouldn't rule it out if I were you.'

'I wonder if Jade got the part in the college musical,' I say, changing the subject. (I'm also wondering if Fletch got in, but I don't tell her that.)

'I expect so,' says Kiki. 'Miss Duke owes her one, doesn't she? Well, she owes her dad, at least.'

I feel sick at the thought of Fletch and Jade together, getting close during rehearsals, practising love duets, working on kissing scenes . . .

'Nettie? You OK?'

'Er, yeah, fine.' I shake the images out of my head as we head towards the tube.

At the end of the second week of term, when everyone has dashed off to get ready for the weekend (Friday night always sees Soho

183

crawling with Duke's kids), I linger in the foyer, pretending to look at the photos on the wall. I'm planning to practise on my own in the studio theatre, like maybe trying it in the only place I've managed to sing will help me find my voice. *The Room Where It Happens*, as it were.

There's music playing from the other side of the folding doors as I walk in. Damn. I was hoping to find the room empty. It's 'Roxie' from *Chicago*. I'd recognize that vamp anywhere.

It's the mystery pianist, I know it. I can't help wondering if I'd secretly been hoping they'd be here.

I'm deliberating whether or not to sing, when a girl begins speaking the opening monologue. It's a loud, piercing voice. *Almost* a shriek. The comic timing is all off. And the American accent is . . . East London with a Texan twang?

It can only be one person.

Jade.

I'm in such shock that I'm rooted to the floor for the entire monologue. I always suspected it was her, but deep down I still hoped I was wrong. This time there's no doubt it's her.

When she starts singing the verse an octave higher than it should be (well, *almost* an octave, and sometimes slightly more), it's more than I can bear. I creep out and head up to the changing room. Seriously, how can she play so well but not even be able to hold a tune?

I sit on a bench, Jade's strident squawking still ringing in my ears. This cannot be happening.

Knowing what Jade's like, I can't understand why she'd even *bother* playing for someone else. I get that she'd play for her own singing, but, as Kiki said, she'd never help anyone else out. It doesn't make any sense. The painted brick wall I'm leaning

184

against cools my shoulders but does nothing to calm me.

The door bursts open. It's Jade. Obviously I've been up here brooding long enough for her to finish the song.

'Oh. It's you.' She strips off her neon-yellow crop top and shorts. 'I thought I was the only one here.'

'Just came back for something. What are you doing here this late?' Casual.

'Practising.' Jade removes her shoes and socks. She's now standing with her hands on her hips, completely naked.

'Oh? I didn't know you played piano.' I feel like I must sound completely obvious, although picking up subtleties is not Jade's strongest point. Maybe I'll tell her it's me she's been playing for all these months. That'll wipe the smug look off her face.

'I don't,' she says, looking at me like I've just grown a third head. 'Anyway, much as I'd love to stay here all evening talking to a pathetic first-year, I've got to have a shower. Laters.'

She grabs a bottle of shampoo, turns her back on me (revealing, annoyingly, what can only be described as an absolutely perfect bottom), and heads into the shower. I sit there for a couple more seconds, thinking about what she just said. Then I grab my bag and make for the stairs. Something's just occurred to me.

When I reach the studio theatre, I start singing the first duet that comes into my head, which is 'You Matter to Me', from *Waitress*. It's not ideal that I'm singing the boy's part, but I've started now, so I'll have to commit.

The piano comes in almost immediately. Oh my God, my knees are shaking. I'm not sure I can do this.

One thing I am sure of – it's not Jade playing. And I think I know who is.

I'm so relieved the sound comes out, I almost have to grab the

185

barre for support. I sing the first verse alone, but as I reach the end of the chorus, another voice joins me.

It's him.

It's Fletch.

I hold my breath for a second, pulse pounding in my ears. I can't imagine how I ever thought it could be anyone else.

I might be imagining it, but our voices are really good together. Almost like it's meant to be. It's like the plot of an MGM musical, or it would be if he didn't have the hots for someone else and I wasn't weird about singing.

The last note rings out, and the piano fades.

What shall I do? Shall I make myself known? There's a voice in my head urging me to burst through the doors.

I'm going to do it. I'm going to tell him.

But as I pick up my bag and make my way to the folding doors, I hear another door the other side of the studio opening.

'Well, hello,' says a shrill voice. It's Jade.

I freeze.

'Hi, Jade.' If there was any doubt before, hearing him speak has confirmed it's Fletch.

'Whatcha doin'?' she says, all sickly-sweet.

I shudder.

'Just going over some music,' he replies. It sounds like papers are being shuffled. 'Finished your shower?'

'Yes, baby. So, are you going to walk me to the station, O new love of my life?' She emphasizes these last words as if she's relishing every syllable. I stand there, rigid.

He laughs. 'Sure.'

She does a ridiculous high-pitched giggle. 'Who was that singing with you, by the way?'

'No one.'

No one. I'm no one.

Wait – I guess he doesn't know it's me.

God, this is messed up.

'Oh,' she says. 'Are we still on for later?'

'Sure,' he says, closing the lid of the piano. 'What time?'

'Seven thirty at BKB. Can't wait to spend time with my *new man*.'

I turn and run as fast as I can, out into the foyer, past the signed, framed photos that now seem to be taunting me with their simpering smiles, laughing at me from on high. Then I go out on to the street, through Soho Square and up the steps of the music hall.

Alec and Leon are watching Kiki dance a very elaborate hip-hop solo. She's alternating between fast, jerky movements and steps that look as if she's wading through treacle. She finishes before the music does, breathless and panting.

'That's all I've got so far.' Gasping, she bends double, holding her knees. 'What do you think?'

'Love it, babe,' says Leon.

'Just the bit where your arms came up . . .' muses Alec. 'Do you not think it might be better to take that round to the back? Incorporate the turn you did straight after?'

'What – like this?' Kiki tries out the new move.

'Yes. Gorgeous. Much better.'

'OK,' she says. 'It's in. Nettie, what are you doing here?'

'I—'

'Goodness, child. What's wrong?' Seeing my thunderous face, Alec swoops over and puts his arm around my shoulders. 'Leon, grab the tissues from my bag, will you, pet?'

'I'm not going to cry,' I say quickly.

'*I* might, though,' says Alec. 'This looks like it's going to be emosh.'

We all sit down in the corner of the studio and I tell them what's just happened.

'So, there *was* someone else?' says Leon.

'Wait, and it was *Fletch* playing in the studio with you?' says Kiki. The others stare at her. 'What, I'm not allowed to know something you don't know?'

'So you've been singing with him for months, and you didn't know?' says Leon.

'Never mind that,' says Alec. 'What a bastard, leading you on like that when he was getting with Jade.'

'Cheat,' agrees Leon.

'Nothing actually happened between us,' I say. 'So he's not a cheat.' The last word stings my eyes, and I blink furiously.

Alec hands me a tissue.

'I don't need it.'

'Take it.' He waves it in my face.

I take the tissue (which actually I do need). 'I've never cried so much in my life as I have at Duke's.'

'Darling, we all cry at Duke's,' soothes Leon. He puts his arm around me. 'It goes with the territory. Incredible pressure, unbelievable competition, teachers telling you you're crap all the time and that you'll never work—'

'They don't tell *me* that,' say Alec.

'They will.' Leon rolls his eyes. 'Just for your attitude, if nothing else. Nettie, it's hard enough here without everything you're going through. I think you're allowed a little cry.'

'You've got to forget about him now.' Kiki strokes a strand of hair away from my face. 'Concentrate on getting your beautiful voice better. She's welcome to him. Personally, I would find anyone who's prepared to spend even a minute of their time with Jade Upton a massive turn-off. Come here.' She gets her thumb and rubs my smudged eyeliner away.

'Bar Soho's got happy hour till seven,' says Alec. 'Come on, Nettie – we're young, talented, beautiful . . . it's Friday night. I promise I won't make you do karaoke again. Just the four of us.'

'OK,' I say. 'Thanks, guys.'

'Nettie,' says Alec, as we all head out on to Wardour Street. 'You've got to be done with him now.'

I take a breath. 'Do you know what? I think I *am* done.'

I cannot give Jade even a smidge of satisfaction. So I keep away from her and her 'new man' (*ugh*), work hard in class, try to sing, fail, try a bit more, and save the tears for my pillow at night when it's just me, the memory of Mum, and the thought of what could have been with Fletch.

'Fancy some more songwriting after college tonight?' Fletch catches me one afternoon in the corridor after I forget to take the back stairs after tap. I've been changing my routes as often as I can when I know he's in the vicinity. You'd think he'd have got the message by now.

'I'm meeting someone later, sorry.'

He actually looks wounded. Like he's got *any* right to be.

'Oh. OK, well, another time.'

I feel a stab of satisfaction.

He tries another tack. 'You know, we really should rehearse our song for the awards.'

'I'm sorry, Fletch, but I'm not going to be able to do that with you,' I say. 'You should find someone else to partner you.'

189

'But we wrote it together. It's our song.'

Have it. Nothing is ours any more.

'Well, I give my full permission as co-writer for you to find another singer.' I say it in a chipper voice. 'Maybe Jade?'

'Jade?'

'Seems ideal. Gotta rush – like I said, meeting someone later. See you.'

I nearly add 'around' but leave it off, thinking that might be overegging it. He leans in to give me a hug, but I turn it into an air kiss and scarper, my cheek still burning from his touch.

After that, I don't respond to any of his messages. In the end, he leaves me alone. If I didn't have to endure watching Jade fawning over him in MT class, loving herself sick, I'd almost be OK.

The musical is announced the following week. There's a big notice up in the foyer, written in pink and blue Sharpie.

THE DUKE'S IN-HOUSE MUSICAL
GUYS AND DOLLS
AUDITIONS THIS FRIDAY
PLEASE BRING TWO CONTRASTING LEGIT
MUSICAL THEATRE SONGS AND A MONOLOGUE
OF YOUR CHOICE TO THE MUSIC HALL AT 4 P.M.

As I'm reading the sign, Steph comes and looks over my shoulder.

'You should go,' she says.

'I can't,' I say. 'What would I take? Two contrasting loads of nothing?'

'Can you come and see me after lunch today instead of your usual slot? I've got to sort something first.'

My heart sinks at the prospect of having to go to ballet instead. 'Uh, sure.'

'Great. I've got something to show you that I think might help.'

Millicent Moore's in a bad mood, predictably. As I take my place at the barre, I wonder if she's just one of those people who's always grumpy, or if it's the sight of me that puts her in a bad mood. I try to keep my head down and make myself unnoticeable (not literally down; if I did that, she'd have me by the throat).

Still, it's not that easy to stay below radar when you're the worst in the class. I'm not some secret Darcey Bussell-esque prima, my talent languishing in the corner of the room while a jealous teacher abuses me. No. I'm genuinely fairly bad, compared to all the other girls in my class, anyway. But not bad enough to stir actual hatred in her. There *must* be something else.

She singles me out four times at the barre, the last time for redoing a hairpin between exercises. I ignore her, hoping she's done. Maybe I'll have a better time in the centre exercises.

I mistakenly think I'm doing well after the *port de bras* because I haven't had a comment from her for at least seven minutes. It doesn't last. She comes up behind me while we're doing *adage* and pinches me in the back. I gasp.

'Well, if you were pulling up properly in *arabesque*, I wouldn't be able to grab so much.' She speaks quietly, so the rest of the class can't hear.

'What are you talking about?' I mutter. 'You're literally pinching skin.'

She squeezes harder.

191

'No, I think there's some fat there, too.'

'Whatever.'

'You know, Antoinette, I've never met a student so brazenly sure of herself.'

Of course she prefers her students insecure; it gives her more power over them.

'I was raised to have confidence in my body,' I say.

'By a self-centred, talentless bitch,' she snaps, still in my ear. 'Your mother was a nasty piece of work who only got where she got by sleeping her way there.'

I'm determined not to let her see she's got to me. Smiling to hide the fact that my cheeks are burning with rage, I finish the exercise breezily, as if I haven't heard. She leaves me alone after that.

But I'm still dwelling on it long after the class finishes. What had she meant, '*sleeping her way there*'? It's true I've got no idea about Mum's past, sexual or otherwise (and, no desire to, either), but sleeping her way to the top? Was that how she'd done so well as a dancer? I'd seen her mucking about, but I'd never really seen her dance. I just assumed she was amazing, after the career she'd had. And the way she spoke . . . She never showed off, exactly, but there was a confidence in the way she held herself that made me think she'd been at the top of her game. It didn't sound like Mum to get something that way. That wasn't the Mum I knew. But . . .

But the more I learn about her, I'm beginning to wonder if I ever really knew her at all.

CHAPTER 17

I'm subdued as I make my way to my lesson with Steph that afternoon. I knock on the door quietly. There's no answer. I knock again, less feebly. Still nothing. So I try the handle and, as it's not locked, I go in to wait for her.

After some minutes, she bursts in, face flushed.

'Nettie! I'm so sorry I'm late.' She smooths her already sleek hair. 'Left something over at the music hall.' She waves a memory stick at me. 'I think you're going to find this interesting and, I hope, helpful. How was your day?'

'Erm, fine.' I can't really be bothered to say anything else.

'That good, huh? Well, let's kick some ass. I want you to see something.'

She pulls a laptop out of her bag and inserts the memory stick. 'Takes a while to load . . .' She smiles. 'I had to get the boys in IT to do a little work on it. OK, here we go.'

It's a video of an empty stage, taken on a (probably old) handheld camera. The picture's a bit fuzzy. A young woman walks on to the stage, her hair in a bun, wearing rehearsal clothes. It's maybe the late 1980s, judging from her high-cut leotard. The woman takes a position on the stage, and music starts to play. It sounds quiet, distant.

'Sound quality's not great,' says Steph. 'I got the vocals removed. Do you recognize the song?'

I do. It's 'No One Is Alone'. Mum's favourite song. I

suddenly realize who the girl dancing is.

'Where did you get this?' I say faintly, not taking my eyes off the dancer as she moves across the screen. 'We never had any videos of Mum dancing. She said there weren't any.'

'The college video archive,' says Steph. 'I believe it's from your mum's graduate show. So she would've been about twenty-one?'

'Nineteen.'

The figure moves around the stage with beautiful artistry; her movements sustained and polished, her technique impeccable.

Steph's watching me. 'She was good, huh?' She smiles.

I smile back and nod. She was more than good. I think of Millicent Moore's comments earlier. Whatever had happened, what she said wasn't true. Mum was brilliant.

Not that it really matters to me how good or not good my mum was at dancing. She'd been the best mother, and I know she was prouder of that than anything she'd done in her career. *You're my best dance, Nettie*, she used to say. It was just the way Millicent Moore phrased it that bothered me, like Mum was some sort of fame whore or something.

'Is it upsetting you?' Steph says. 'I was worried it might.'

'No! I feel . . .' What do I feel? 'Happy.'

Steph clears her throat. 'I'm going to play it again, Nettie, and this time I want you to sing. Let her be here with you. Get lost in it.'

She plays the film again. 'No One Is Alone' is the song I tried to sing in my audition. I haven't been able even to listen to it since. I swallow and take a breath.

My voice is quiet for the first few lines. I'm shaking uncontrollably. But I put all my energy into the figure on the screen – and by the third line, something in me releases.

I'm singing. In front of an *actual* human. In the same room. Who I can *see*.

I concentrate on Mum as I sing, never taking my eyes off the ghostly figure weaving its way around the stage. I glance at Steph halfway through the song, hardly daring to believe what's happening. She's smiling widely, her eyes bright. I carry on singing, all the way to the end. *All* the way.

I let out a huge 'Ha!' as the music finishes and Mum runs to the front of the stage for her bow. Steph wipes her face and joins me in celebration, pulling me in for a huge hug – me laughing hysterically, Steph half crying, half giggling at my infectious mirth.

'I think we can call that a breakthrough,' she says eventually. 'How did that feel?'

'Kind of . . . *normal*, I guess – like the old me,' I say.

She wipes underneath her eyes. 'Old is good. Now, I don't want you to expect miracles. What you've done today is great – fantastic. But we're taking baby steps, Nettie. Don't do anything you're not ready for.'

I bound down the stairs and knock on the boys changing room. A tall boy with huge muscles answers the door, dressed only in his jock.

'Yes?'

'Is Alec there?'

He lets the door slam on me. I hear him yell, 'Alec! It's one of your hags.'

Alec appears. 'Hi, darling. What's up?'

'I sang.'

Alec swoops me up in a cradle lift and swings me around until I'm dizzy.

195

'You go, girl! I've got ballet now. You've got MT, right? See me after for chats.'

Oh, no. I'd forgotten it was MT next. I usually get there early these days to avoid seeing Fletch in the corridor.

By the time I've galloped down the stairs and sped over to the music hall, he's already there, talking to Jade in a corner of the studio. Oh, hi, anxiety, you're back. You'd left me alone for ten whole minutes there. I sit down in the opposite corner and hope not to be noticed.

He looks over, mouths '*Hi*', and lifts his hand. Jade notices what he's doing and scowls. I pretend I haven't seen them.

Michael St. John breezes in, glancing over to see who's here before launching into one of his big speeches. It would never do to perform to a half-empty house.

'Darlings. I want to talk to you about the college musical, which, as you may or may not know, was announced earlier today. This year, we're doing *Guys and Dolls* – does anyone know it?'

Most hands go up.

'Of course you do. Wonderful show. I want everyone in this room to audition. All of you. Now, as most of you know, Miss Duke herself requested a few second- and third-years to audition for the leading roles, but the ensemble is open to all. So, first-years . . . Do I have any first-years here? A few, I see. Well, auditions will be this week and next. We start rehearsing a week Friday, so be prepared to be called at any time from then. That's right – no Easter holidays for anyone involved. You'll need to prepare two legit MT songs and a monologue – and be familiar with the script because we may ask you to read. You can get the sides from the college office.

'Today, I'd like you to learn one of the songs from *Guys and*

Dolls. It's 'I'll Know' – the first duet between Sarah and Sky. We've already cast these roles, but it's such a great song that I thought it would be good to have a go at it in class. Some of you are already familiar, I know.' He smiles over at Fletch and Jade, who are now sitting next to each other (she might as well be on top of him, the way she's snuggled up to him). Jade titters. I don't run over and rip her eyes out. But I *really* want to.

We learn the song altogether. After the third time through, Michael St. John claps his hands joyfully and says, 'Great! Let's have a bash through in twos. Who's first?'

Michael selects a couple of second-years who have raised their hands. They perform the duet together, in front of the class. Two by two, Michael goes round the class until everybody has got up.

Everybody except me. A crest of panic is rising up my body. My palms are sweaty and I've got that funny twitch in my left cheek again. Jade's watching me with sly amusement. Someone must have told her I can't sing. Was it Fletch? The thought of him betraying my trust like that makes my throat ache.

I set my jaw in defiance.

You can do this. You literally just did it, upstairs with Steph. This is no different. Just stay calm.

'Who hasn't been? Nettie?' Michael St. John looks at me quizzically as if to let me off the hook, but I nod through gritted teeth and get myself to the front.

'We need a boy. Have you all sung, boys? I need someone to come and sing again.' He looks around the room.

Anyone but Fletch. Anyone but him. *Anyone*.

'Fletch, would you mind? Thank you.'

Oh, God.

The thought of singing love songs with Fletch is bad enough,

197

but the idea of everyone watching us and listening – and judging – is horrendous. Fletch comes up to the front next to me. As I look into his eyes, I already know I can't do it. I turn to Michael and shake my head.

'Actually, can we swap Jade in for Nettie, please?' Michael says breezily.

Fletch looks confused; Jade leaps out of her seat quicker than Simone Biles off the beam. I shrink back into my seat, cheeks burning. There are a couple of murmurs; people are clearly wondering what's going on.

'Sorry, everyone – it's just that we're running out of time, and I want you to see these guys in action. Most of you know by now that Jade and Fletch have been cast as our Sarah and Sky –' (so Natasha wasn't bullshitting for once) – 'although I don't know how you're going to have time, Fletch, with all the writing as well! We've roughly blocked our way through this – perhaps we could go back a few lines leading in, Jade? Thank you.'

As Fletch sets himself in his position on stage left, he catches my eye, concerned. I do my best attempt at a smile.

Jade reminds me of Lina Lamont trying her hand at talkies in *Singin' in the Rain* – OK to look at but a disaster when she opens her mouth. The worst thing is, she doesn't seem to know or care. It really is a shame to pair something as haunting and melodious as Fletch's voice with her screeching cackle.

Miss Duke must be getting a *lot* out of Jade's dad to give her this part. I could reel off at least twenty first-years who could've done a better job on their first day. Even Michael looks like he's wincing. Talk about a sell-out.

But Fletch is in the moment. He's looking across at Jade adoringly as he sings his verse, his voice effortlessly beautiful. The class is spellbound. If it weren't for Jade's awful mugging catching my eye from stage right, I'd totally be in the moment with him.

The song reaches its close. The pair of them are now face to face, almost touching for the last note.

Please don't.

They draw closer. Fletch puts his hand on the small of Jade's back.

Urgh. Please no.

Their lips meet for the most tender kiss I've ever seen. It's textbook – the kind of kiss you dream about when you're fourteen. The kiss I thought would be ours. I'm nearly sick in my hand as I watch through my fingers, the rest of the class applauding and whistling. Jesus, will they ever break the moment?

Jade looks around the room, grinning. There's *no way* Michael St. John set the kiss. That's got to be their own direction. Fletch scratches his neck and looks to Michael, who responds with a loud, 'Thank you! It's a work in progress. But lovely, guys. Great work today. Rehearsals will be *out of college hours*.' He raises his voice over the clatter of scraping chairs. 'So no social life for anyone who is successful.'

He makes his way over to me, clearly wanting to talk, sympathy in his eyes. I speed out of the room before he can catch me.

'Blimey. Talk about *draaama*, Nettie,' Alec says. I've just filled him and the others in on the day I've just had. 'You seem to attract it.'

We're sprawled out in the halls common room, which is thankfully deserted. Kiki's finishing off a big tub of ice cream while Leon throws Haribos up into the air for Alec to catch in his mouth.

199

'What *is* it with Millicent Moore?' says Kiki. 'Did she know your mum?'

I pinch a Haribo from Leon. 'I don't know. She must've done, but Mum never mentioned her. Doesn't help me either way though, really. She still hates my guts.'

'Maybe you should get her class taken off your timetable altogether,' says Leon.

'And let her win? No way. I'm sticking it out.'

'Maybe it's just an envy thing,' says Alec. 'Your mum had an amazing career. Millicent Moore never got out of the *corps de ballet*. I think the work dried up eventually. She's been here for the last twenty-odd years. She's just bitter and twisted.'

'Don't pay any attention to what she said,' says Leon. 'Your mum was amazing. Way better than Millicent Moore.'

'What do you mean?' I say. 'You saw her? I'd never seen her dance before today.'

'We had archive DVDs at ballet school,' he says. 'One of them had your mum dancing on it. She was in a white dress with a blue sash. Beautiful.'

'You had a DVD of her? I've searched online and never found anything.' I think about Leon's description of Mum's costume. White dress, blue sash . . . it must be from *Oklahoma* – the production Mum was in with Miss Duke all those years ago. I'd do anything to get my hands on it.

'Well, admittedly, not *all* her,' says Leon. 'It was mixed footage on an archive film. One of my father's biggest clients is high up at the Opera House, got me loads of stuff illegally from the library. All the greats on there. Sylvie Guillem, Darcey Bussell, Antoinette Sibley – Oh, God in Heaven, are you named after Antoinette Sibley?'

200

'I know, hilarious, right?' I say. 'I can't even hold my leg above ninety.'

'That's the most fabulous thing I've ever heard,' says Leon. 'The name, not the leg.'

'How did you not know that?' says Alec.

'How did you not tell me?'

'Any*waay*.' Kiki's clearly tired of this. 'What about Jade? How was she?'

I make a 'meh' face.

'Shocking, I expect,' says Alec. 'It's OK, Nettie. You don't have to say it. It'll just look like sour grapes. We've heard her sing before. We know exactly how talented she isn't. So, they sang together and that was it?'

'Yup.' I don't feel much like talking about watching Fletch and Jade making out. 'So, are you guys ready for the Duke's Awards?'

'Alec's been ready since September.' Leon throws him a sly look. 'Kiki and I are just about there. What are you doing, Nettie?'

'I'm not doing anything. I can't sing, can I?'

'But you have to enter,' says Kiki. 'Everyone has to have their name down for something.'

'I co-wrote the song they're singing, so I guess that's my entry,' I say. 'It says that composition counts as participation without performance. At least that gets me out of doing anything else. Although maybe I should do a nice little ballet routine. Moore'd love that.'

03:00

Fletch:

Nettie

I keep thinking about you

03:45

Have I done something to upset you?

03:51

Are you there?

04:02

Oh, just realized it's ridiculously early. Sorry.
Couldn't sleep. Hopefully see you later in college.

07:30

Not upset, just busy. See you later.

Want to have lunch today?

• • •

I can't, sorry.

OK. ☹ Maybe another time.

We're in registration. Kiki nudges me and indicates that Fletch is coming over. I tuck one side of my hair behind my ear and arrange my face into a neutral smile as Kiki sidles away.

'Hi.'

I look up. 'Hi.'

'Long time no see,' he says in an I-know-everyone-says-that-but-what-else-is-there-to-say kind of way.

'Yeah.'

'So, I was wondering . . . unless you've changed your mind about singing with me?' (I shake my head) 'Would it be OK if I sang our song with someone else for the Duke's Awards?'

'Sure.' I try to sound carefree. 'Who?' Go on, say it. I dare you.

Fletch takes a prep breath. 'Uh, Jade, actually.'

He looks embarrassed. He will be when everyone hears them together.

'Michael has asked us to do something together, sort of leading up to the college musical.' He's speaking in a hurry now, like that makes it sound less bad. 'I think it's come from Miss Duke. If you'd rather she didn't, I can—'

'It's fine – I don't mind,' I lie.

'You'll be credited as co-writer.'

'Great.' Fantastic. Amazing.

'OK, great.' He seems unsure whether to be relieved or sorry. 'Thanks.'

'I've got to go.' Get me out of this hellish conversation.

'OK. See you around?'

He says that to my back. I'm already halfway out of the door, wiping the corners of my eyes.

CHAPTER 18

The thing about singing is that it's super emotional. Even without all the other stuff I've got going on right now, it would be hard. I swear I see the following happen outside one or other of the music rooms at least three times a week:

> 'Yeah, that was a great vocal lesson, thank you.'
> [Student turns around; weeps in despair.]

It's kind of impossible to sing without putting a *little* bit of yourself out there, exposed. Turning yourself inside out and letting people get to the core of you. Letting your guard down, leaving yourself open to criticism.

Leaving you open to hurt.

I *am* hurt. Ugh. It feels horrible to say that. I'm hurting about my mother's death; at the shame of not being able to sing; at realizing the one person in the world I *could* sing to was the person I love, only to find out that they're with someone else.

Fletch told me he couldn't play the piano. Does he really believe that? He *is* a perfectionist, I suppose. I should know – I've written songs with him. His guitar playing's amazing, and he's fairly modest about that. Maybe being surrounded by virtuosos all day makes him extra critical of himself.

I'm missing singing. With him. I'm missing singing with a guy I didn't know I was singing with. That's completely messed up. Now that I know it was Fletch there with me all along, I can picture him playing, his hands moving effortlessly up and down the keys, his eyes firmly on the sheet music. It's like having access to a movie I only had the audio description for before – it's altered my memory of what happened. 'The Movie in My Mind', if I'm going to get all *Miss Saigon* about it.

I'm trying to stay cheery when my friends are around, but I *know* they know I'm putting on a front. Alec distracts me with hilarious tales of his sexual exploits. I'm sure some of them are embellished (especially the one about the threesome with two TV presenters in Torquay). Kiki keeps asking me to watch her solo for the Duke's Awards. My opinion's not worth much, but I appreciate the effort.

Leon does something amazing for me. He gets someone in the year below him at school to film the school DVD footage of Mum dancing on their phone and send it to him. We watch it together in silence.

'Do you know why I'm named after Antoinette Sibley?' I say.

'I assumed it was because of her talent.'

'No. Mum said she was kind to her after she stopped dancing. Most people weren't.'

Leon lies back on my bed and does a *grand rond de jambe en l'air* with a ridiculously arched foot. His feet are the only thing about him that Alec's envious of. 'Why did your mum stop?'

'I don't know. I wish I knew.' I also wish I knew why she didn't want me to see her dance. It's comforting to watch her, but it doesn't glue up the enormous rend in my heart. I swear I can actually feel it aching sometimes. Is that a thing?

Just googled it. It's a thing.

*

The first round of the Duke's Awards is in the studio theatre, the absolute *last* place I want to be right now. I can't even go past it without cringing at myself. Cecile Duke, Michael St. John and the other heads of department are going to pick through the competition and compile a list of finalists. The finals will be held in a West End theatre – the Novello, I think – where Miss Duke invites directors and choreographers to come and be guest judges. If I hear the phrase *This is a huge opportunity for all the finalists* one more time, I think I'm going to be sick in my mouth. It's unlikely *I'll* ever get to the finals, seeing as how I still can't even sing in front of my MT class without having a breakdown.

I walk into the studio theatre, this time with the sliding doors fully open to reveal the stage area and the whole college piled on to the pull-out raised seating to watch the first round. My eyes scan the audience and locate Alec sitting at the back, waving.

He hisses in my ear as I sit between him and Kiki, 'This round of the competition takes *two days* to complete. Two days. Did you know that? My section's not until last thing this avo. My bum's going to flatten horrendously if I don't keep squeezing it.'

'Ugh, I know,' whispers Kiki from the other side of me. 'I can't wait to get back to class again.'

Personally, I'm glad of some time away from the scrutiny.

Alec, predictably, sails through to the finals at the end of day one with his beautiful contemporary ballet solo. Even the third-years can't touch him. Leon and Kiki also scrape through in the jazz rounds the following morning, which apparently is 'almost unheard of for first-years', according to literally everyone. I'm happy for them and selfishly pleased that I've managed to land myself three of the most talented people in the year as best mates.

Luca performs an original song he's been working on with

one of the third-year girls. I get why Michael's poached him for MT. His voice is lovely. He's amazing on the piano, too.

'It definitely *could* have been Luca,' murmers Kiki in my ear. 'My theory had everything going for it.'

Apart from the aforementioned good bits, I spend most of the time dreading the singing round. I wonder whether I could slip out before it gets to Fletch's turn. Possibly. But I won't be able to do it without it being really obvious and, as Kiki points out as we sit down together for the final afternoon, 'That'll just make Jade well smug.' So I'll have to endure it.

Fletch steps on to the stage with his guitar, dressed in a dark grey suit that makes him look so gorgeous that Kiki has to whisper a sharp 'Stop it!' in my ear. Argh. *Why* does he have to be so hot? I put my head in my hands. It's bad enough that I'm going to have to *hear* him. I can't *watch* him as well.

Fletch stars to play the first few chords. His beautiful voice singing the words we wrote together brings huge waves of nostalgia crashing over me.

Our song.

It takes me straight back to those early days, when it was just us, writing together in the library, laughing, talking, making excuses to stay longer. Before Jade stole him from me.

I *have* to hold this together.

Alec nudges me. I look up. Jade has appeared, sashaying on in a ridiculous cerise ball gown with her hair piled up on top of her head like a basket. Kiki reaches over me and hits Alec on the shoulder as he begins to shake with laughter.

As Jade takes a breath in to sing, I can't help wishing it's her last. At least, her last at Duke's.

It could be, from what happens next.

The second a note escapes her mouth, there's a titter from the audience. People are laughing at her. And I can kind of see why.

It's not just a bit bad. It's *awful*. Worse still, she's got *no idea*. She thinks she's incredible.

'Ob-*liv*-i-ous,' I hear Leon whisper from the other side of Kiki.

Necks are craned to see the teachers' reactions. Michael St. John is smiling kindly with sadness in his eyes, the way you might if someone told you they had to put down their aged dog. Cecile Duke's face has a grim tightness about it that I've never seen before. People start muttering to each other, and laughs are suppressed. Alec leans in and whispers in my ear.

'*Schadenfreude.*'

He's right. It helps my heart that she's bad. More than anything else, I'm now annoyed to hear the song Fletch and I wrote together murdered buy Jade's awful wailing. The way I feel right now, I'll take that over sad every time.

'She won't put that through,' says Alec. 'Gorge song, though, Nettie,' he adds. 'Well, at least my butt's had a pumping up from all the clenching. Just a shame about Jade. I could've almost forgiven that fright of a dress she's wearing, if she'd at least been good. She's got nothing on you, babe.'

Then why has he chosen her over me?

I go up to see Steph the next morning. It's been a week since I've seen her (she's also been watching the Duke's Awards). I fill her in on my terrible MT class last week.

'Breakthroughs are tricky.' It's a kind way of not saying *I told you so*, and I love her all the more for it. 'You mustn't beat yourself up for having a setback. Let's see what we can do today.'

We scrabble about a bit trying to recreate what happened the other day. It's a struggle. So far we've been at it an hour, and nothing.

Steph stops playing. 'Nettie, you seem distracted today.'

'Sorry. I am a bit.'

'Anything I can help with?'

'Not really.'

'Boys?' she says.

I sigh slowly. 'Yeah . . . boys. Sounds juvenile when I say it. But . . . boys.'

'Someone let you down?'

'Kind of.'

'OK. Let's try this song.' She pulls some sheet music off the shelf. It's 'Burn' from *Hamilton*.

I try to disguise my fear by giving a small laugh. 'That's kind of heavy.'

'Exactly.' Steph unfolds the sheet music briskly and starts playing the intro before I have a chance to protest any further.

As I begin the first verse, I realize how much this song reflects my feelings for Fletch. How strong our connection was when we first met, how I relished those evenings we spent together riding through town on his bike, how we just 'clicked'. How I thought he returned my feelings. Then, how it all came tumbling down after I realized the truth about him and Jade; how he was happy to flaunt their relationship in front of the entire college without giving me a second thought. It's the saddest and most angry song about betrayal ever – and today, it works. I forget all about singing . . . and suddenly I'm singing. Finally.

As my voice soars over the end section, I hit notes that I've only been able to dream about for the last twelve months. Through the pain and rage of the last verse's lyrics, I feel utter exhilaration, a pleasure that only exists in hearing your voice belt Ds and Es with a zing, or executing the perfect turn, or nailing a really difficult piece of Shakespeare; and flooding back to me comes that heady mixture of passion for the piece I'm performing, and the elation of doing it justice.

The song ends, and – surprisingly – I feel calm. Not wrecked and charred like I have been for the last year. I smile at Steph.

'Wow, I really felt the emotion,' she says.

If my life was a movie, this would be the part where I say, 'Me too, Steph. Me too.'

The list of finalists for the singing round of the Duke's Awards goes up on the wall in the foyer. Alec, Kiki and Leon have all been put through. So has mine and Fletch's song, but weirdly, Fletch's name appears alone, without Jade's. Alec nudges me and says in a low voice, 'Looks like Madame Screech has been given a consolation prize.' He points to the list of commercial dance finalists posted yesterday. Jade's name has been added at the bottom.

Kiki makes a noise of exasperation. 'But she didn't even do a commercial solo.'

I don't blame her for being annoyed. I'd be irritated if she'd been bunged into my section.

'Miss Duke's in a difficult position,' says Alec. 'She needs to keep Jade's dad sweet, at least until the new wing's built. But she can't put that monstrosity we heard yesterday through to the finals. Can you imagine all those industry people listening to that? Cecile Duke's got her reputation to think about. Looks to me as if Fletch will perform on his own, and Jade's been given a place in the finals as a dancer. Clever.'

'But that's not fair!' says Kiki.

'That's showbiz.' Leon appears behind us. 'Well, at least she's not singing your song any more, Nettie. Congratulations to the four of us, I say, for making the finals at all. You with your writing, Nettie, and us for our spectacular moves.'

It's a fairly quiet week. Until Friday, that is, when I see my name on the noticeboard. I've been summoned to see Miss Duke. With a hammering heart, I climb the stairs to her office and knock on the door.

'Enter.' Because 'come in' would sound too inviting.

I push the door open. Cecile Duke's sitting at her desk, writing what looks like a letter, by hand. She's using a navy-blue-and-gold fountain pen, and there's a bone china teacup and saucer sitting by her right hand.

'Antoinette, a couple of things have come to my attention,' she says without looking at me. She doesn't ask me to sit down. I wait without saying anything. I mean, what could I possible say that would help at this stage?

'Miss Moore tells me you have been insubordinate in her class.'

Yeah, well, she pinched me til I bled and called my mother a slut.

'I'm sorry, Miss Duke.'

'You will apologize at the soonest opportunity.'

'Yes, Miss Duke.'

She puts her pen down and looks up at me with deliberation. There's obviously something else.

'About your singing, Nettie,' she says. I feel smaller and

smaller under her gaze, to the point where I wonder if I can run under her desk and hide without even having to stoop. 'Term two and no improvement. You're still not singing in MT class; I noticed you didn't put your name down to sing for the Duke's Awards; and when I last questioned Miss Andrews, she seemed to think you weren't "quite there yet".'

'I've—' I begin.

'As such, I have no choice but to exclude you.'

'Exclude me?'

'Duke's is the best performing-arts school in the country, possibly the world. So you'll understand why I can't keep a student who isn't up to scratch.'

Exclusion? I can't be excluded.

My mind races through several scenarios: I picture my friends sympathetically watching me pack; Jade and Natasha reaching new heights of smug; I see myself waving goodbye to Fletch, the thought of never seeing him again making my heart ache; my grandmother, stern-faced and judgemental; Millicent Moore spitting on me as I leave Duke's behind forever; Steph . . .

'Steph?'

'Miss Duke!' Steph is panting in the doorway. 'Miss Duke, I came to say that Nettie—'

'It's too late, Miss Andrews. I've explained to Antoinette that she has to go.'

'But you don't understand—'

'I understand perfectly well.' Miss Duke sits back in her ornate chair. 'Antoinette has underperformed for the best part of two terms, and it's time for her to say goodbye. It's obvious your sessions aren't producing anything.'

Steph looks at me with such despair in her eyes I feel like I've betrayed her. Why couldn't I have got my act together sooner? There's nothing I can say to save myself. She's right. I've been here fraudulently, on borrowed time. I don't deserve my place at Duke's.

I turn to go.

'Nettie *sang* last week,' blurts out Steph. 'And this week. She's made a breakthrough.'

Miss Duke looks surprised, but interested, and I feel hope burgeoning.

'But when I asked you last week, you said there had been no change.'

'I didn't want Nettie to feel too much pressure.' Steph tucks a strand of hair behind her ear. She looks nervous but committed. 'She went straight to MT and tried to sing again and I think it was all too much for her – but I *know* I can help her, Miss Duke. If you'll let her stay and we take baby steps and do it in our own time, I know you're going to see one of the best singers we've ever had here.' She seems younger when she's speaking to Miss Duke. I guess most people do.

Miss Duke shifts her gaze to me. I immediately arrange my face into an expression of sombre and contrite agreement (as opposed to confused and terrified).

'I'm not used to being bargained with, Miss Andrews,' says Miss Duke. 'Since our conversation about Antoinette last term, I've shown infinite patience. I've removed her from as many "trigger situations", as you call them, as possible; I've got all the staff hand-holding beyond anything we've ever seen at Duke's; and I've even changed the rules of the Duke's Awards, in which no student has ever been allowed to enter simply as a writer and not a performer. I've overlooked it all, on your recommendation,

213

giving you space to nurture this girl as you see fit. Well, I'm tired of being lenient.'

'*Please*, Miss Duke.'

Miss Duke removes her glasses, leaving them to hang from their chain. 'You have until the summer. I need to see some evidence of improvement by then. If you can't produce anything, Antoinette is not welcome back in September.'

'Thank you, Miss Duke,' says Steph. She clasps her hands together as if in prayer, or maybe as if she's about to take a musical theatre bow (why would *that* pop into my head at a time like this? Seriously). 'We can do it. I'll leave Duke's myself if we don't.'

'Yes, you will,' says Miss Duke.

We head out to the corridor together. Neither of us dares speak until we are out of earshot.

'Steph, I'm so sorry.' There are probably better things to say, it's just that I can't think of them right now. 'And . . . thank you.' That was it. Thank you. Thanks for saving my ass.

'Nettie, I know you can do this.' Steph holds my shoulders as if it will force me to understand more. 'We've already made a huge step. It's only going to get better from here.'

'But if it doesn't, you'll lose your job.'

'Who needs a job?' she says, with a wave of her hand.

'Er, everyone?'

'Jobs are for losers. Anyway, we're going to do this. You owe me. So no pressure.'

I'm not sure those are the words I need to hear right now, but to be honest, the pressure couldn't get much worse. So I give her a nod as if to say 'I'm game', and we go our separate ways.

I'm still thinking about it after college when I go to meet Alec at

Munchies. I take a seat outside, knowing that Alec will be late, and watch the hundreds of people walking up and down New Row.

Alec turns up about a second after my cup of tea arrives. 'Jesus, what do you call this place?'

'Cheap.'

He sits down on the metal chair, then stands straight up again. 'Where's the bog? I need to sort my hair out if I'm sitting outside.'

I point across the road in the direction of a pub.

'I've got to go across the road? To a *sports pub*?' He looks genuinely horrified.

'Yup.'

'Seriously? No toilet?'

'It's part of its charm.'

Alec huffs and storms off to the pub. I chuckle, before remembering I'm in massive trouble and I shouldn't be laughing. At all. About anything.

Miss Duke is right. I've got to get my act together. I WILL get my act together. This has got to be the punctuation point in my life. I've proven I can actually still sing, with Steph. I've just got to do it in public now.

But I've finally worked out the problem. I'm scared of what happened in my Duke's audition happening again. I'm not worried how my voice might sound; I'm scared of how it might make me *feel*. After what happened with Mum and the voicemail, and then Fletch – I'm scared to feel *anything*.

'Nettie?'

Ugh, ugh. Heart in mouth. What's *he* doing here?

'Hi, Fletch.' Let's keep this business-like and casual. (Not easy

215

when all I can think is, Oh God, is my hair a mess and WHY *Munchies*, of all places? It's got to be the least glamorous place in the whole of the West End, apart from . . . no, Munchies wins.) OK, let's just style this out. Pretend I'm sitting outside Café de Paris. I cross my legs elegantly. One of my heels gets stuck on the metal table leg, so they end up in a sort of half-crossed position that I will now just have to hold with the power of thigh.

'Whatcha doing?'

'Just waiting for Alec.' That's right, Fletch. I just happened upon this joint on the way to somewhere more chic.

'How are you?'

'Good,' I say. 'I meant to message you, actually, to say congratulations on reaching the finals of the Duke's Awards.' We both know that I meant to do nothing of the sort, only he doesn't know why, and I do.

'Thanks. I'm singing it alone, though. Miss Duke shifted Jade on to the jazz finals.'

Hearing the word 'Jade' pop out of his mouth makes me want to reach up and rip his lips off, but I smile instead.

'Well, you were great. Our song sounded great.' *Our* song. Take that.

'I wouldn't have picked Jade,' he says quickly, 'but Michael St. John wanted us to—'

'It was great.' He's not going to get me to slag off Jade, however much I want to.

'Nettie, I wanted to ask you—'

But Alec is bounding back like a large puppy and cuts him off.

'Hi, gorgeous. Shall we go? They're waiting for us at Floridita's.' Omg, he's sticking to a plan I couldn't have imagined he would guess. 'Oh, hi, Fletch. Lovely singing last week. Shame about Jade.'

I actually *love* Alec right now. Fletch looks the most mortified anyone could look, ever.

'Uh, yeah. It didn't sound great.' His guitar slips off his shoulder. He only just catches it in time, almost stumbling in the process. It's an awkward move.

'What? Oh, no, she was fab, darling. I mean it's a shame they moved her on to the jazz finals. Anyway, gotta fly. Bye, Fletch!' Alec takes my hand and whisks me out of New Row like Fred Astaire dragging Ginger Rogers off to dance (who, let's face it, always looked a bit surprised to be prancing around in the middle of her movie).

'Bye!' I shout to Fletch, who looks completely confused and utterly miserable.

CHAPTER 19

'Which one looks best?'

Kiki's examining herself in the full-length mirror on the inside of her wardrobe door. We're judging a tiny piece of grey material she's holding up versus a tiny piece of pink material.

'What's it for?' I'm lazing around on her tiny bed. Reluctantly, I lift my head up.

'Guest teacher for hip hop tomorrow. Ryan Gale. Gotta impress.'

'Pink.'

'I think the pink one's a bit chub-making.' She turns sideways and starts flicking the skin below her armpit. 'Look at this disgusting bit under my arm.'

'I can't even.' I roll my eyes and shift on to my back. 'Wear the grey one if you're going to be uncomfortable in the pink. But please don't say that about yourself, Kiki. It's . . .'

'True?'

'Omigod. NO, it's not true. It's . . . *rude*. You wouldn't say that to me, would you? Call my body disgusting?'

'No, but—'

'Well, there you go, then. Be kind to yourself.'

She smiles. The trouble is, she doesn't believe it. And she's not alone. Half the college are starving themselves. It seems to be an accepted way of being around here. Self-hating and hungry.

'It's easy for you to say. You're well skinny. And Miss Moore says you're fat all the time. How do you think that makes *me* feel?'

'She'd say anything if she thought it would upset me,' I say. 'Anyway, you're gorgeous. I've literally never met anyone as beautiful as you.' I put my arms around her neck and rest my cheek against hers.

Kiki smiles at me in the mirror. 'That's why I love you,' she says.

After two jazz classes, a session with Steph and a contemporary lesson that leaves my face looking like a wet tomato, I have the quickest shower known to humankind and run across Soho Square to MT in the music hall.

We're learning an ensemble number, so there's no chance of me having to test my theory of being-brave-and-going-for-it-alone. I try not to make eye contact with Fletch AT ALL, although I have a couple of near-misses when I'm blatantly watching him and he looks up. Fortunately I'm faster than he is and I turn my attention back to Michael St. John quicker than you can say, '*The 25th Annual Putnam County Spelling Bee*' (which is what we're learning, not just a random phrase).

The class finishes, and Fletch makes his way over. 'Hi, Nettie.'

But it's like the angels are looking out for me and at that *exact* moment Michael St. John calls across the room.

'Nettie! Can I have a word, darling?'

I've been avoiding Mr St. John since that dreadful class where I had to sit back down and watch Jade and Fletch making out in front of us all. I'm not keen to talk to him if he's going to make me relive the whole thing. But, two things: Number one, since my meeting with Miss Duke, I am in my new empowered phase; and number two, I would rather have a deep and meaningful

219

with Michael St. John than spend any time with Fletch. And anyway, Jade is all over him like gin on Miss Hannigan as soon as she gets a whiff that he might be coming within five feet of me. So I scoot over to Michael before Fletch even has a chance to get close.

'Hey, girl,' says Michael. That phrase is way too hip for someone of his age to be saying, but he says it so kindly that I forgive him. After all, he does spend his entire professional life with students. I'm surprised he hasn't broken out an ironic 'lol' before now.

'Hi, Mr St. John,' I say.

'Michael, please.'

'Michael.' Now would be a good time to start repairing the damage I've done. 'I'm really sorry about the other day.'

'Don't apologize. I know you're going through some rough stuff, Nettie. But something's got to give. I'm worried about you. Miss Duke told me you're now on probation. I've said I don't think that's the way to go with you, but when Miss Duke gets an idea into her head . . . well, you know.'

I do know.

'So,' he says, 'what I really want is for you to audition for *Guys and Dolls*.'

'I can't—' My default phrase these days.

'I get it.'

I'm not sure he does get it. Singing aside, I really don't think I can sit through rehearsal after rehearsal of Fletch and Jade doing underscored snogging to rapturous applause. But I can't say that, so I just let him think he gets it.

'So, I was thinking you could audition for me now, while there's no one else around.'

'What, here?' Obviously that's an absurd comment because we're in a musical theatre studio, the perfect location for an audition.

'Sure, Nettie. Why not?'

'Er, well, because . . .'

'Nettie.' He sits down on an old leather sofa behind him and gestures to me to do the same. 'Your mum would have wanted you to get over this. She would have wanted you to sing. We were close, for a time.'

I'm torn between wanting the conversation to end so that I can escape, and desperation to hear a morsel about my mother. The latter wins.

'You were close friends? She never mentioned—'

'After Anastasia left the business, she cut all ties. I think she had to, to survive. Those of us who really loved her knew she would come back to us eventually, but sadly it wasn't to be. When I saw your application for Duke's, I was sure she would reach out. But then, it was all so sudden and—' He stops abruptly, tears filling his eyes.

'Nettie,' he says. 'I miss her, too.'

I spontaneously hug him (which should be uncomfortable given that he's my teacher, but let's face it, the whole thing went beyond weird ages ago, so it's kind of OK).

What did he mean, though, 'she had to, to survive'? I'm about to ask him when he suddenly shifts gear.

'Nettie. What happened in your audition? What made you run out like that?'

I straighten up. 'I – I got a voicemail from Mum. Like, a mistake, or something. She must've left it for me before – before she even got sick. It was just a message about picking up something for me from the supermarket. But for some reason it came through just before I went in to sing and it – it messed me up. The shock of it, you know? I couldn't speak for weeks. Then gradually my voice came back, but I still couldn't sing. Until—'

'Until what?'

There's no point going into the saga with Fletch. 'Until . . . Until Steph got me to sing last week. That's why I wanted to get up and sing in your class. I'd just had a breakthrough with her. But I guess I wasn't ready.'

'Nettie, you should have told me. I can't begin to imagine what you've been coping with these last few months. We're all here for you.'

'Why?' I feel a sudden rage well up inside me. 'Why are you all so hell bent on holding my hand through this? Making it easy for me? Because if it's because of who Mum was, then you can all stop bothering, thanks. I know I only got in here because of Mum's friendship with Miss Duke. I know you've all got some weird debt you feel you need to repay her. Well, please don't, not on my account.'

Michael looks shocked. 'Is that what you think, Nettie? That you got into Duke's because of your mum?'

'Well, that's it, isn't it?' My throat feels tight again. But this time, it's got nothing to do with singing.

'Let me tell you something, Nettie.' He takes my shaking hand. 'On the day of your audition, I came out into the foyer to call you in. You weren't there, but I knew you'd been signed in, so I went to look for you. I went through to the corridor outside the ground floor changing room, and heard you singing in there. It was thrilling, Nettie. I stood there listening, with shivers going up my spine. You were wonderful. I ran back into the studio and

222

told Miss Duke and the other teachers what I'd just heard. They were keen to hear you, and excited too, after what I told them about your singing. And then . . . Well, now it makes sense, but I just couldn't understand it at the time. Look, Miss Duke and I go back a long way. She trusts me. So she took you on my word.'

So many things are spinning through my brain right now. 'You heard me?'

'"No One Is Alone".'

I feel a bit weird, like I might pass out, even though I'm not a fainter and I don't really know what that feels like.

'You heard me,' I say.

'That's why you're here,' he says.

I put my head in my hands. I'm glad I'm sitting down because my legs feel wobbly.

I'm not a complete fraud, after all. Millicent Moore can say what she likes about me and Mum. I deserve to be here. I look up at Michael.

'So. Shall we?' He says. He gestures to the piano. Predictably, my heart starts pounding. Michael seats himself on the stool and opens a book of music.

'"Light",' he says. 'Do you know it?'

'From *Next to Normal*?' I say. 'Isn't that a duet?'

He nods. 'I'll sing it with you. Moral support.'

Those are the words I need.

He plays the intro (beautifully), and I relax into the song almost straight away, a feeling I haven't had for nearly a year. Despite the difference in age, our voices blend perfectly. He looks back at me and smiles, and I smile back. I think he hears it, too. Wait . . . am I . . . *enjoying myself*?

The song's over brfore I know it. Michael closes the lid

dramatically and folds his hands on top of it.

'I think we can say you're in. Congratulations, Nettie. You just got yourself a part in the college musical. You're wonderful.'

I want to run around the piano and hug him, but I feel that we've done all the hugging we need to for today and so instead I smile and thank him politely.

'No solo singing,' he says, 'just ensemble. Maybe a couple of featured speaking lines. We'll build your confidence slowly. Does that work for you?'

I nod thankfully. He does get it.

The finals of the Duke's Awards are this weekend. For me, it's a chance to get dressed up and have a night out with no pressure, but for my three pals, it's all stress and nerves, as they're competing. I feel a bit abandoned because I'll have to sit on my own, but let's not make this all about me.

Kiki is the ultimate stress-head, practising her solo and trying on her outfit and doing different make-up 'looks' and trying to decide which one is the best. She's only allowing herself to eat gherkins and chicken breasts.

'You've lost loads of weight,' I observe.

She takes it as a compliment. 'Thanks!'

I meant it more as an opener.

'Are you sure that's going to give you enough energy?' I say tentatively, watching her prepare a slice of ham and two tomatoes for dinner.

'It's fine, babe. I've been doing it all week. I've lost six pounds already.'

'I just mean, aren't you hungry?'

'Yeah. I am. But I kind of like feeling hungry. I think I thrive on it. It makes me feel like I'm achieving something.' She shakes her pale auburn hair out of a bun she's somehow done without any fastenings.

'That sounds kind of . . . messed up,' I say.

Kiki puts down her plate and sighs through her nose. I brace myself.

'OK – yeah,' she says, surprisingly reasonably. 'It *is* a bit messed up. But this is the life I chose. Whatever you say, Nettie, and I really appreciate your kindness, I *am* a bit heavy for the sort of work I want to do. This is just how it's going to be for me.'

'Until when, though?' I say.

'I guess until the industry accepts more than one body shape. Or until I give up and have babies. And I'm OK with *that*.' The look on her face tells me it's the end of the conversation.

Leon's been quiet lately. I think he's nervous. I wonder if Alec's getting to him. At school they probably weren't in competition. In any case, I reckon Leon probably had his grades to fall back on. At Duke's no one cares how clever you are. Talent is the currency here. Leon's incredibly talented, and they're really different, but he still kind of sits in Alec's shadow. Everyone talks about Alec all the time, and – let's face it – he *is* amazing. Leon never says anything, but I think he feels the pressure.

Alec's like a spaniel, racing around college looking for spare studios to drill his routine in. He knows he's the favourite to win the classical section and he's loving the attention.

I spend Sunday morning alone at the halls while Alec, Kiki and Leon go to the theatre for rehearsals. The dress code for the evening is 'cocktail'. I've gone for a backless sequinned dress in black.

Alec knocks on my door at two o'clock, freshly showered and

225

dressed in a grey marl tracksuit with a sports bag slung over his shoulder. He's also carrying a suit bag.

'Wow, Nettie. Gorge.'

'Thanks. Are the others OK?' Kiki and Leon have stayed at the theatre to get ready, but Alec doesn't take long about such things, being effortlessly beautiful (by his own admission).

'I think so. Leon's a bit stressy, but he'll be fine.'

We tube it to the theatre, getting off at Holborn and walking down Kingsway. It's a chilly March afternoon, but the sun is bouncing along the wide road and dappling the tall buildings through spring trees. The Novello sits small and proud on the corner of Aldwych and the Strand, resplendent in the sunshine. I instantly fall in love.

'Bye, darling.' Alec pulls me in for a hug. 'Wish me . . . Nah, don't need it.'

I roll my eyes and kiss him on the cheek as he saunters off to the stage door. Where should I go to kill a couple of hours? The Nell's just across the road. It's maybe not the venue for a sequinned cocktail dress, but then again it *is* always rammed with theatre types, so I guess anything goes there (actually, I think *Anything Goes* did go there a few years back, at the Drury Lane Theatre opposite). Also, Mum would've loved it.

It's dark inside after the brightness of the street. The barman looks up from his newspaper long enough to get me a drink, and I settle down in a corner with my notepad of lyrics. Half an hour passes quite peacefully as I scribble away, the ice slowly melting into my Coke.

'Bitter shandy, please, Brian.' I recognize Fletch's voice instantly. I'll ignore him. No, dammit, it's too late; he's seen me.

'Hi, Nettie. Wow, you look amazing,' he says. He's looking

down on me in my seat and can probably see right down my front. I silently dare him to so that I have a reason to be cross with him, but of course he doesn't. 'What are you doing here this early?'

'Came over with Alec,' I say. 'That's why I'm wearing this. For the finals later.' In case you thought I usually went out in March in a sequinned gown, Fletch.

'Hey, I'm not complaining,' he says. 'You look beautiful.'

My treasonous heart skips a beat.

'Do you wanna sit down?' I *swear* the only reason I say this is that the alternative would be for him to sit at the next table, which would be more awkward than us sitting together.

'Sure.' He seems happy to join me. 'What are you doing?'

'Oh, nothing.' I reach for my notepad to put it away. 'Just some lyrics.'

'Can I look?' he says.

He needs to see that I don't give a damn. I push the notebook towards him. Just my luck – it's a song about not being with someone you love. I watch his face as he reads my words, hoping he thinks they're about someone else.

'These are brilliant,' he says. 'Nettie, why did you stop writing with me?'

Er, because of Jade? I want to yell. Instead, I pretend to read the lyrics while my eyelids secretly deal with the leak springing up under them. Fortunately his phone rings, breaking the moment and getting me off the hook.

'*I'm just going to the loo,*' I mime, keen to make my exit before he sees me crying.

In the toilets, I grab a paper towel and blot the tears before they leave my eyeballs. I look at myself in the tarnished mirror above the sink – my reflection's a little fuzzy – but what *is* clear is the outline of someone who needs to get a grip. He can't know how I feel. I've got to hide it.

I take a deep breath and walk back out into the bar.

'Hey,' says Fletch. He's irritatingly hot. 'I've got to go for a final soundcheck.'

'Have a good one,' I say, ignoring the hotness. 'Are you still singing on your own?'

'Yes.' He stands up, stretching. 'I entered as a writer/performer, so I have to do a song with the same original writers credited, i.e. you *and* me. They wouldn't let me enter one I'd written by myself. That's partly why I've been so desperate to write with you over the last couple of weeks. It's not perfect as a solo, but it'll do, I guess. Unless . . .' He looks at me uncertainly, as if he's trying to gauge my response.

'Unless what?' I say, before I remember that I'm not supposed to be interested.

'Never mind. See you at the party afterwards.' He grabs my waist and gives me a peck on the cheek before I can do anything to avoid it, and dodges out of the pub.

Two hours seems to pass quickly; the scribblings I make in the back of my notebook reading more like an outpouring of emotion than lyrics. I cross over to the theatre and stand among the crowd of students and industry people queuing to get in. A couple of nice second-years start chatting to me and ask me if I'd like to sit with them. The students have to sit in the top two tiers and at the back of the stalls, all of which give rubbish views, but Miss Duke likes to save the best seats for her important guests. I'm just about to accept when I hear Steph calling me from the front doors.

'Nettie! Over here!'

I excuse myself and squeeze through the crowd to join her.

'Wow. Nice frock. I've got a spare ticket. Do you want to sit with me? It's in the dress circle.'

'Yes, please! Thanks.'

We filter through to the foyer, show our tickets and follow the surge of people up the stairs. I hope that I'm not stuck in a section with all the other teachers. That would be embarrassing.

Fortunately our seats are in a group full of actors and casting people. I feel a little self-conscious. Steph looks at me.

'How do you feel? Not singing your song, I mean.'

'I'm OK, I guess.'

'Michael St. John tells me you sang with him. He's given you a part in the college musical, is that right?' she says.

I nod, glad that for once we've got some good news to talk about.

'That's amazing news, Nettie.' She pats my arm. 'You're making strides.'

The lights dim. It has immediate effect – like someone's turned the volume down on the audience.

Kiki comes out busting some fab moves, and gets herself runner-up in the girls jazz section, leaving Jade Upton looking furious in her luminous-green catsuit when the judge hands out the awards. I think it's like a rule or something that Jade has to hate anyone associated with me. Leon does well but doesn't place (some of the third-year boys are FIERCE at jazz), and Alec marks himself out as the future of contemporary dance by thrashing everyone in the classical section and winning hands down. I know he's cocky. But in all seriousness, he's *so* talented.

After the actors have finished, the singer-songwriter round

begins. There's some stiff competition. Students are singing, some at the mic stand, others accompanying themselves on various instruments. Luca's song is particularly good and gets a huge cheer from the back of the stalls.

Finally Fletch comes on to the stage. I sense Steph looking at me – not because she knows anything about how I feel about him – but because she knows I co-wrote the song. He was right. It isn't going to be as good as a solo. I know that before he's even started. Even after everything that's happened, part of me wishes I could get up there and sing it with him. He seats himself at the piano (wait – piano? This song was written on guitar) and pulls the microphone over.

'Hi, everybody,' he says warmly, as if this isn't at all a scary thing he's doing, more of an impromptu recital for friends. 'I'd like to dedicate this song to two people who aren't here any more but who I'm sure would've loved to have heard it.' He waits for a second, gathering himself. I feel a lump in my throat that is nothing to do with Fletch.

'Tonight I'm going to sing you a new song, written by myself and Antoinette Delaney-Richardson. Nettie, I hope you'll forgive me.'

What? What does he mean? My mind is racing, thoughts of Mum and Danny flashing through my brain. Fletch starts the intro. I don't recognize it. It's definitely not our song. Is he just using my name as an excuse to get something different into the finals? He'll get disqualified. Maybe he doesn't care. What on earth is going on?

He starts singing, and it takes me a moment to realize.

It *is* our song. Not the original one we wrote; another song.

A song I didn't know I'd written.

230

He's singing my lyrics, the ones I showed him in the pub. I reach into my bag and grab my notebook, flinging it open, not caring that Steph is giving me suspicious looks. He's ripped the page out. He's stolen my lyrics and put them to music. How dare he? How *dare* he be so arrogant?

I'm raging so much that I miss the first half of the song.

'Nettie, this is beautiful,' whispers Steph.

Her comment throws my attention back to the stage, and for the first time I listen – I mean, *really* listen. Steph's right. Even through my anger, I can hear he's made a beautiful song. I never knew this melody before. Now I feel like I've always known it.

My lyrics that were just words on a page have a life. Even if I wanted to, I couldn't un-hear it. It's part of me now.

There's an interval while the judges confer.

The house lights go up, and Steph says to me, 'Nettie, you didn't tell me you'd written another song for the finals.'

'I didn't,' I say. 'I just saw Fletch in the pub. He asked me what I was doing and I showed him some lyrics I was working on. He must have stolen them when I went to the toilet.'

'Wow. You two are like a dream team.'

'Yeah.' Apparently.

Someone is trying to get our attention from the aisle.

'Antoinette Delaney-Richardson? Here you are,' he says in a stage whisper that the entire dress circle can hear. 'Come with me, please. All finalists should be backstage.'

'I'm not a finalist,' I say, confused.

'You are. You're credited as co-writer. You have to go backstage now before the results.'

Muttering a hundred *sorrys* and *excuse mes*, I awkwardly step over everyone in my row and follow him downstairs, crossing the gilt-and-mahogany bar, passing through several long passages and ending up at a little wooden door with a keycode next to it.

'Silence, please. This is the pass door,' he says.

I don't know who he thinks I'm going to be chatting to. He punches in the code and leads me through to the stage left wing. I follow him silently through to the backstage corridor, which is a narrow, split-level thing, full of finalists from the last two categories, milling around and talking. Fletch is waiting at the top of a little staircase but I don't go over to him because:

a) It's too crowded and I can't get over there, and

b) What do I say? 'Erm, I'm so angry at you right now but also overwhelmed with love and gratitude for making my lyrics sing?' Barf.

We're herded on to the stage, behind the curtain. A stage manager lines us up. She's speaking to someone through her cans as well as us. It's hard to tell who she's speaking to.

'Over here, please. Yes, you. Upstage left, next to the tower. No, not you. You stay here. I told you – it's upstage . . . Who are *you*?'

I'm pretty sure this last bit is directed at me. She's looking straight at me, anyway, and seems to be waiting for a response.

'I'm Nettie?' I've no idea why I phrase it as a question.

'What are you doing here?' she barks impatiently.

If I'm honest, I don't know. I start to go red.

'She's with me.' Fletch raises his hand from the other end of the line.

She motions me over to him and scurries off the stage, just in time for the curtain.

As it lifts, thunderous applause hits me first, then dazzling light. The audience is going for it. I think it might be the first time I've stood onstage in a packed theatre, but *obviously* I can't enjoy it because I've literally done nothing to deserve it. I stand there uncomfortably with all the other performers as Kenneth Brannagh (one of the judges, not just randomly there) does a little talk from the dress circle about the talent at Duke's and how we're the next generation of stars, blah blah blah. I stand there next to Fletch, unable to move. Kenneth Brannagh's voice goes all fuzzy, like the teacher in Charlie Brown, and it's several seconds before I realize that he's said my name. Fletch's hand in the small of my back guides me forwards. There's a stampede of feet coming from the upper circle. The Duke's students are going wild.

Jesus, this is weird.

Standing onstage with a guy I'm in love with, but who doesn't love me, taking credit for a song I didn't know I'd written. I look up at him. He looks back at me and mouths '*I'm sorry*'. I mouth back '*It's OK*', and I think maybe it is, at least that part of it. He puts something in my hand.

It's the folded-up page of my lyrics. And at the bottom he's added another word.

Netch.

233

CHAPTER 20

I'm physically at the party, but my mind is totally somewhere else. But Jade's gone home in a huff at not getting placed and Natasha's gone with her, so I should at least *try* and enjoy a social occasion without them breathing down my neck.

I can't relax, though.

I haven't seen Fletch. Even if I did, I wouldn't know what to say to him. As soon as the awards were over, Alec swept me off back to the bar. He's all excited at winning but trying not to seem it, which is very cute (*obviously* I'd never tell him that, not unless I wanted to live the rest of my life without him). I haven't told the others yet about Fletch and the lyrics – or, more specifically, what he wrote underneath them. I don't want the evening to be all about me. But it's there, tugging at the corner of my mind, and I can't seem to shrug it.

Where is he? I try surreptitiously to look-but-not-look over Alec's shoulder.

'Oh, Nettie. First Night Eyes, much? Am I boring you?'

Sprung.

'Sorry.' No point trying to deny it. 'It's just Fletch.'

'And I thought you were eyeing up a potential agent,' he says. 'Jokes. Oh, Nettie, what now?'

'Did you hear his song?'

'Actually, no.' He pushes his hair back. 'Sorry, treasure. I should've supported you. I was prepping for the party, actually.

234

When I heard Fletch's introduction over the backstage tannoy, I rushed down, but there are so many stairs in this damn theatre that I went below stage level by accident (it's grim down there, by the way; don't ever do it), and by the time I'd found my way back, he'd finished.'

'It's fine.'

'Soz.'

'Really, fine,' I repeat. 'I wasn't asking you so you'd give me compliments. Listen, I saw him in the Nell earlier.'

Alec turns his mouth down in disdain. 'I hope you didn't speak to him.'

'Not for long, but long enough for him to somehow steal some lyrics I was working on, put them to music and perform it onstage just now.'

He whistles. 'Cheeky fucker. How did he get them?'

'I went to the loo and left my book on the table. He must've ripped the page out then. I didn't notice when I came back.' After Fletch had left, I went straight to the back of my notebook to write. That's where I scribble all my thoughts before I turn them into lyrics. It's a mess back there and I can't read most of it, but Steph says it's good to get it out.

'Are you angry?' Alec arranges my fringe for me, a thing he likes to do a lot, like I'm his own personal doll.

I hesitate. 'I was, but the song was good. It felt . . . *right* listening to it.'

'Nettie,' says Alec, abruptly serious. 'You've got to stop this.'

'What?'

'This going all gooey-eyed every time Fletch does something you think is remotely nice. Let's not forget that he took you on a date and totally made you think he liked you, NEARLY

235

kissed you, then started seeing Jade Upton with no apology or explanation. And now he steals your words and not only puts them to music without your permission, but does it in front of the whole college and half the industry. Did he even say sorry?'

'Sort of,' I say awkwardly, although even *I'm* not sure that mouthing it in front of eleven hundred people when I can't properly answer back is acceptable.

'And then . . . there's this.' I show him the ripped-out page of lyrics with the word 'Netch' added at the bottom.

'That's *my* word, anyway, so it's not just your stuff he's stolen.' He rolls his eyes. 'You two are messed up. Look, shall *I* just talk to him?'

'No! Don't do that.'

'I think you need answers,' he says. 'Or you're just going to spend your entire time at Duke's pining over him. Nettie, this has got "player" written all over it. Which, you know, would be fine if you were on the same page. But you're not. Your feelings for this guy run deep.'

'Please, Alec.' I grab his arm urgently. 'Please don't. Please.'

'Oh, for God's sake,' he says. 'OK. But stop this, all right? Or outright ask him. Just stop torturing yourself.'

I point to the bottom of the page. 'Do you think he means the writing? Or us?'

Alec shakes his head. 'I don't know, Nettie. No one knows. Maybe even *he* doesn't. But you can't just hang around while he gets all cryptic. Have some self-respect. Jeez, how old is he? Fifteen?'

Steph comes over, thus ending my bollocking.

'Hi, guys.' She smiles at Alec. 'Beautiful dancing. A worthy winner.'

236

'Thanks, Miss Andrews.'

'You should come to see me in second year. You know, add another string and all that. What's your voice like?'

'Pretty good,' says Alec thoughtfully. 'Not good enough, though.'

'I like your attitude.'

'Thanks. I like your hair.'

Steph's immediately besotted, just like the rest of us. He's irresistible. She turns to me. 'Nettie. Great song. I mean really fantastic. You're even good when you don't know you've written it.'

'Thanks.' I haven't really earned the compliment. Has this ever happened to anyone before – that they wrote a song without realizing it?

The evening drifts on but I don't see Fletch anywhere. I keep scanning the crowd when no one's looking. He's completely disappeared. Maybe he's gone home with Jade. Yuck.

'Hey, Nettie.' Luca finds me alone at the upstairs bar, staring out of the window. It's a semi-circular room with windows all along the curved side looking over the Aldwych.

'Hey,' I say. 'I haven't seen you for ages.'

He smiles and sits next to me on the window seat. I feel like a hobbit next to him. He's over a foot taller than me even sitting, with enormous shoulders and arms.

'Congratulations on your win. You guys work well together.' He raises his glass and I chink it with mine in response, even though I don't feel like a worthy winner.

'Thanks. Your piece was beautiful.'

He smiles. 'It works better in context . . . I was looking for

237

Fletch – has he gone with Jade? She was in a bit of a state the last time I saw her. Had half the second year trying to calm her down.'

'I don't know.' They must have left early for a cosy night in. Ugh. Change the subject. 'How busy is it tonight, by the way?'

'Half the West End's here,' he says. 'I think that's why Miss Duke always holds these awards on a Sunday night. Maximum reach. I thought he might've stayed – winning an award and all.'

'I haven't seen you in MT.' I'm desperate to talk about anything other than Fletch. 'I thought you were joining my class.'

'They put me in another group because of timetable clashes,' he says. 'But I'm doing *Guys and Dolls*. You're in the cast, aren't you?'

I don't know how he knows that because no cast list has been posted. Maybe he's just assuming because I do MT. 'Yeah. Should be fun.'

'The college musical is always the best thing in the whole of the Duke's calendar,' he says. 'And the parties are off the scale. Last year, the lead got alcohol poisoning, and the cover had to go on for him for the last two days. You can imagine how Miss Duke reacted.'

'Omigod. Was he all right?'

'As in, is he still alive, or did he ever work again?'

I laugh. 'Both, I guess.'

'Well, he did survive. Miss Duke was determined to make his life difficult, though. She tried to chuck him out.'

'She *tried* to kick him out?' I say.

He nods. 'Yup. Three weeks before graduation.'

'But didn't *actually*?'

'He got a call the same day from Frank Associates saying he'd got the juve lead in *The Boy Friend* revival. So he called her bluff and never looked back.'

The thought of someone having the bollocks to stick two fingers up to Miss Duke is kind of thrilling.

'Wait,' I say. 'Not Jamie Baker?' He's the hottest new thing in the West End right now.

'Yes,' says Luca. 'So for all Miss Duke thinks she controls us all, she doesn't really.'

'Well, not if you're *Jamie Baker* . . .' I say. He's amazing (and a boy, which automatically gives him a head start).

'Yeah, I get that,' says Luca.

Alec sashays over, a gin and tonic in his hand.

'Well, *hellooo*, Luca.' He ignores me completely. I kick his ankle. 'Ow. I was just getting to you. Leon wants to go. You coming?'

I down the dregs of my drink and jump up from the window seat.

'Nice to talk to you, Luca,' I say.

He stands up to give me a kiss. I have to stand on tiptoes and lean on his shoulder to reach his cheek.

'Ooh, you're *sooo tall*,' Alec says. I swat him.

'Hopefully we'll see more of each other over Easter,' says Luca. 'You know, in *Guys and Dolls*?'

Alec drags me out on to the staircase, grabs my shoulders and gets right up in my face. I think he's a bit worse for wear.

'Oh my actual freaking God, Nettie. Luca Viscusi has got the hots for you.'

I push him away. 'No, he hasn't.'

'Babe.' He pulls a serious face, but his eyes are struggling to focus. 'I know a crush when I see one. You should go for it.'

'There's nothing to go for!' I say. 'And anyway, I'm off guys. I've got my college career to think about. I'm on probation, don't forget. Did you know that Miss Duke threw someone out last year just for getting pissed?'

'Jamie Baker?' he says. 'Yeah, everyone knows about that. Didn't do him any harm, though, did it?'

'Yeah, well, I'm not taking any risks.'

Alec and I stumble home, along with Kiki and Leon. They sit down in the common room while Kiki makes toast ('Thank God I can eat again now'), but I don't much feel like it, so I feign tiredness and go up to my room. I wonder what Fletch is doing. Immediately my warped brain conjures up a GIF of him and Jade shagging against a wall. Worse still, the soundtrack I've given it is 'You Can Be as Loud as the Hell You Want (When You're Making Love)' from *Avenue Q*. I need help.

Sometime after I fall asleep, my phone bleeps.

Fletch:

I'm sorry, Nettie. That was unforgivable. Are you angry?

Yes

I just don't know why you would do that

They were really good lyrics ☺

And I had to do something to get your attention

???

We haven't spoken for weeks. I had to get you to talk to me. I just felt like we were so close. And then . . . we weren't.

• • •

Look, I'm not presuming to be on your radar. You've got a lot going on.

Well, it worked. You have my attention now. So . . . ?

What happened?

?

Between us.

What do you mean? There IS no us. Look, Fletch, what do you want?

• • •

I want you and I to write together again. I miss us.

I don't think Jade would be too happy about that.

What's Jade got to do with it?

Nettie:

• • •

I just don't think it's a good idea right now.
We've both got a lot on.

Maybe after I've finished *Guys and Dolls*?

Maybe.

I'm secretly pleased to see the surprised look on Fletch's face when he sees me on the first day of *Guys and Dolls* rehearsals; even more pleased to see the horrified look on Jade's face. Get used to it, babe. You've got two solid weeks of me.

Kiki's got a dancing role as one of the Hot Box girls. Apart from us and a boy called Harry, it's been cast solely using third- and second-years, so we've both done well to get in at all. I recognize Lauren Rose as one of the other dancers, the girl Miss Duke sent home on the first day for not wearing any make-up (she's been applying it with a trowel ever since). Michael St. John has given me the part of Waitress/Salvation Army girl, which I'm happy about because it means I don't have to do much. Less pressure.

But I'm not having him treating me with kid gloves, so I come to rehearsals with what I hope is an air of calm professionalism. It's different. Not like being at normal college – more like being in a proper company. Michael has us doing all sorts of exercises to break the ice, including one where we have to pass an orange down the line with our chins. I'm stationed next to Luca in the line. I can't see how that's going to work, given how I'm pretty much waist-height on him.

242

The room's falling about with laughter *anyway* at how ridiculous the game is. Someone who had just come in would think we were all taking turns to snog each other. But when it gets to Luca's turn to pass me the orange, the comedy reaches all-new levels.

We try several ways – with Luca bending as low as he can and me standing on tiptoes – but the height difference is too great. I look at Kiki, who's got tears streaming down her face.

Eventually I say to Luca, 'Lie down on the floor.'

He does as I say through peals of laughter and gets down. I follow suit and we get the orange passed by writhing around on the floor together. I'm not going to say I don't notice how firm his pecs are. That happened.

When I finally get the orange, everyone cheers. The line collapses in hysteria, and Luca high-fives me and picks me up in his big arms to whirl me around. I catch Kiki's eye, and she cocks her head to the other end of the line, where Fletch is standing. He's not laughing as much as everyone else.

Despite Jade and Natasha, rehearsals are fun. Ros Kamba-Smith comes in to guest-choreograph and immediately singles out Kiki, putting her front and centre for every number. Michael works hard on the music and direction. The main thing I concentrate on is ignoring my feelings for Fletch, which isn't easy, given that I have to sit and watch him being annoyingly talented all day long.

Jade spends most of the day looking stressed or angry – even with Fletch sometimes.

'I saw them have a heated word about a scene the other day,' says Kiki, after day five of rehearsals. 'They don't seem to be too coupley. Maybe it's over . . .'

'Do you think?' I say.

'Yeah – or maybe it was only ever a casual thing?'

'She called him the love of her life, remember?' I say. 'Anyway, I'm not even going to entertain that thought. I've got a voice to mend and a show to put on.'

I'm not going to let it distract me. But I can't help feeling hopeful when I see Jade storm out without Fletch that afternoon, after a particularly fraught session ending with Michael cutting her verse of 'I've Never Been In Love Before'.

Maybe it *is* over.

Or maybe I shouldn't be thinking about it at all, after everything that's happened.

At our last rehearsal in the studio, Miss Duke comes in to watch. She looks tanned; people whisper that she's got a house in the Caribbean, and she seems happy and relaxed. More relaxed than Jade, who seems to be freaking out about having the principal watch her. I'm not surprised, after Miss Duke banned her from singing with Fletch in the finals of the Duke's Awards and shifted her to the jazz dance section. I'd be crapping myself. Jade's huddled in a corner with Natasha, sipping water compulsively, refilling her bottle every ten minutes.

Miss Duke takes a seat at the front of the studio, bang in the middle, in plain view, lest we forget she's there. (Like we could.) The rumbling of low-level chatter is replaced with terrified silence.

Jade gets through her first scene without any major mishaps. Then comes the mission scene.

Sarah and Sky, the two leads, have an intense first scene and duet that starts with an argument and culminates in a kiss. Jade stumbles through her verse. It's the worst I've ever heard her sing, and that's saying something.

'I think the nerves have finally got to her,' whispers Kiki in my ear.

Miss Duke is *so* not impressed. The rest of the cast, who are sitting around the edge of the playing area, are dividing their attention between Miss Duke and Jade; it's way more interesting to see how much trouble Jade's going to be in if she doesn't pull this round than watch what's happening onstage. As poor Jade gets worse with every breath, Miss Duke's top lip gets thinner. I can't help feeling sorry for Jade. (I mean, obviously I still hate her. But she does look like she's going to explode with nerves.)

I exchange a glance with Kiki, who hisses, 'She's drowning in all that water. She's going to barf.'

Omigod, she *is* going to barf.

Well, not so much barf as projectile vomit, right next to Miss Duke's foot. I mean, it's *huge*. It's the most colossal amount of sick I've ever seen. Miss Duke glares at her – and Jade, horrified at what is happening but unable to stop it, clamps her hand over her mouth as cascades of watery vomit escape through her fingers. She runs out of the room, mortified, followed by a fussing Natasha Bridgewell, who calls back to Michael, 'She's had about a gallon of water. For her voice.'

The room erupts. Cast members start talking loudly to each other, speculating about what has happened to Jade, what Miss Duke is going to make of it all and if we're going to get an afternoon off now that one of the leads is incapacitated. Over the top of it all Michael St. John shouts for silence.

'That's enough, everyone. Martha, go down and phone for one of the cleaners to come over. Tell the office they need to call the nurse for Jade. Everyone else, I think we need to move downstairs to the other studio until this has been cleared up.' He indicates the sorry pile of puke on the floor, which has spread from Miss Duke's feet to the entire downstage area.

We all pile down the rickety wooden stairs, through the plyboard-walled changing room and into the other studio, putting ourselves back in roughly the same positions in the new room, still speculating, but now in mutters and whispers. This room is what's left of the original auditorium, after the circle was converted into the upstairs studio, and still has the original gilt paint and ornate lamps on the walls. I feel like I've gone back in time. I wonder if Mum ever came here, back when she was training.

Miss Duke waits until we're all settled and then enters from the back, making sure we can all see her. The usual ritual happens – we stand up dutifully, a minion grabs her a chair, and we all sit back down on her cue.

'I was timing the run this morning.' Michael holds up his stopwatch. 'Let's just busk through the end of the mission scene, then we'll break. Can someone fill in for Jade? Just the end, please? Nettie?'

What? WHAT?

'We'll go from after Sarah's verse,' he adds hastily, seeing the look of abject panic on my face. Making me sing in front of Miss Duke right now would not be a good idea, what with me being on probation and everything. 'Starting from Sky's verse, through to the dialogue and his exit. You know the blocking, don't you, Nettie?'

I nod. Miss Duke watches me, unsmiling. I look over at Fletch, who is busy writing something on his script.

'Great. OK, let's go from there. You're both stage right. Thank you, Andy.'

Andy, the rehearsal pianist, starts to play as Fletch prepares to sing. All I have to do is keep acting and move to the right place at the right time. Should be easy, right?

The audience seems more silent than usual, as forty pairs of eyes devour the scene. Fletch continues singing to me. I concentrate on not passing out from the stress.

At this point, the stage direction is for Sky to caress Sarah's face, which Fletch does. I shiver involuntarily. He's looking right into my eyes.

I'm sure he doesn't look at Jade like that.

Fletch eventually breaks the moment to move stage left for his next line.

God, this is weird.

He walks back over to me, singing his last few lines. Jade's harmony was cut from the end of the song in an earlier rehearsal (Michael's attempt at damage limitation), so I don't have to join him. I'm so busy feeling relieved that I completely forget what happens next in the scene.

Then I remember with a jolt.

The kiss.

He takes my hands, which (as per stage directions) are clasped down in front of me. His fingers are charged. Or maybe it's mine. I don't know. Michael's in my peripheral vision, watching intently, cradling his stopwatch, head slightly on one side, as if he's thinking deeply about something. The music itself seems to be underscored by an eerie tension stretching the length of the room, keeping everyone enthralled. As Fletch looks into my eyes again, I feel savagely thrilled. This is the kiss I've been longing for, isn't it? The kiss I've fantasized about forever, since the first day we met?

BUT NOT LIKE *THIS*.

Not a *stage kiss* in front of all my peers, my teacher and the scariest principal *ever*. I think I'm going red. Of *course* I'm going red; this is *the* most embarrassing thing to happen to anyone, ever. Is he going to know? What if everyone realizes how I feel about him and I become a laughing stock? Just what I need, after the year I've had, to be the college joke. How can I do this with everyone watching me?

He leans in to kiss me and I forget everything else.

I feel his hand on the small of my back, the other cupping my face. As his face nears mine, I smell that familiar scent of leather and mint that makes my insides ache with longing. I can barely hear the accompaniment for my pounding pulse.

His lips brush mine. They are soft and warm. He pulls me in tighter. It's *real*, it has to be. We're kissing.

Er, kissing to *romantic music*, in a room *full of spectators*. This is beyond weird.

I'm aware that the music is running away and we should have broken apart by now. I can't break the kiss – it has to be Fletch who does that. But he isn't showing any signs of going anywhere.

The door creaks. It's only a tiny sound, but among this hearing-a-pin-drop crowd it's the equivalent of shouting through a megaphone. Fletch breaks the kiss and seems to glance to my right.

Then I see Jade out of the corner of my eye, back from pukesville and standing in the doorway, giving us the evilest evils in the history of dirty looks. Fletch loses concentration for a second and drops his hat.

I come back to earth with a crash. It's all pretend. We're no more together than we were the night he told me he had feelings for someone else. Of *course* it isn't real. Jade's still got something

248

over him. He was *acting*. Humiliation courses through my veins.

Trying to stay in character, I watch him pick up his hat, but my hands are shaking. He smiles at me, and I immediately raise my right hand and *wallop* him one across the face. The music stops.

He looks at me in surprise, says his line, and exits stage left.

The scene is over. Michael starts the applause, and the room joins in readily. A couple of people whistle. And what's that? A smile from Miss Duke? Fletch looks at me bemusedly, rubbing his cheek. I'm not sure what to do, so I smile demurely at Michael and go and sit back down in my place.

(Let me back up a bit and just say that the slap is *supposed* to happen. It's in the stage directions.)

Michael had said earlier in rehearsals that it needed to be a real slap because in an intimate environment like the studio theatre a stage slap would look fake. Still, I know I hit Fletch too hard. I just couldn't help it. I felt real, red-mist anger.

Now I know what they mean by 'method acting'.

CHAPTER 21

'So tell me again,' says Alec, pulling a half-sucked Kit Kat finger out of his mouth as suggestively as only Alec can. 'You kissed for *how* long?'

I'm sitting in Alec's room at the halls with the others, drinking tea and eating chocolate (well, Kiki's 'not eating' again, but we are). It's the night before college starts again for the summer term and the boys are back from their holidays.

'It was at least thirty seconds,' says Kiki, who'd watched the whole thing. '*Waay* longer than they were meant to.'

'And did he slip you the tongue?' says Alec.

'No.'

'He *so* did!' shouts Kiki exultantly. 'You know, that's what everyone was talking about for the rest of the day. Jade was furious.'

'Let's not forget the fact that if you slip someone the tongue during a stage kiss, it's basically mouth-rape,' says Leon seriously.

'What?' says Kiki. She takes a square of chocolate, nibbles a tiny corner of it and puts it back quickly. Alec eats the rest.

'It's an unwritten rule that you don't do tongues onstage,' says Leon. 'Unless it's like some sort of porn production.'

'How do you know?'

'Everyone knows that.'

'It's OK. No tongues.' I say.

'What happened afterwards?' says Leon. 'Did you speak to him?'

250

'I couldn't because Jade Upton ran up to him crying about puking on Miss Duke's foot and he was all over her, comforting her.'

'She was only doing it to stop him from talking to you,' says Kiki. 'I saw her whispering with Natasha just before. There was nothing wrong with her, apart from being a massive twat, which we all knew anyway.'

'Well, it worked. I haven't heard from him since,' I say. 'I just feel like . . .'

'Spit it out,' says Alec, eye-rollingly.

'I feel like . . . like he couldn't kiss me like that and not mean it.'

'Isn't that what Lina Lamont says to Don Lockwood in *Singin' in the Rain*?' says Leon. 'Just before he tells her he's the greatest actor in the world.'

'And we all know what happened to *that* relationship,' says Alec.

We're to perform the show three times altogether, on consecutive nights in the studio theatre. The rest of Duke's is back after Easter break now and lessons have resumed.

Miss Duke comes into registration, unannounced. Students shuffle uncomfortably, giving each other ominous looks. It's never a good thing when Miss Duke appears.

'I strongly encourage the rest of the college to come and support the cast of *Guys and Dolls* this week,' she begins. 'They've been working hard over the Easter holidays, and I know they would appreciate your support.' She looks around the room slowly. I get the distinct feeling she's scanning each student to check they've cancelled their lives and booked their ticket.

'One more thing: this year, the musical will be completely in-house,' she says. 'No guests allowed. We will not be inviting casting individuals, nor will any directors or choreographers be coming. The Summer Showcase later this term, of course, will be open to the public. I trust you will respect my wishes on this matter.' She marches out into the foyer, followed by students in dribs and drabs.

Some of the third-years start complaining.

'Why does it have to be in-house?' says one boy.

'Isn't it obvious?' says Lauren Rose. 'She doesn't think it's up to scratch.'

'Or doesn't think *everyone's* up to scratch,' says Kiki pointedly.

Jade exits quietly out of the back door.

We spill out into the foyer. Miss Duke's still there, talking to Miss Paige, the secretary. Her face looks murderous.

'Well, you'll just have to un-invite them,' she snaps to Miss Paige. 'I'm not having anyone of note witnessing that monstrosity.' Miss Paige cowers her way back into the office.

'Oh, and, Hot Box girls,' calls Miss Duke, as some of the *Guys and Dolls* cast drift out of the studio theatre. 'I don't want to see any rolls of fat hanging out from under those gingham cropped shirts tomorrow. So lay off the carbs. Especially *you*,' she adds as Kiki walks past her.

Kiki turns and runs upstairs to the empty changing room. I follow her but she shuts the toilet door in my face.

'Kiki—'

'Just leave me alone, Nettie.'

'She was pissed off about Jade. She was looking to upset someone. You were just in the firing line.'

'She thinks I'm going to look big in that skimpy costume.'

'She would've said it to anyone who was nearby,' I say. 'I swear, Kiki. Please open the door.'

People are starting to come in to get changed for their first class.

The door opens a crack.

'Are you coming out?'

'You come in.' She's crying.

She opens the door a little more to let me squeeze in. Kiki sits on the toilet and I lean against the sink.

'It's just . . . It's on my mind all the time.' Kiki pulls off a piece of loo roll to wipe her eyes. 'So when someone else says it, it just reaffirms what I've been thinking.'

'You know you're gorgeous, right?'

'I know I'm the biggest girl in that Hot Box line-up.'

'You're beautiful.' I rub my lower back where the cold edge of the sink has started to dig in uncomfortably.

'Why can't I be thin like you?' She blows her nose loudly.

'Do you think I don't sometimes wish I looked more like you?' I say. She looks at me disbelievingly. 'Look, Kiki. I promise you that not one person in that audience is going to look at you and think anything apart from, "Wow, she looks hot." You're the best dancer on the stage—'

'I'm the only one who can't sing, so I should be the best dancer.'

'Michael let you in the show, didn't he?'

'Only because I told him I might do musical theatre next year.'

'Come here.' I take her in my arms and hug her. 'You're stunning. Like, the most beautiful person at Duke's. Sometimes I find myself staring at you because you're so gorgeous.'

'Shut up,' she says, but she's laughing.

'I'm not even joking.'

'I'm just exhausted thinking about it all the time.'

'Maybe allow yourself fifteen minutes a day. That's what I do when I'm thinking about Mum all the time. When it's getting out of control, I let myself have fifteen minutes in the morning and five more before I go to bed. Otherwise it just takes over.' What I don't tell her is that lately, thoughts of Mum have been replaced with constant thinking about Fletch and I've done nothing to stop it, so I'm not exactly practising what I preach, am I?

'I just don't know if I've got the energy for it anymore.'

'Then don't *give* it your energy.'

'Miss Duke—'

'Can piss off. How dare she say that to you?'

There's a harsh bang on the door.

'Come on, I need the toilet,' says a voice I vaguely recognize as belonging to one of the third-years. 'What are you doing in there?'

'Probably getting off with each other,' says another voice.

Kiki mouths '*Natasha*' at me.

'So what if we are?' I say, opening the door.

'Dirty lesbians,' says Natasha. 'Do your disgusting stuff somewhere else.'

I'm about to retort when I notice her looking over my shoulder to Kiki in horror.

'That'll make a nice end to my Instagram story,' says Kiki. She's been videoing Natasha.

'Delete that now,' says Natasha.

'Only if you apologize for your offensive and prejudiced remarks,' says Kiki, still holding up her phone.

The changing room's gone quiet. I can tell they're on our side.

'Oh, fuck off,' says Natasha, and she storms out.

254

Kiki's distracted by the other girls begging her to see the video and asking her if she's really going to post it.

'Nah, not worth it. I don't want hate on my story.'

'You're gonna let her sweat, though, right?'

'For a bit.'

Guys and Dolls opens to a small but appreciative audience. Apart from Jade, everyone in it shines. Luca's playing Big Jule – it surprises me that he can act so well, considering he's on the writers and MDs course. He's funny. Sophie McDonald, a third-year, plays Adelaide opposite a second-year called Kieran Potter. Along with Fletch, they're working really hard to make up for Jade. They *almost* do.

Kiki smashes it in the Hot Box numbers. I watch her from the wings during 'Take Back Your Mink'. She's the most dynamic dancer on the stage. Peeking out from behind the curtain at the final performance, I see Miss Duke smiling at her approvingly, oblivious to the damage she's caused. I wonder how many other girls have been messed up over the years by her comments.

Most of the cast members go for a drink in the Nell before the after-show party, which Seb, Fletch and Luca are hosting. Luca's already at the bar when Kiki and I arrive.

'Hey, well done, Luca,' says Kiki. 'You were really funny.'

'Thanks,' he says. 'You guys were great, too. I've got to say, I've never clenched my arse so hard as I did tonight.'

'Was that when Josh stole your seat at the end of "Sit Down, You're Rockin' the Boat"?' says Kiki. 'You looked really uncomfortable.'

Luca grins. 'Ended up with one cheek on the chair, one off, and the corner wedged in between.'

'That must have smarted,' I say, laughing.

'Let's just say the chair and I are on first-name terms now.'

'Nettie?' Fletch has appeared behind me. We haven't spoken since our very public kiss. The laughter subsides.

'Hi, Fletch.' I make room for him between me and Luca, who shuffles closer to the bar. It's all a bit cringe-making, especially as no one is now saying anything. 'Er . . . how's it going?'

'Good, thanks. Are you . . . coming to the party?'

'I—'

''Course,' says Kiki, without waiting for me to agree.

'Great!' says Fletch. 'Do you want to grab a cab with us? We've got to be there to let everyone in.'

'Also, you might want to hide your vinyl in case anyone's sick on it, mate,' says Luca.

'Already did this morning, after you'd left,' says Fletch. 'Along with four guitars, a keyboard, a trumpet and twelve pairs of thigh-high boots.' (Kiki throws me an impressed look – I think about anyone having that many thigh-high boots, rather than Fletch's tidying skills.)

Luca checks his phone. 'Our Uber's here.'

We finish our drinks and leave the pub. Luca gets in the front, leaving the rest of us to sit in the back.

'Nettie, you're—' begins Kiki.

'Yes, I know – small. I'll go in the middle,' I say.

I slip in next to her. Fletch puts two guitar cases in the boot and gets in beside me. As the car pulls out of Catherine Street, I'm aware of his leg next to mine, and it's all I can do not to push my thigh against it. I sit forward abruptly.

'Nettie, you all right?' says Kiki.

'Yeah . . . just don't want to squash you guys,' I say.

256

'Don't be silly.' She pulls me back into my seat. Unfortunately at that very moment, the car turns left, flinging me pretty much into Fletch's lap. So much for avoiding him.

'Sorry,' we both say. I laugh nervously.

Kiki side-eyes me and pulls me back up.

'Centre, Antoinette,' she says, in a perfect impression of Miss Moore.

I punch her arm. 'Core strength never was my thing.'

We arrive at the flat. Seb flings the door open and leans up against the frame, one leg in a high *développé* against the opposite side. He's wearing a Ramones T-shirt, skinny jeans, heavy lashes and five-inch red patent-leather stillettos. I hand him a bottle of vodka we've managed to pick up on the way and he lifts his leg over my head by way of admission.

'Hi, kids,' he says. 'Nettie, I am *living* for that *crêpe de Chine* tea dress. Is it vintage?'

'Forties,' I say.

He nods approvingly. 'Of course. Kiki, you beautiful goddess, I've got to say, your dancing in the show was –' He licks his thumb and puts it on his arse, making a *tssss* noise and throwing his head back in mock-ecstasy. 'You're gonna be a star, babe. This way to the *partaay*.' He leads us through the narrow hall to the kitchen, Luca and Fletch following behind. *In the Heights* is blaring out over the speaker.

'Luca, honey, I couldn't move your drum kit, but I've covered it,' he yells over his shoulder. 'And, Fletch, the sheet music's all locked in my room.'

'Thanks, Seb,' says Fletch.

'Anything for my favourite straight boys,' says Seb. 'Now, drinks. What's this? Amazing.' He grabs the vodka bottle from my hand and pours five large shots.

'OK, down in one.' He indicates that we should all take a glass. 'On eight – *five, six, seven . . . eight*!'

We drink. Kiki's a lot better than I am – with four older brothers, she's had to hold her own from an early age. I cough.

'Seb, she'll be on the floor in ten minutes if you carry on like that,' says Kiki. 'There's not much of her.'

'Jesus, you're right.' Seb downs another swig from the bottle. 'Nettie, take your shoes off and stand next to Luca. I *have* to get a picture of this. If you two ever get a job together in *The Greatest Showman 2*, I'm taking commission.' He moves Fletch out of the way to get a better shot. 'Smile!'

We oblige.

'That's great – now Luca, can you pick Nettie up with one arm so that she looks like she's as tall as you? That's it, so her feet are dangling. Omigod, this is *gold*.'

Fletch squeezes past and leaves the room. I figure he's just gone to the toilet, but half an hour later he still hasn't come back. Every time the door opens, I can't help looking over to see if it's him. So much for forgetting about him and having a good time.

Luca's right; the party's pretty wild. As the night goes on, the breakfast bar in the kitchen becomes a kind of club podium, led by Kiki looking stunning in a red strappy bodycon dress. Girls and boys dance on it in less and less as the night goes on, with bigger and wilder moves. Even some of the guys from the actors course are having a go (although Kiki says they probably shouldn't). Kiki pulls me up there with her and encourages me to copy her moves. It's lucky I'm too pissed to care that I'm drunk-dancing next to the best freestyler in the college. I don't even want to imagine this sober.

'Whoah!' Kiki grabs the back of my dress, saving me from stacking it and falling off the bar onto a couple of stage managers. 'Maybe this isn't such a good idea, Nettie.' She helps me down and drags me into the lounge, where Seb's got everyone else involved in a debauched game of spin the bottle that involves the entire room downing shots each time a couple is picked. I sit next to Kiki, relieved to be off my feet. There could be twelve of us playing, it could be twenty-four. I don't know because I can't see any more. I look around and feel a dull disappointment. Fletch is nowhere to be seen.

Kiki gets handed the bottle.

'Boy or girl?' shouts Seb.

'Girl!' yells Kiki. She spins the bottle, and it lands on Emilie Drake, who stands up and beckons to Kiki with her finger.

'It's on – drink, everyone!' says Seb.

Oh, God, another swig might finish me off. I pretend to drink while they kiss to a lot of whooping and cheering and downing of shots. Where's Fletch? He can't have gone home because he *is* home. He's missing the party.

'Nettie?' Someone's speaking to me. 'Nettie, it's your turn.'

My eyes barely focusing, I set the bottle down in the middle of the circle and give it an almighty spin. It lands on Luca.

'Luca! *Lu-ca, Lu-ca, Lu-ca,*' chants the circle.

I look at Kiki, and she shrugs in a kind of *go for it, he's hot!* way. She's right, I guess. Stumbling a little, I cross over to him. As we face each other, the entire room bursts out into laughter, remembering the orange-passing game.

I giggle. 'This might be tricky.'

'Nah,' he says, and picks me up.

I put my arms around his neck, straddle him with my legs,

and we kiss. The room goes wild, shouting and whistling, and I push my face harder into his. At one point, Kiki yells, 'YES, NETTIE!' and a rumble of foot-stamping starts up, led by Seb's stillettos. The snog goes on for a long time, egged on by the crowd, until I start to feel dizzy and pull away.

A huge *BOOO!* goes around the room, followed by applause. Laughing, Luca puts me down, holding my shoulders because I think he senses me swaying.

'That was amazing! *Tell* me someone got that on their phone.' Seb hands me another shot which I take, but don't drink, because I've just seen something over his shoulder that sobers me up straight away.

Fletch is standing in the kitchen doorway, looking at Luca like he's just punched him in the stomach.

CHAPTER 22

'He doesn't get to be jealous, Nettie. It's not like you've ever been together.' Kiki and I are walking down Wardour Street together on our way to college on Monday morning.

'But do you think he was?' I sidestep a delivery van. 'He looked really hurt.'

'I just don't think he has the right to be, after the way he's treated you.'

Yeah. I need to remember that.

The rest of the evening is hazy. Kiki whisked me home shortly after I kissed Luca because she said I looked like I was going to spew. I've got a secret feeling of dread that I might have clung on to Fletch for a little too long when we said goodbye, and also that I did this in front of Luca, having just snogged him. It's too embarrassing to think about, so I try not to for the rest of the journey.

I change the subject. 'So, kissing Emilie Drake. How was that?'

Kiki thinks for a moment. 'It was . . . nice.' She stops walking to face me. 'I've kissed girls before, actually.'

'Do you think that's the way forward for you?'

'I don't know,' says Kiki, smiling. 'Maybe, yeah.'

'Is Emilie . . . ?'

'I think she was just caught up in the moment. It's cool, though.' Kiki links my arm as we cross Soho Square. I put my head on her shoulder.

Fletch approaches me after registration. 'Hi, Nettie. Can I talk to you for a second?'

'Uh—' I look around for my friends, but Alec and Leon have disappeared and Kiki's already slinking off in a *don't mind me* kind of way. I follow him out into the foyer.

'Good party on Saturday night,' he says.

I don't know how he knows that. He missed most of it. 'Great party. Huge hangover, though,' I say.

'You and Luca seemed to be getting on well,' he says. When I don't reply, he continues awkwardly. 'I, uh, haven't had a chance to ask you – how did the show go for you?'

'Fine, thanks. You?' I can't bring myself to give him a compliment, even though he was completely brilliant and melted my heart every time he stepped onto the stage.

'Yeah – not bad, thank you.' To be fair, I don't think he's after one. 'We should get together some time, you know – to write.'

'Is that what you brought me out here to say?' I say. I can feel Kiki's eyes boring through the studio window at me.

'No! Well, sort of. I wanted to apologize.'

'What for?'

'For everything.' He puts his hand up to his hair and grabs a handful, something I've noticed he does when he's uncomfortable. 'I've been a total knob. The Duke's Awards, stealing your lyrics . . . I'd go mad if someone did that to me. And at Christmas – what I said.'

'What did you say? I can't remember.' Obviously, I've been thinking about nothing else since, but I'd rather eat my own feet than admit that.

'About – about having feelings for two people . . . I thought that was why you were annoyed with me,' he says. 'After that, you just stopped talking to me.'

'Nope . . . just busy.'

'Anyway, I was wondering if you'd consider writing with me again? Maybe we could meet for a drink to talk about it?'

'What about . . .' I can't bring myself to say Jade's name.

'Look, that's over,' he says, rolling his eyes, I think at himself. 'I'm embarrassed even thinking about it.'

He should be. But I won't just come running now that he's got bored of her. 'I'm busy working on something with Steph for the next few weeks,' I say.

'Oh. OK. Maybe after that?'

'Maybe.'

Steph has put me on a regime of no alcohol, no caffeine, no dairy and lots of water and sleep. She gets me singing in every session. It's so huge for me that I don't know how to thank her, apart from hugging her every time.

'Just keep singing, Nettie,' she says. 'That's the only thanks I need.'

The Summer Showcase is approaching. It's to be a compilation of lots of different pieces and the whole college is involved in some way, whether it's with music, or performing, or writing, or in the technical department.

Michael St. John has put the Havana section from *Guys and Dolls* in – all Jade has to do is act drunk and get thrown around the stage, which she actually doesn't do a bad job of with her long limbs sliding around like Bambi on ice. (No singing involved.) Alec's in all the third-year numbers, despite being a first-year, and Leon and Kiki have got into a special piece for all the dance

263

finalists of the awards choreographed by Clair Patterson, who Kiki tells me is a big deal in the commercial dance world.

One of Luca's songs has made it into the showcase. I spot him after college one afternoon sitting on one of the benches in the foyer, packing up a clarinet.

'Hi, Luca. Congratulations on getting your song selected. That's brilliant.'

He looks up. 'Thanks. How are you? I haven't seen you for weeks.'

'I've had a lot of vocal coaching lately,' I say.

He closes the clarinet case. 'I don't think I've ever heard you sing.'

'There's a story about that, but I won't bore you now.'

'Well,' he says, 'we never did get that coffee. I'm a good listener.'

'I've got a lot going on at the moment,' I say. 'And Steph Andrews has banned me from caffeine. But maybe when things are less hectic, I'll go for a water with you?'

He stands up. 'Seriously, Nettie. I'd love to spend more time with you.'

For a second, I don't know what to say. 'Oh – it's just – there's kind of . . . someone else.' Kind of.

'Is it Fletch?'

'Why – has he said something?'

'No, but I've seen the way you look at him. If it is, I'd rather know. I don't want to step on a friend's toes.'

'Well . . .' I hesitate. 'Yeah, kind of. But I'd prefer you didn't—'

'Yeah – I mean, I won't. Thanks for telling me.' He picks up his things. 'I'd still love that water some time, as friends, if you're up for it.'

I hug him. 'Sure.'

It goes around college that Jade's dad has been in to see Miss Duke to demand she let her sing in the Summer Showcase.

'Can you believe it?' says Kiki. We're walking back to our changing room after jazz, drenched in sweat as usual. She looks around to check no one is in earshot. 'I mean, if you were Jade, wouldn't you just tell him to stay out of it? She must know that everyone thinks she's a terrible singer.'

'I don't think she cares.' I say it quietly to avoid a group of passing second-years overhearing us on the stairs. 'She's got really thick skin.'

'She's gonna need it after the reviews she gets in the showcase,' says Kiki. 'They get the press in for first night. Listen, I've got to rush off for physio. See you back at the halls?'

'Sure,' I say.

I jump in the shower and stay there for ages, enjoying the fact that everyone's gone home so I can spend longer than two minutes in there. The showers in the halls go cold after about thirty seconds. I pootle around in my towel, dry my hair and get dressed, before sauntering down to the foyer.

There's someone playing the piano in the studio theatre.

Fletch?

It kind of sounds like him, if a piano *can* sound like a person.

Should I go in? He'd be none the wiser. But *I* would know, and that would make all the difference. It'll be like a test. I slip in through the door.

He's halfway through the first chorus of 'Fly, Fly Away' from *Catch Me If You Can*. But as the door closes behind me, the piano stops. He knows I'm there – well, he knows *someone* is there. It's been a long time since we did this. He might not even want to accompany me.

I decide I don't care, picking up where he left off.

Nothing happens for a few seconds. Then I hear a scuffling of sheet music, and he's with me.

It's just us, like it was last year, before everything went wrong between us. God, I've missed this.

I realize something else as well.

I don't need them any more, these secret sessions in the studio theatre. I'm finally free.

As soon as the song finishes, he closes the piano lid. I pick up my bag and head to the door. Opening it, I hear him say quietly,

'Goodbye.'

CHAPTER 23

Goodbye, he said. That's odd. Did he mean he wouldn't be coming back? I'd kind of made up my mind that I was finally done with it, that I didn't need it any more, but a tiny part of me wishes I could go back to the studio again just to see if he's there. I guess I'll never know now. And he'll never know it was me.

It would be too much hassle to tell Alec I've agreed to go out with Fletch tomorrow. He's been reminding me of all the reasons I shouldn't be with Fletch for the last few weeks and steered me away whenever he's seen him approaching. I just . . . well, I just want to hear what he has to say. Who knows – maybe we can repair our friendship. Maybe something could even happen between us.

I'm in the changing room after lunch the next day – the day we're meant to be meeting. It's packed and there's barely any room to move, let alone get changed. Jade and Natasha are over the other side, by the mirrors. Ever since Kiki videoed Natasha's peculiar anti-lesbian outburst, they've left us alone. As people leave and it gets quieter, I hear Natasha whisper to Jade.

'So, you two are back on?'

'Yeah,' says Jade under her breath.

'What did Fletch say?'

Jade glances over at me (I pretend not to be listening). 'I'll tell you tonight, afterwards.'

It's back on?

I feel sick.

I wait until they've gone before I get my phone out to text Kiki. A banner flashes up on the homescreen alerting me that Fletch has messaged me. Of course. It's going to be him cancelling tonight because he's seeing Jade. How could I let him do this to me again?

I throw the phone as hard as I can. It smashes against the mirror and lands on top of a pile of paper towels in the bin. Kiki walks in just as it happens.

'Nettie, what's wrong?' She fishes my phone out of the bin and hands it to me. A piece of glass from the smashed screen cuts my finger. Great.

'Let's just say nobody had better mess with me today.'

Ballet with Millicent Moore does nothing to help my mood. I warm up at the barre and try not to make eye contact with Natasha Bridgewell, who looks smugger than if she'd just been offered a two-year contract on the *Mamma Mia!* world tour.

Miss Moore sweeps in, her chiffon teaching skirt trailing behind her. She's pissed about something.

That makes two of us.

Without even so much as a greeting, she starts making up a complicated *plié* exercise and cues the music immediately. We all fumble into position, each keeping an eye on the best girl at the front of the barre because most of us haven't a clue what comes next.

Today she's ignoring me. That's weird. Usually I have to endure little digs all the way through class. I do the best I can – although it makes little difference whether I make maximum effort or not – if Millicent Moore is out to get me, she will have me, whatever I do.

As we leave the barre she goes over to the piano and lights up a cigarette. I see a few raised eyebrows – there were rumours she smoked in class, but no one really believed them. When one girl goes to open a window, Miss Moore snaps, 'Leave it!' Instead, she comes over to the window nearest me and flings it wide open. It's pouring outside and water starts coming in.

I struggle through the *adage* section while hard rain batters the backs of my legs. At one point I slip on a puddle. Millicent Moore comes over.

'Not like that, Antoinette. We can't have our foot trailing down there, can we? Even stubby legs like yours should be able to cope with simple moves like these. I guess the talent didn't run in the family.'

'I thought you said my mum didn't have any talent,' I mutter through gritted teeth. I might have apologized, but I still haven't forgotten.

'Shut your mouth, you little bitch,' she snarls in a whisper. 'And get your *développé* higher. Maybe we need an incentive.'

She gets her half-smoked cigarette and holds it under my leg. I'm at the back, so no one can see what she's doing. Even if they could see in the mirror they wouldn't dare turn around. She moves it closer to my thigh, forcing me to lift it higher, which is impossible because it's already about as high as it can go. My leg is shaking with the effort. The heat burns through my ballet tights, giving off a smell of melting fabric. She pushes the cigarette into my thigh. There's a searing noise. A second later, I feel the pain.

'What do you think you're doing?' I yell, breaking position and heading for the door. 'Is there *actually* something wrong with you?'

She follows me. 'Come back here now, or I'll tell Miss Duke about your little outburst.'

'Like hell, you will.' It's hard to think straight through the burning pain my my thigh.

'Probation period finished yet, has it?' She says this loudly so that everyone can hear. 'I thought not. Well, you'll have to go home to Granny and tell her you don't have it in you to be as good as Mummy.'

'What exactly is your problem with my mother?' I say. The music has stopped now, the rest of the class not even bothering to pretend they're not listening. 'Is it the fact that she was way more successful than you, or just that she was more talented? Are you still jealous of her, after all these years?'

'Anastasia was delusional,' she says, shaking with rage. 'She was wild. She drank and slept her way to the top—'

'I DON'T CARE!' I shout. 'I don't care if she slept with the entire orchestra of the Royal Opera House. I've seen her dance. She was amazing. She had more talent in her little finger than you've got in your whole body. And do you know why? Because her soul was beautiful, and it came out in her dancing. All that's ever come out of you is bitterness and resentment.'

'Well, guess what?' shouts Millicent, right up in my face. 'She's dead.'

I look around the class at the stunned faces (including Natasha's; for once she has nothing to say), then back at Millicent's, twisted in hatred.

'Go fuck yourself,' I say. And I storm out.

That's it. I'm out. As soon as she tells Miss Duke what I just said, I'm expelled. Right now, I don't care. I meant it.

I run up three flights of stairs to the changing room and pull on my clothes. I don't have a coat, but I'm barely bothered by that. I'm too angry. I grab my bag and go downstairs.

It's the last period of the day. Classes are still going on in most of the studios – except the studio theatre, which is oddly empty. I look through the window and see Jade and Fletch at the far end of the room. He's holding her face gently in his hands. She's looking blissfully into his eyes. They turn and see me.

'Oh, for God's sake,' I spit.

I turn and run out of the studio, through the foyer, out into the rainy Soho streets, sobbing as I head into the square.

'Nettie!'

It's Fletch. He catches up with me and grabs my arm. It's four o'clock in the afternoon, but the rain has left the streets deserted.

I try to shake him off. 'Leave me alone.'

'Nettie, it's not what it looks like.' He lets go of my arm.

'Classic response. Hilarious, Fletch. Really funny.'

'No, it's not. We were rehearsing.'

'Is that what you call it?'

'*Yes*,' he says. We're both soaking wet, and it's hard to hear what the other is saying because of the torrential rain clattering over the trees. 'Michael St. John was in the studio with us. Didn't you see him? He's rehearsing us for the summer show. Our duet's back on after Jade's dad went and threatened Miss Duke last week. He said he'd pull out of the new building if Jade didn't get a song in the show.'

'Michael was in there? Really?' I say skeptically.

'We were rehearsing,' says Fletch. 'Nettie, honestly.'

I remember what Natasha said to Jade earlier: *So, you two are back on?* Could she have meant the duet? I briefly wonder if he's telling the truth. Then anger burns back through. He's done

271

nothing but mess me around.

'I thought we had something,' I say through tears. I don't care if he knows how I feel any more. 'We were so close. I thought we had a connection.'

'We did. We *do*. Nettie, I'm so into you. But you keep pushing me away.'

'That night you told me you had feelings for Jade, I thought something was going to happen.'

'Jade . . . ? What—'

'And then the next thing I knew, you were together and singing the song we wrote with her. *Our song*, Fletch.'

'You didn't want to sing it with me! I kept asking you. I thought it was your way of telling me to get lost. That really hurt, Nettie.'

'I *couldn't* sing!' I shout. 'Anyway, what do you care? You moved on pretty quickly to Jade!' I tuck my sopping hair behind my ears.

'Moved on to Jade? What are you on about?'

'You told me you had feelings for her. At Christmas.'

'You thought I meant Jade?'

'There's someone *else*? Great, Fletch – that's just great.'

He stares at me. 'I was confused. I told you, I've been a prick. It wasn't real. It's not real.'

This is ridiculous. I don't even know what to say now. I stand there, drenched, staring at him.

'Nettie, *say* something,' he says.

I don't say anything.

I start to sing.

I sing, in the middle of Soho Square on a Friday afternoon in the pouring rain with tears streaming down my face. I sing the song we wrote together all those months ago, full pelt, at him. I sing *us*.

For a while, he listens. Then he runs over to me and holds my face, staring into it as if he's searching for something. Before I know what is happening, we are kissing. I can taste the rain on his lips and the mint in his mouth and together they're the most amazing thing ever. I throw my arms around him as he grasps my wet hair tightly in his fingers.

Then I remember something, and I pull away.

'I can't do this,' I say. 'Not if there's someone else.'

And before he has a chance to say anything, I turn and run.

CHAPTER 24

The first thing I do when I get back to the halls is go into my bag for my phone. It's all smashed up and won't switch on. I lie on my bed, my mind racing with everything that's just happened.

Fletch likes me. And not Jade. But someone else? . . . Although that might be over and not real anyway. What does that even *mean*? I wish I hadn't run off. I wish I'd stayed and asked him. Argh, I can't even message him now. What if he's called me? Surely he would have called me. Christ, I'm so confused.

The next thing I know, Alec, Kiki and Leon are banging the door down, trying to get in.

'All right!' I say, opening the door for them to barge in.

'OK, spill,' says Alec. 'What happened in ballet? Miss Moore went home halfway through a class and everyone's being saying that you had a row.'

'Did she go home?' I say. 'Well, at least she didn't go straight to Miss Duke. Maybe I've got another day of not being expelled.' I tell them what happened.

'Nettie, that's abuse,' says Leon. 'She'll never tell Miss Duke. If she does, she'll have to admit to burning you. Did anyone see her do it?'

'No. But they all heard me telling her to go fuck herself, *and* I'm on probation.'

'Just keep your head down from now on,' says Alec. 'Don't go to any more of her classes. Anyway, what happened with Fletch?'

'Nothing.'

'Er, well, if by "nothing" you mean having a blazing row in Soho Square in the pouring rain, then snogging each other *majorly* passionately, then yeah.' He does a *Pippin* with his hands on the word 'yeah'.

'How do you know?' I say, amazed.

'Let's just say the rehearsal in Studio Four stopped for about ten minutes while everyone watched out of the window. Nothing like a good matinée on a rainy afternoon.'

I groan. 'Everyone saw us?'

'Babe, we opened popcorn,' says Alec cheerfully. 'Well, me and all the third-years.'

'And first-year jazz on the second floor,' adds Kiki.

'I seem to have been the only one who missed it,' says Leon. 'Let me know when it's on Netflix, will you?'

'Come on, then,' says Alec.

I tell them everything – from yesterday in the studio theatre, to seeing Fletch and Jade, to our row in the square, to the kiss, and finally me running off. They don't say anything, even when I've finished talking.

'Christ,' says Alec finally. 'I thought *my* life was complicated. What are you going to do? Have you heard from him since?'

'No. I threw my phone against a wall and it smashed.' I feel a little like I overreacted now. 'There is one good thing to come out of all this, though . . . I can sing again. The tightness in my throat has gone. It feels normal again.'

'Go on, then,' challenges Alec. 'Sing us something.'

So I do.

And it's good.

275

It seems Millicent Moore hasn't told Miss Duke what I said to her and fortunately no one else has said anything, either. I'd better do as Alec suggests – stay out of trouble and keep singing.

It's working. I haven't sung like this since before Mum died. Her image is clear now, not sketchy and intermittent like it was at the beginning of the year. It still hurts that she's not coming back (I don't think that'll ever go away), but in a weird way, when I sing she *is* back. She's there with me through every note, and I never want to lose that feeling again.

If it weren't for the row I'd had with Fletch, I'd be on cloud nine. I don't see him at all. He's busy rehearsing all the stuff he's in for the Summer Showcase, and seeing as my phone is going to take a week to be fixed, it's not likely that I'll hear from him, either. I wonder if he's tried to call? Maybe he's gone off with this other girl, whoever she is. It's hard to know what to think any more.

The following week is spent back and forth between Duke's and the Novello theatre, doing tech and dress runs of the show. I'm in two numbers – Michael has added me to a second-year number as well – which is more than most of the other first-years are in, so at least Miss Duke will see I'm doing well, even if she hasn't heard me sing yet. All the teachers are so busy this week that I wouldn't be able to pin any of them down for five minutes to listen to me, even if I tried. I'll just have to hope I get an opportunity before the end of term.

Natasha Bridgewell has managed to get herself a position as assistant dance captain to one of the third-year girls. She's loving her life, bossing everyone around and finding fault – especially with everything *I* do. I've got to grit my teeth and bear it because

Miss Duke's sitting in the audience somewhere with the God mic and she won't be afraid to use it if I start an argument with Natasha. Getting notes is fine, but when Natasha says stuff like *Nettie, that move is on three, not four* (after blatantly telling me it *was* four) and *Nettie, you're in the wrong place – you're standing in front of the projection video* (when *she* put me there not five minutes earlier), it begins to feel like sabotage.

'Nettie, we're using a live feed for close-ups at this point,' she says on the second afternoon of tech rehearsals at the theatre. 'If you stand there, you're blocking the camera. It doesn't need a close-up of your feckless arse.'

I start to lose my temper. But it seems that Leon, Alec and Kiki have taken it upon themselves to take shifts in watching over me to make sure I don't get expelled, and when Leon catches my eye from the wings, I manage to rein myself in.

I can't talk to Fletch. He's always onstage. Even when he's not, he's talking to Michael about the band arrangements. Despite being on the writers course, he's now starring in at least six numbers. I get it – he's amazing. But I bet the MT boys are pissed off. He only joined in with a few MT classes this year because Miss Duke forced him to. Now he's singing more solos that the rest of them put together.

We're in the theatre all day and back at college to rehearse in the evenings, which makes it impossible to go and pick up my new phone. Argh. What if Fletch has messaged me and I've missed it?

After the dress rehearsal on Saturday morning, we get a half-hour break before the notes session. It should be long enough to slip out to the phone shop.

Bad decision. By the time I've fought my way through the

Covent Garden shoppers, I'm four minutes late back to the theatre. This is not going to go down well with Miss Duke when I'm already on probation.

One of the crew is having a cigarette outside a side exit. He doesn't look especially approachable.

'Excuse me?'

He looks me up and down. 'Yeah?'

'Erm, is there any chance I could . . .'

'Sneak in? You late?'

'Er, yes.' This was a mistake. He's going to bollock me.

But he doesn't. He looks up the road towards stage door, then nods. 'Go on, then. Just make sure you sign in.'

I thank him and slip through the crack of door he's left for me. It wouldn't be good for me to be discovered here during a break, but it's better than being officially late. I can always say I forgot to tick myself in, or get Alec to do it. He probably already has. I steal along the passageway and open the auditorium doors. It's completely empty. They must have delayed the notes session. Good, I've got time to sign in. I slip through the pass door, which leads me straight into the wings.

Miss Duke and Jade are there, standing in the middle wing. I duck behind a curtain.

'No, Jade. Do it again. *Da daa dada dada* – I don't know the words, but you do. Come on.'

'I–is it flat?' stammers Jade.

'*And* sharp,' snaps Miss Duke. 'Do it.'

Jade tries again, twice, but it gets worse each time.

'This is precisely why I didn't let you sing onstage in the Duke's Awards finals.' Miss Duke uses the phrase 'Duke's Awards' very comfortably, despite it containing her own name.

'I fully appreciate what your father is doing for us, with the new building. But I cannot let you disgrace the whole college. We open tomorrow, Jade, and I've already delayed the press until the following show, an embarrassment in itself. Sort it out by tomorrow night or I'll have to cut the whole number from the remainder of the run.'

'Yes, Miss Duke,' says Jade quietly.

Miss Duke leaves. Jade bursts into tears and crosses the stage.

I get up to the dressing room and tell Kiki what I've heard.

'I'm not surprised,' says Kiki. 'Did you hear her in the dress rehearsal this morning? I think my ears were bleeding.'

'I kind of felt sorry for her.'

'Are you kidding me?' says Kiki.

'It's just – I know how frustrating it is not to be able to sing.'

'That was completely different! You lost your already-good voice because of stuff you were dealing with. Jade can't sing in tune, yet forces her voice upon us all every chance she gets and even gets her dad to buy her *more* opportunities, taking them away from *actual talented people*. It's not the same thing.'

We head back to college as soon as the notes session is over. Miss Duke isn't happy with several of the numbers and makes us rehearse all afternoon. Kiki, Leon, Alec and I sit on the sweaty tube together, too tired to speak. It's all we can do to get up the stairs at the other end. God, I need a shower.

I've just finished rinsing out the shampoo when my door goes. I run to get it, throwing a towel around me and squeezing out my dripping hair, expecting it to be Alec.

It's Fletch.

'Hi,' he says.

279

'Er, hi.' I'm half naked and soaking wet. Not how I envisaged this conversation.

'Sorry to drop by unexpectedly.'

'I would ask you in, but . . .' I look down at the puddle on the floor.

'Right. Of course. Sorry.'

He stands there, staring at me. I adjust the top of my towel where it's tucked in under my armpit.

'So . . . ?' I say. I'm not starting.

'Oh,' he says, remembering himself. 'Yeah. I wanted to . . . er, give you something.'

'What?'

'Did you get my messages this week?'

'Oh,' I say. 'No, sorry. My phone broke. I haven't had it all week. I've got it back now, but it hasn't charged yet.' Wow, Nettie. Thrilling conversation.

'I was hoping you'd say something like that.' Apparently he's easily pleased.

'What do you mean?'

He looks awkward.

'Just, you know, as opposed to something like, "Fuck off, you twat." I thought you might say that.'

'It's been on my mind,' I say.

'Yeah, well.' He reaches into his jacket and pulls out a white envelope. 'I deserve it. But if there's any chance you can forgive me, Nettie . . . Here. This is for you. Please read it.'

'Can't you just tell me?' I'm desperate to squeeze the ends of my hair into the corner of the towel but I can't because it's a short towel and I'm already flashing enough at him.

'No. It's too embarrassing,' he says. 'Look, just read it and . . .

let me know what you think?' He sounds nervous. I notice he's grabbing his hair again.

'OK.'

'OK. See you tomorrow, Nettie.' He turns and heads off down the corridor.

Screw the wet hair. He's written me a letter? I make a leap on to my bed to tear it open and read it.

But in the process, I slip on the wet floor. My feet go flying up in the air, throwing me back with a heavy thud as my head bangs on the wooden floor. Everything goes black, and I pass out.

I can hear something vibrating. It's fuzzy at first, but becomes clearer. Are there workmen outside?

It's my phone.

Groggily, I press accept.

'Nettie! Nettie, are you OK?'

It sounds like Alec. Alec's digging up the road? What?

'Nettie, where are you? You missed warm-up, and we're just about to get the half.'

I stand up quickly. The effort makes me nauseous.

'Oh God, I'm going to be sick.' I stagger to the toilet, taking the phone with me.

'Nettie, what's happened?' says Alec down the phone. 'Are you spewing? You weren't drunk without me last night, were you?'

I rub the back of my head, feeling a huge bump and quite a lot of dried blood. 'I think I knocked myself out.'

'How on earth did you manage that?' says Alec.

'I fell.'

'If it's bad enough to make you vom, you shouldn't do the show today.'

The show.

'I have to,' I say.

'Nettie, you've clearly got concussion. You should be in hospital. The show can wait.'

The show *never* waits. The show must go on. Especially when you're on probation and likely to get expelled if you don't turn up.

'Nettie—'

'Gotta book an Uber. Bye.'

Except I can't book an Uber because none of my apps have downloaded yet. I'll have to flag down a cab. Dammit.

Tentatively, I get myself under the shower. I've got to wash all this blood out of my hair. I'll have to be extra gentle.

Despite the pain, I manage to get myself washed, dressed and ready in seven minutes. The unopened envelope lying on the floor reminds me of the visit from Fletch last night. I grab it on my way out.

I try to stay the waves of nausea as I sit in the back of the cab. OK, where's that letter?

> *Dear Nettie,*
>
> *The first thing I have to do is apologize to you for being a total and utter knob. I won't blame you if you tear this letter up and never speak to me again. (Please don't. But if you do, I get it.)*
>
> *I need to explain this from the beginning.*
>
> *That first day we met, upstairs in the common room, I couldn't believe my luck. I met an amazing person – beautiful, clever,*

282

funny – who understood what I'd gone through with Danny.
When you helped me with the end of my song, I felt that we
had a connection. And as the weeks passed, this grew, and I
knew I had feelings for you.

But all the time there was something else going on that I
never told you about. I've been a total dick.

The first day back at Duke's, I was in the studio theatre, and
someone walked in and sang. A girl. I was blown away,
Nettie. She was breathtaking. I'd never heard a voice like
that before. It happened again and again. And every time
it happened, I got more and more drawn in. I felt this
connection so strongly with her – similar to what I was
experiencing with you, only this was an anonymous musical
connection. It was huge for me.

I felt like I was living a double life. And although there was
nothing happening with the other girl (we'd never actually
met), I felt guilty, because I was spending so much of my
time thinking about her. That was when I told you. I was so
attracted to you, Nettie, but I was obsessed with her voice. It
didn't feel right starting something up with you when I had
all that going on. I kept thinking I would just walk through
the studio doors and find out who she was, because deep down I
knew that if I did, then it would all be real, and it would stop
all the feelings.

But I was afraid. I was afraid to end what I had with her.
Losing Danny has affected me deeply. A musical connection

with someone is one of the things I've missed the most. You and I had it with the writing, but then you stopped wanting to work with me. I couldn't understand why.

I didn't think for a second that it could be you singing with me, Nettie. You told me there was something prohibitive going on with your voice – the problem you were having – and it didn't even occur to me that it could be you I was meeting in the studio theatre every night. When did you know it was me?

I think I know. It was when Jade walked in on us. Did you think we were together? I keep thinking about that now. Was that why you stopped coming? I was devastated. I felt I had got what I deserved. I'd messed you around, and you were (quite rightly) mad at me. I'd lost you. And now I'd lost the singing girl as well. I should have put two and two together.

When you came and sang last week in the studio, I'd already made up my mind that it would be the last time. I knew it was you – the real you – that I wanted, and I had to let this other girl go. I didn't know I was letting you go.

I can't tell you how many times over the last week that I wish I'd told you. Or you'd told me. We could have spared each other so much heartache.

Can you imagine how I felt when I heard you sing in the square? The two people I was obsessed with were one person. One perfect, amazing person. And I'd messed it up with both of them.

284

Nettie, I meant what I said when I told you that I was over the other girl – I'd finally realized what a knob I'd been, and I wanted to tell you – but you were asking me about Jade and then you were singing and I was distracted and confused and then, well . . . I'm sorry that instead of explaining myself, I just threw myself at you – I don't know what I was thinking. It's all I can think about now.

I hope you can forgive me. I love you, Nettie. I've loved you since that first day.

Yours, forever, in hope,

Fletch x

CHAPTER 25

So it's been me all along? *Both* mes? I try to get it straight in my concussed head.

I should be happy.

But I can't help feeling annoyed that he liked the 'me' behind the studio doors more than the real me.

Also, it's a bit weird, falling for a voice.

Maybe I'm being harsh. I think hearing him sing, that first time in the library, was what sealed it for me, so in a way, we're the same. If I'd just been able to sing that day, none of this would have ever happened. Maybe we'd be together.

It just never entered my head that he could be attracted to someone he'd never met before. I was so convinced he was with Jade. And I'm sure that's what *she* wanted me to think, as well.

We're like a sort of Georg and Amalia in *She Loves Me* – unaware that their colleague is, in fact, their mystery pen pal they've been in love with the whole time. Or Stephanie and Michael in *Grease II* – where she's in love with him, but only when he's in disguise as a hot biker. I realize that makes me the hot biker and Fletch the Pink Lady, but hey. We're a musical theatre plot gone wrong.

But musical theatre love stories generally have happy endings. So why shouldn't ours?

The cab stops in traffic. Oh god – the show opens in twenty-five minutes. Miss Duke will be prowling the corridors making sure everyone's sufficiently nervous. I definitely cannot afford to be late. If I don't make it for the fifteen minute call, they won't let me onstage.

'I'll just get out here, thanks,' I say to the cab driver. It looks as if there's more traffic ahead. It's not easy to run with a broken head, but it's quicker.

As I cross Tavistock Street to the stage door, Natasha Bridgewell jumps out at me from behind a car. What's she doing here? She should be inside.

'Hi, Nettie.'

'What do you want?'

'Hi.' Now Jade's appeared. Of course.

'We just need to ask you a little favour,' says Natasha. She and Jade hold me by the elbows outside the stage door to stop me going in. 'As part of my duties as *assistant dance captain –*' (Christ, she just loves saying that) – 'Miss Duke has asked me if I can give you a little extra task in the Summer Show.'

'What?' I say, irritated. I need to get signed in. I try to free myself, but Natasha tightens her grip.

'You see, Jade's really suffering from a terrible throat.'

Terrible voice, more like, but I'm not going to go there.

'I am,' says Jade.

She sounds perfectly normal to me.

'You know the booth in the wings?' says Natasha. 'For backing vocals?'

'Yes,' I say. I can't get rid of them, so I might as well humour them.

'Well, there's another one, under the stage,' says Natasha. 'It's not been used this year, but I've had it all wired up and ready to go. We're going to need you to go in there during Jade's vocal number with Fletch and sing her part.' She says it quite casually, as if she's just asked me to go and grab her a Diet Coke from the newsagent's.

'What are you talking about?' I say.

'I'll show you,' she says. 'It won't take a minute.' She pushes me through the stage door and drags me down under the stage to a caged-in area with a microphone set up on the back wall. It's cold and smells of mice. Alec was right about it being grim down here.

'All you've got to do is sing into here,' she says cheerfully. 'You'll have cans so you can hear the orchestra. And there are three monitors. The first screen shows the MD in the pit. The second shows the stage right wing – I'll be there – and you'll see Jade and Fletch on the live-feed monitor here, so you can match Jade's mouth. I've wired the booth mic up to Jade's radio mic channel. It'll go straight out front.'

'Hang on a minute.' The realization of what they're asking slowly seeps through. 'You want me to sing for Jade while she mimes onstage? No way.'

'Miss Duke's asked especially for you,' says Jade, 'so you have to.'

'Miss Duke's never heard me sing,' I say. 'So, that's rubbish.' I go to leave but Natasha stops me by putting her arm across the entrance of the cage.

'*We* have,' she says. 'And we think you're the person for the job.'

'You haven't heard me.' I wrack my brains for a time where they might have overheard me. Upstairs with Steph? No, they'd have been in class. When, then?

'Your little friend Alec showed us a video of you singing on

New Year's Eve,' says Jade.

Oh god. 'Well, I'm not doing it,' I say.

'You will do it,' says Natasha. 'Because if you don't, you'll be expelled.'

'Miss Duke's not going to expel me for refusing to be part of your sick plot to make Jade look good.'

'No,' says Natasha. 'But she might expel you for telling one of her longest-standing teachers to go fuck herself.'

Of course. Natasha was in the class with Millicent Moore. Naturally she's been waiting for an opportunity to use that one. I *can't* get expelled now. Not after everything that's happened.

I'm cornered. I know it, and they know it, too. Natasha moves her arm to let me go, calling after me, 'See you here at the top of Act Two!'

I trudge up to the dressing room. Kiki's not there, so I go and knock on the first-year boys' door. Alec answers.

'Hi, darling. You're here.'

'What the hell did you think you were doing, showing Jade and Natasha that video of me?' I say angrily.

'What video?' He looks at me blankly.

'The video of me singing in the karaoke bar,' I say. 'I specifically told you not to share it after you showed Steph.'

'Well, technically, I didn't – *after*,' says Alec. 'I'd already shown them. They were bitching about how you never did anything and how you were such a shit singer that you ran out of MT. I wanted to shut up their smug faces. Anyway, what does it matter now?'

'This is a disaster.' I put my head in my hands. It's still throbbing from the fall.

'Why?' says Alec. 'It was ages ago.'

I tell him what's just happened under the stage. He stands,

289

thinking, for a few moments while I wait expectantly for him to come up with a brilliant solution as usual. But instead he says,

'You'll just have to do it.'

'What?' I can't believe he's saying that. Whose side is he on?

'Nettie, they've got you over a barrel. You've just got your voice back, haven't you? You don't want to be expelled now. Not after everything you've been through. And *I* need you here, darling girl. ' He takes my hand in his and kisses it affectionately.

I snatch my hand away. 'What, you're saying I just get on with it?'

'I'm saying exactly that. It's only one song.'

'*Two* songs.'

'Whatever. Just get over yourself and sing them. Then you can move on with your life. Look, I've got to go. See you after?'

And with that, he disappears. Fuming, I storm back to my dressing room.

I avoid speaking to anyone during Act One. I sit in my place with my headphones on listening to 'No Good Deed', enjoying the way it feeds my anger at Alec (but secretly hoping he bursts through the door with a plan). Kiki mutters something about going down to rehearse something during the interval. She doesn't come back. On the five minute call for Act Two, realizing that Alec's not coming, I head down under the stage to the secret booth.

Why am I doing this – letting Jade win? I could just *not* do it. The satisfaction of seeing her fail might just outweigh being hauled into Miss Duke's office with Millicent Moore to explain my actions. But then I imagine that scenario. Miss Duke would never believe me over one of her longest-serving staff members. I'd be booted out on the spot. And then Jade and Natasha would *really* have won. No, much as I hate to admit it, Alec's right – I'm just going to have to suck it up and sing.

I step into the booth, put the cans on over my head and listen to the sound of the audience through them. When the show starts again I guess I'll be able to hear the orchestra or whatever foldback they've got onstage. I watch the monitors. The one focused on the MD just shows an empty seat at the front of the pit and a few people milling around with ice creams in the stalls behind it. The onstage monitor currently shows the iron. On the screen displaying the stage right wing, I can see students flitting about, chatting, grabbing props, warming up. Natasha's there in the background, going over some choreography with someone off-screen.

Then I see Alec. He looks like he's waiting for something or someone (in the splits, but still waiting). Fletch walks past. Alec jumps up and calls after him. Fletch turns back and they start talking. What's he up to now? Whatever he's saying, it seems to be pretty interesting to Fletch. Oh God, please don't let it be about me. Not before I've had a chance to speak to him myself. Alec puts his arm around Fletch's shoulders, and they stand there whispering to each other for a good few minutes. My stomach has a knot in it that has nothing to do with singing.

The MD appears on the second monitor, raising his baton, as the house lights go down behind him. On the backstage monitor, Alec and Fletch disband – Fletch on to the stage for his number with Jade, and Alec melting into the darkness of the wings. A figure I think is Michael St. John appears next to Natasha and starts talking to her. Surely he wouldn't be in on it? The orchestra starts up. I can just make out Luca on the far left of the MD, picking up his trumpet.

The lights go up onstage. As the curtain lifts, I see Jade and Fletch in position, ready to begin. Oh God, am I really doing this?

I take a simultaneous breath with Jade and begin singing. It seems to work. I can sort of hear myself coming through the cans in addition to hearing my voice coming out of my own body. Jade's miming muggily, grinning at Fletch wherever she can. His face isn't showing a flicker of recognition. I get that once you're up on the stage, it's a bit awkward to just stop if something feels weird – but it's like he hasn't even noticed. Oh, God, please tell me I don't sound like Jade.

The song ends and Jade stands there with a satisfied look on her face as the audience goes mad. The applause is so loud I have to take one side of the cans off my ear. I can't believe she's taking the credit for my singing. Jade and Natasha are going to blackmail me forever with this. I see the next year at Duke's, the two of them swanning around college having a wonderful time while I run around being their bitch.

Then something else occurs to me.

I just got my voice back, and it's been stolen from me.

I've become a ghost singer.

Marni Nixon, move aside. There's a new kid in town:

Nettie Delaney-Richardson.

There's no time to think about it any more because the music's just started for the second duet. It's the song I wrote with Fletch, to add to the misery.

Behind Jade and Fletch, the big screen at the back of the stage is projecting a black-and-white film of 1940s London. I start to sing again, all the while hating myself for what I have done. Jade looks so smug I can't even look at her. So I concentrate on the MD. It'll all be over soon. Just watch the MD.

292

I hear talking in the audience. It gets louder. The people I can see on the screen in the front row are nudging each other and pointing.

Then I see it.

On the screen behind Jade and Fletch, large as the entire backdrop, is my face, projected live on to the stage. I see the look of terror in my own eyes, and oblivious grin on Jade's face as she carries on miming.

What the—?

Then suddenly, from behind, someone grabs me and stuffs a hand over my mouth. It's Leon. Alec slips into my place and carries on singing, his voice an octave lower. Suddenly the audience is divided between gasps and confused chatter. The band eventually stops, led by a mystified conductor.

'Miss Duke, everyone, my apologies,' says Fletch. Leon has let go of me now as I watch the monitor, dumbstruck, too absorbed in the drama unfolding to check my horrified expression now being projected to eleven hundred people. 'But there is something you need to know. The voice you're hearing does not belong to the person you're watching.'

Jade looks at Fletch in fury but says nothing.

Miss Duke's voice materializes through the speakers. 'What are you talking about, Fletch? Can someone please tell me what's going on, and why I've had a show stop of two and a half minutes?'

'Nettie's downstairs singing in the booth,' says Fletch. 'Jade and Natasha forced her into it.'

'Bring her up here,' demands Miss Duke.

Leon and Alec drag me up to the wings and push me on to the stage.

'Well?' says the disembodied voice. 'Antoinette? Was that you singing?'

'Yes,' I say, but I have no mic on, and she doesn't hear me.

'What? Speak up!'

Fletch comes over to me and points to the radio mic on his cheek. 'Speak into here,' he whispers, holding it so he won't be heard.

'Yes, Miss Duke.' I say it to Fletch's cheek, which is glistening with sweat.

I look out to the audience. I can pick out some faces in the dark, but I can't see Miss Duke. People in the crowd start murmuring. I look to Alec in the wings, who's rather unhelpfully standing with his hands clasped in excited mini-applause. Then in the dark I see Miss Duke step through the pass door and into the wings. She walks on to the stage with her mic.

'My apologies for the show stop, ladies and gentlemen,' she says, perfectly calmly. 'But it appears we have a bit of a situation going on here.' She turns to me.

'Antoinette, was that you we just heard?'

I nod.

'Can you do it again?'

'I – I think so, Miss Duke.'

She turns to Jade.

'Get out of my sight, before I turn you out of this theatre *and* out of my college. You disgust me.'

Jade flees into the wings, mortified. A couple of people in the audience boo her as she goes offstage.

'Before this descends into the realms of pantomime,' says Miss Duke, 'I wonder if you'd indulge me in hearing that last song again. With its rightful star.'

A soundman runs on from the wings and fits a radio mic on me quicker than you can say Debbie Reynolds. Miss Duke strides

294

over to where I'm standing with Fletch on centre stage.

'Antoinette,' she says to me, smiling, 'I think it's about time you came off probation, don't you?'

The audience cheers.

She drops the mic down to her side and adds quietly, 'Anastasia would have loved this. Make her proud.'

She steps off the stage, leaving just me and Fletch. He takes my hand and mouths '*Ready?*' at me. I nod, and the MD strikes up the band again. Alec and Leon are dancing together in the wings like the couples do at the end of *Strictly*, and I think I can make out Kiki jumping up and down by the sound desk at the back of the stalls. Shouldn't she be backstage?

'They're playing our song,' says Fletch, laughing at his own cheesiness.

It *is* the cheesiest line ever, but today it also happens to be true. By the time we reach the end of the chorus, half the college has rushed on to the stage and is dancing with us. The audience is up in the aisles. Theatre etiquette seems to have gone out of the window.

The applause is thunderous – more so because there are at least a hundred students on the stage applauding as well. There's been so much going on that I've almost forgotten all the stuff that's happened with Fletch. He tilts my chin. Do I want to do this with all the cheering and whooping and students onstage?

All of that melts away as his face nears mine and he kisses me softly.

And this time I *know* it's for real.

295

CHAPTER 26

There's a party atmosphere in the air long after the finale has finished. Everyone piles into the Nell to celebrate an unusually high-drama first night – even by Duke's standards. Students are spilling out onto the road by the time I leave stage door. Fletch takes my hand and we walk together, like a couple. It feels a bit strange, seeing as we haven't talked about any of this yet.

Alec, Kiki and Leon bound up to us at the bar.

'Aaaaaaagh! You guys were amazing!' yells Kiki, throwing her whole self around me and spinning me around until I can't see. 'That was the most awesome show, like, in the history of Duke's! It's going to be one of those shows that people wish they were at, for hundreds of years.'

'And you were responsible for making it happen,' says Leon to her.

I look at him, confused.

'I distracted Natasha with loads of questions about Clair Patterson's number,' says Kiki. 'I knew it would work. Natasha's so far up Clair's arse I'm surprised she can even see the choreography.'

'It was the perfect ruse,' says Leon.

'Then I snuck through to front of house to hijack the guys on the live-feed desk,' says Kiki. I can tell she's proud of this.

'And they let you?' I say.

'We'd already told them what to do,' says Alec.

'Also I think the bloke in charge fancied me,' she says.

I'm confused. 'When did you do that? And how did you convince them to set up an extra camera in the booth?'

'I just told them it would be a good marketing opportunity,' says Alec. 'The show's gone viral, Nettie. It's already had a hundred thousand hits on YouTube. Did you notice they'd put their name at the bottom of the screen when it flipped to you?'

'I was quite distracted, if you remember.'

Alec laughs. 'Well, it's been great advertising for them.'

Michael St. John comes over, a little tipsy. He grabs my cheeks and kisses me on the head, sloshing his drink all over the floor. 'I knew you could do it, Nettie.'

'Wait, how did you know?'

'Darling girl,' says Alec. 'I know I'm the most capable person on the planet, but sometimes you need a bit of authority on your side. I had to enlist Michael.'

'*You* were in on it?' I say.

'We had to keep Natasha busy after Kiki went front of house,' he says. 'Let's just say I had a lot of notes for her.' He drains his now nearly empty champagne glass. 'I love a theatrical drama, and this was irresistible. So, as I think we can safely say you're cured, Nettie; Miss Duke and I would like you to reclaim the role for the rest of the run.'

Alec and Leon do a Disney Channel high five, and Fletch puts his arm around my shoulders.

'I knew there was something going on between you two.' Michael does a mini-point at both of us.

'Omigod,' says Kiki. 'They're, like, *meant to be.*'

Well, this is embarrassing.

Fletch looks down at me and says, 'Wanna get out of here?'

'Yup.'

We turn and leave the pub. People congratulate us and pat us on the back as we go (I must do at least six high fives). We come out on to the quiet street. It's a warm evening, and Covent Garden smells of cigarette smoke, garlic and restaurant grills. I feel like I'm on holiday.

'How did Natasha and Jade force you to go in the booth?' says Fletch.

'They were blackmailing me.'

'What reason could they possibly find to blackmail you?'

'I told Miss Moore to go fuck herself. It's a long story.'

'I've got all night.'

We start walking, heading down to Waterloo Bridge and across the river. The last of the day is fading over Westminster and the first stars are twinkling in the sky. At the South Bank, we stop and sit on a wall near the National Theatre – tonight illuminated by a giant rainbow projection.

'So, you got my letter?'

'I did.'

'When did you know it was me?'

'Only after Jade came in, like you said. I actually thought it was her playing until then.'

Fletch almost chokes with laughter. 'Jade? Seriously?'

'Yeah, and I thought you were together.'

'Why would you think that?' he says. 'Aside from anything else, I can't believe you thought I would go for a girl like that. She's pretty mean.'

'Well, she did say you were the "new love" of her life, and that she couldn't wait to spend time with her "new man".

What was I supposed to think?'

'Er, that we'd just been cast as the romantic leads in *Guys and Dolls*?' says Fletch.

'Well, it sounded like more than that,' I say. 'Fletch, can I ask you something?'

'As long as it's not, "How can you fall in love with a voice?"' he says, rolling his eyes with embarrassment.

'Er, yeah – it was that.'

'I really don't know.' He winces. 'I feel quite embarrassed about it now. Believe me, I've asked myself the same question. Maybe I kind of sensed it was you, even if I didn't *know* it was you . . . Nettie, can I ask *you* something?'

'Sure.'

'Why *didn't* you fall in love with my terrible piano playing, and how much practice do I have to do to ensure you're mine forever?'

I laugh. 'Your piano playing is really good. Why did you tell me you couldn't play?'

'I guess it's not my strongest point. I have to practise – a lot. Michael's been coaching me, but he's never happy. I think it rubs off.'

He takes my hand and I get a small whoosh of adrenaline. The good kind, not the kind that freezes you with fear and stops you doing things. God knows I'm the expert.

I smile. 'It's OK – I'm a sucker for a guitar.'

'Thank God for that.'

We walk and walk, eventually coming back over Charing Cross footbridge, up Villiers Street and through Chinatown. Fletch has his arm around my shoulders; I'm leaning into him. We find ourselves back in Soho Square, looking down Frith

Street, past Duke's towards Old Compton Street. It's 4 a.m. and the last hardcore partiers are toppling into Balans for breakfast before catching the first train home to bed. I think about the last time we were here. So much has changed since then.

'Duke's is different at night,' says Fletch. 'Like a dark theatre.'

We walk up to the front doors and stand there together, looking in.

'From now on, it's us, OK?' says Fletch. He holds me around the waist and draws me towards him. 'I can't lose you again, Nettie.' He kisses my eyes, one after the other.

Then he picks me up and kisses me on the mouth, and it feels like a first kiss – tender and warm and soft and new. Around us, Soho carries on noisily, ignoring the couple locked together on the corner of the square, oblivious to everything but the sound of their own music.

THE END

EPILOGUE

I close the door and lean against it, feeling the early-morning sun on my face. I'm so tired but can't imagine ever being able to sleep. What a night.

I'm standing on something. It's a square envelope with my name on. I bend down to open it. There's a memory stick inside. Who's sent me this?

Curiosity wins over tiredness, and I go straight to my desk and plug the memory stick into my computer, yawning as I wait for it to load. It's a video.

Should I play this? What if it's a virus, or something illegal? But as I peer at the blurred figure in the middle of the screen, I realize something.

It's Mum.

I press play immediately. She's onstage, somewhere big. She's dancing in a white tutu and headdress – it looks like she's playing Odette in *Swan Lake*.

But there's something not right. She's wobbling, falling out of her turns – at one point she crashes into a *corps de ballet* girl upstage left, who in turn falls off her *arabesque*, scowling. Wait – is that Millicent Moore? I rewind it and watch it again. Yes, it's definitely her. Oh my God. I knew she hated Mum, but I'd no idea they'd worked together. Well, *that* explains a few things.

As I watch, my feeling that there's something weird about Mum is confirmed.

Is she . . . *drunk*?

She starts a series of turns heading downstage and it's obvious she's not in control. She's going too fast. As she reaches her seventh turn, she misses her footing and stumbles, but the momentum she's built up forces her forwards. Too far forwards. With a shriek, she falls off the stage and lands with an almighty crash in the pit. Gasps and screams come from the crowd, people stand up to see, and whoever's holding the camera finds their view blocked. Amidst the panic, the orchestra stops playing and I hear someone yell,

'Call an ambulance – she's unconscious!'

Then the video stops. I replay the end again – twice, but that's it. I sit there, stunned.

Is this why Mum never told me about her career? Is this what she was hiding? Was it a one-off, or was she always drunk? I never saw her take even a sip of alcohol in my lifetime. My mind is spinning.

Occasionally people would approach Mum and ask her if she was Anastasia Delaney-Richardson. She always denied it. I thought it was because she didn't like the attention. But maybe she was trying to hide something from me.

I've got to find out. There are people at Duke's who know – Michael St. John, Miss Duke . . . Well, I'm not going to stop until they tell me.

I won't stop until I know what happened to Mum.

ABOUT THE AUTHOR

Vanessa Jones was born and raised in Kent. After training at Laine Theatre Arts, she went on to be a Musical Theatre actor in West End shows, including *Sister Act*, *Grease*, *Guys and Dolls*, *Annie Get Your Gun* and *Mary Poppins*, where she met (and married!) a fellow chimney sweep. She now lives in East Sussex with her sweep and their two children. *SING Like No One's Listening* is her first YA novel.

ACKNOWLEDGEMENTS

As a person who is frequently required to stand on a stage and thank people, it's a relief to be able to write these acknowledgements without the added pressures of an audience, the fear of not finding the right word in the moment, or just plain nerves . . .

To my fantastic agent, Jane Willis, I am so grateful for your support and how you championed my book from the very start. Along with Hannah and the rest of your team you have helped me grow wings. Thank you from the bottom of my heart.

To my editor George Lester, who is not only an incredibly talented man of words, and *the* most enthusiastic person I have ever met, but who, in a strange twist of fate, is now a musical theatre student at his own *real life* Duke's (I like to think you read *Sing* and thought, yep, that's the life for me!). It's beyond lucky – and a little hilarious – that I get to work with someone who *completely* gets the world I'm describing. I could thank you every day for the rest of my life and it wouldn't be enough. You had me at 'Seasons of Love' . . .

The hugest thank you to all the glorious people at Macmillan – to the wonderful Venetia Gosling, for believing in Nettie's story and taking a chance on her, and to Simran Sandhu and Cate Augustin for working with me to polish *Sing* into something lovely.

To Kat McKenna, Amber Ivatt and Emma Quick, I am so

glad that you are the fabulous people getting this book out into the world. You have *all the ideas*!

To Rachel Vale for designing the beautiful cover – I could never have imagined I would see *Sing* looking so utterly showbiz. My stagey heart thanks you.

To my gorgeous pal Lucy Dawson, for helping me with everything from 'how to do a first edit' (seriously), to guiding me through how to make the kids' tea when I was on deadline and the cupboard was bare ('But I don't even have *toast*'). Thank you for your patience with my many questions, and for your unwavering friendship. It means the world to me.

Huge thanks to copyeditor Veronica Lyons for helping me to find clarity in my writing, and to proofreader Emily Thomas – especially for checking my optimism when it comes to how long train journeys take! Thank you also to Tracey Ridgewell for setting the text, and to Viki Ottewill for taking in all the corrections.

To the amazing Keris Stainton, *the* biggest thank you for introducing me to the wonderful world of YA, and for giving me the motivation to get to the end of my first draft.

Jo Stocker – when a random stranger walked into the YA department of Waterstones in Tunbridge Wells, asking ALL the questions, and you not only answered every one and gave advice freely, but also kindly offered to read their book. . . your feedback gave me the courage to submit to agents, and I cannot thank you enough.

To George Stiles and Anthony Drewe, for allowing me to use your lyrics on Kiki's wall – I wanted your work to be an inspiration for her like it has for me in my life, both as a performer and a writer. Thank you.

To the amazing Tim Federle and Cheri Steinkellner, thank you for encouraging and inspiring me in those early days of *Sister Act*, when all I had was a secret blog and a vague thought that I might actually be able to do this one day. Your kind words were *treasure* and I still carry them with me.

To my husband Howard, you are everything. That is all. I love you.

To my parents, for supporting me through two very risky careers – first showbusiness, and now writing. Thank you for believing in me and never insisting I get a sensible job.

To Charlotte Parsons, for explaining technology to me (I will be making GIFs forevermore in your honour). Thank you to The JPA Company, my talented people, for helping me find emotionally appropriate songs for Nettie, and for the 'teen lingo' help (eg. not allowing me to write phrases like 'teen lingo'). You are all awesome.

To Eleanor Prescott, I don't know where to start. Thank you for teaching me how to hone my words, how to shape my ideas into a real book, for being ever-encouraging and relentlessly optimistic. I'm so grateful to have you as a mentor and friend. To the NBTs – Nick, Clair, Suzanne, Ros, Kate, Catherine, Emilie, and especially Karl – thank you for your help and feedback, for reading my work at its worst and never judging me.

And finally, this. Once upon a time, I stood on a stage to thank people, and out of nerves I forgot the most important person. It still haunts me. So thank you Emily, for the other thing.

Turn the page for the first chapter of Vanessa Jones's stunning sequel to *Sing Like No One"s Listening*: *Dance Like No One's Watching*!

CHAPTER 1

If my life was a musical right now, it would be that scene at the beginning of *Grease* where Danny and Sandy are frolicking in the waves, chasing each other up and down the sand dunes, laughing and – let's not forget this – *kissing*.

So much kissing.

Fletch and I have been living our best teen-romance lives this summer. And now my head is resting on his lap as we lie on the hill overlooking Crystal Palace Park, the warmth of his thigh under my neck competing with the early evening September sun on my face.

'Should we think about going?' I ask, my eyes still half closed. We're moving all my stuff from my grandmother's house to Alec's flat today, but I wanted to bring Fletch here first, for one last moment of 'us'.

College starts again tomorrow. I'm *ridiculously* excited about going back to Duke's, but it's just been Fletch and me for the whole summer. Everything changes tomorrow: the bubble bursts. Last year, Jade Upton did everything in her power to keep us apart, and it nearly worked. What's to say something like that won't happen this year? The last six weeks have been so good; I don't want anything to change.

'No. Let's stay here forever,' he says.

I laugh. 'You and I both know if we keep Alec waiting that

long, he'll be unbearable.' I sit up, shielding my eyes from the sun with my hand. 'At least we've had today. At least you didn't meet *her*.' My grandmother was only too glad to get rid of me when I moved into halls at Duke's Academy of Performing Arts last year. Now that I'm moving in with Alec, I'll never have to see her again.

Fletch props himself up on his elbows and takes off his sunglasses. 'You mean "Auntie"? She doesn't scare me.' My grandmother insists I call her Auntie because she says anything else is "ageing". It's ridiculous, but not worth arguing about.

'I know, but . . . it's been such an amazing summer. I don't want anything to spoil it.' The thought of only having a few precious hours of the holidays left makes my stomach flip over.

Life has been so good since the Summer Showcase. This could all slip through my fingers. What if I can't live up to people's expectations? The end of last year was kind of a big deal for me: after months of not being able to sing, of nearly getting kicked out of college, I finally managed it in spectacular fashion, onstage in the West End with a thousand people watching. Everyone's heard me now. As Kiki has been unhelpfully reminding me all summer, they'll be expecting things this year.

'You're right. It *was* amazing,' he says, reaching up to trace my jaw with his finger, sending feathers down my spine.

'You're not going to get me like that.'

'Wanna bet?'

He leans in and kisses me softly. My resolve disappears as we fall back down on to the grass together.

'Took your time, didn't you?' says Alec, helping me carry a box of sheet music up the stairs.

Alec's your basic pretty, white ballet boy – talented as hell, and knows it too: there's no better dancer at Duke's, nor one with a bigger ego. Or a bigger heart, as far as our friendship's concerned. God knows how I'd have got through last year without him. I glance down at him; his hair's been naturally highlighted from a month of 'summering' (his word) at his mum's chateau in Bordeaux, and his usually creamy skin is now a golden bronze.

'Sorry,' I say, panting slightly. 'Bumped into Auntie.'

Alec rests the box on the banister for a second. 'Whew. How did that go?'

'Oh, you know. As expected.'

'Did you ask her about the video?'

My eyes flicker to Fletch, who's coming up behind us. Thankfully, he doesn't seem to have heard Alec. 'Yeah,' I mutter, jogging Alec into action again with the box. 'I'll tell you about it later.' I'd like to keep the evening drama-free.

Alec seems to understand. 'Is this it?' he says as we reach the top of the stairs, nodding at the stuff we're lugging.

'Two more boxes.'

'Christ, Nettie,' says Alec. 'It's not a mansion, you know.'

It might as well be. After he begged her all year, Alec's mother finally relinquished her swanky London apartment to him. I have *majorly* lucked out. No flat hunting. No more going to my grandmother's house for the holidays. Don't get me wrong, it was fun living in halls with Alec, Kiki and Leon just down the corridor, but I'm really going to enjoy having a shower that's not glacial, and I *definitely* won't miss Jade Upton lording it over the common room like Regina George and generally making my life hell (if she even comes back to Duke's after the humiliation she suffered at the end of last year). Things are looking up.

'Most of it will go under my bed,' I assure him, as we take the box through to the living room.

'And the rest?'

'I thought maybe it could go in that big cupboard in the hallway? Come on, you owe me.'

Alec cocks his head to one side. 'How, exactly?'

'It's basically down to me that you're even here.'

'All I did was tell Mum how your grandmother treats you—'

'About seventeen times a day for three months.'

'. . . and let her know that she'd be saving you from cruelty and starvation if she let us move into the flat – all of which is true.'

Fletch calls down the hall to us. 'Where shall I put these cases?'

'*Cases?*' Alec looks at me in exasperation. I give him my biggest Orphan Annie grin. 'Oh, for God's sake . . .' He rolls his eyes at me. 'Just put them in the cupboard in the hallway,' he shouts back to Fletch.

Together we heave the last of the stuff up the three flights of stairs. It's a beautiful old building with a wrought-iron Grade II-listed lift, which would be wonderful if it actually worked. Fletch downs a pint of water, kisses me on the cheek, grabs his keys and stretches.

'Off so soon, my love?' says Alec.

'I'm double-parked,' says Fletch. 'Luca'll kill me if I get a ticket.' Fletch usually goes everywhere by motorbike, but today he's borrowed his best friend's car to help me move. 'Be right back.'

'Don't be long,' I say.

'I won't,' Fletch says, kissing me on each eye, working his way down my nose until our mouths meet. God, he's lovely.

4

There's a deliberate-sounding clatter from the kitchen. We both jump. Alec appears with a frying pan.

'Oops,' he says.

Grinning, Fletch takes the hint and leaves.

'Subtle,' I say, following Alec back into the kitchen. He points to the mounting pile of washing-up on the draining board.

'I'll wash – you can dry.' He puts some music on, starts doing a dance with the dishcloth (somehow it's sexy?) and throws me a tea towel. 'So first of all, why didn't you tell Fletch about seeing Auntie? He knows about the video, right?'

At the end of last year, I got a mystery envelope through my door at the halls. It contained a video on a memory stick of Mum dancing the part of Odette in *Swan Lake*, except that instead of being graceful and controlled, as you would expect of a prima ballerina, Mum crashes into another dancer before careering off the edge of the stage and falling into the pit. It's full-on drama – audience screaming, ambulance called, show stopped . . .

I've been watching it all summer. It's almost the only connection I have to her life before I came along. And it's throwing up more questions than answers.

There's so much she didn't tell me: how she was best friends with Miss Duke, how she had this amazing career as a dancer, how she left the business abruptly and never went back, and now this video . . . I feel like I barely knew her. How can you live with someone for nearly eighteen years and not know anything about their life?

'I couldn't,' I say. 'Fletch does know about the video – I showed him the day I got it. But at Auntie's, I made him wait in the car. It just seemed like too much of a downer to end our holiday together on. Anyway, you were right. I learned nothing

5

from her.'

'What did she actually say?' asks Alec.

'That it was none of my business. I didn't even collect Mum's stuff – Auntie threw me out before I could get to the loft and grab it.' I'm kind of kicking myself now that I didn't take Fletch in with me – I could've done with the support, and I'd have the boxes too.

'Ah, sorry. I didn't want to be right about that,' says Alec. 'Well, she's not the only person who knew her. There's Michael, Miss Duke – even Miss Moore, if you're feeling brave.' I can't help a little laugh at that last one. One of the ballet teachers at Duke's, Miss Moore, hated Mum and goes out of her way to let me know it. Not exactly my go-to for a cosy chat.

I take a deep breath through my nose. 'I really don't know what to do. Should I even be looking? What if I find out something horrible about her?'

Alec adjusts my fringe and gives me a cute grin. 'Whatever you need to do, I'm here for you,' he says. 'We can search newspaper archives, look at old ballet programmes, talk to people . . . We'll get you the truth. And equally, if you just want to forget all about it and drown your sorrows, I'll be there with a bottle of JD and my Mariah playlist.'

I smile. He just . . . *gets* me. Maybe the drowning-my-sorrows option would be better. It hurts to admit it, but this might just be one area of Mum's life that she didn't want me involved in, and who says I automatically get a free pass to it because I'm her daughter? She must have had her reasons for not telling me. Maybe I have to accept that.

But Mum was all I had. Although I try not to think about it too much, it's horrible feeling like I didn't really know her.

6

Knowing literally nothing about my dad was just something I accepted growing up. I had Mum, and we were everything to each other. But the more I dig, the more I'm realizing there was this secret part of her that I never got to know, and it hurts in a way I've never felt about my dad. I'm like a jigsaw with so many missing pieces that you can't make out what the picture is. Last year was traumatic, dealing with grief and losing my voice. I grew up so much, and now that I'm finding out who *I* am, I need those missing pieces.

But they're all hidden with Mum.

'Thanks,' I say. 'But I'm going to do it – I'll ask them all. Starting with Michael.'

'Whatever you need.' Alec smiles. He reaches for the other end of the tea towel in my hand and uses it to pull me in to a dip. 'So, tell me all about your gorgeous summer with Sir Hunkalot.'

'It was . . . amazing.' I giggle as he spins me out, Fred 'n' Ginger style, and grab a smooth pearl-grey plate from him that's obviously too posh to bung in the dishwasher. 'We went for walks, lay out in the fields watching the shooting stars, spent days at the beach . . . It was just amazing. His mum and dad were so welcoming, too.'

'And . . . ?' he says.

'And what?'

'Oh, come on. You two have so much drama, I thought there was bound to be something.'

He has a point. The journey to Fletch and me getting together wasn't exactly easy. 'No drama. No fights in the pouring rain. No college mean girls locking me in a cage trying to steal my voice.' I laugh. 'I guess we were too busy having a good time.' My brain floats back to big skies and the feel of his hand in mine.

'Ugh,' he says, rolling his eyes. 'Spare me the gory details. Actually, what am I talking about? I want to know *all* the details.'

I hesitate. Don't get me wrong, I could shout from our rooftop to the whole of Covent Garden about how my spine tingles when my new boyfriend touches me, how I crave being near him on a minute-by-minute basis. But if I tell Alec, then it doesn't belong to Fletch and me any more. I want to keep it for us.

Fletch sounds the door buzzer, sparing me.

I go to my room to unpack all my stuff while Fletch and Alec go to grab a take-away. I check my phone to see that Kiki and Leon have been messaging the group chat.

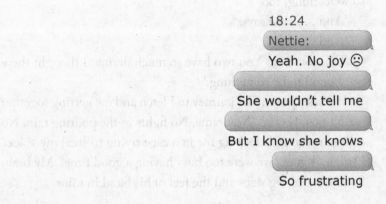

17:53

Kiki:
So?? How did it go at Auntie's?

Leon:
Did you ask her about the video?

I reply quickly.

18:24

Nettie:
Yeah. No joy ☹

She wouldn't tell me

But I know she knows

So frustrating

8

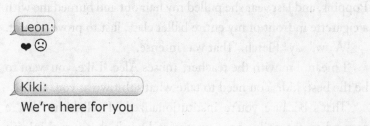

Leon:
❤ ☹

Kiki:
We're here for you

Nettie:
Thanks, friends ❤

CANNOT WAIT TO SEE YOU TOMO!!!

Leon:
xxx

Kiki:
😊 😅 😖 😫

I smile. No matter what this year throws at me, with friends as brilliant as these, I can handle anything.

We spend the rest of the evening chilling with a movie. Alec refuses my suggestion of *La La Land* on the basis that he can't stand Ryan Gosling's hands; in the end we settle on *Whiplash*. As the movie starts and I sink into the soft velvet sofa, I look from Fletch to Alec and it suddenly feels like I've lived here a lot longer than a few hours. Like it's *home* – something I haven't felt since before Mum died. Things are going to be good this year.

The credits roll. I thought *we* had it bad in class, but this drumming teacher makes Millicent Moore look like Mary

Poppins, and last year she pulled my hair out and burned me with a cigarette in front of my entire ballet class, just to prove a point.

'Wow,' says Fletch. 'That was intense.'

'I mean, I'm with the teacher,' muses Alec. 'Like, you want to be the best, kid? You need to take what's thrown at you.'

'That's because you're institutionalized,' I tell him. 'You're so used to the daily abuse we get at Duke's that you think it's acceptable.'

'Duke's is the best college in the country; it must be doing something right.'

'Yeah, creating a whole new generation of bullies.'

Alec turns to Fletch for support, but Fletch's phone buzzes insistently. As he checks it his smile drops a little. 'Excuse me just one sec . . . *Hello?*' He goes out of the room, closing the door behind him.

Alec shrugs. 'You need to toughen up, Nettie.'

He's right – I do need to toughen up. And I plan to. But surely that means taking less crap from people, not more? His logic's completely warped.

Fletch is on the phone for half an hour. By the time he's finished, Alec is getting ready to go to bed.

'All OK?' says Alec, unusually seriously, as if Fletch just had some bad news. Although, from the look on his face, he might have.

'Yep,' Fletch replies shortly.

Alec looks like he's about to say something else but changes his mind. Instead, he kisses me on the head and breezes out the door.

'Sorry about that,' says Fletch, coming to sit next to me on the sofa. 'It was Michael St. John. He wanted to run through a few

10

things about this year with me.'

'Oh,' I say. Michael's the head of Music at Duke's. He's this amazingly talented and all-round nice guy, and everyone basically adores him. I don't know why he couldn't have done that with Fletch tomorrow, though. Bit odd phoning him at night. 'Everything all right?'

'Yeah, course. Why?'

'I don't know. You look stressed.'

'I'm fine.'

I'm about to snuggle in, when something catches Fletch's attention from the other side of the room. He goes over to the huge windows overlooking Pineapple Dance Studios, where a late-night rehearsal is in full swing.

'What do you think they're rehearsing for?' he says, watching them intently.

I follow him over to the windows to see. The dancers are working on a high-octane fusion of jazz and salsa. 'Isn't that the tall dancer from *Strictly*?' I say, squinting. 'It looks like one of those spin-off tours.'

'You really have to give up your whole life for it, don't you?' he says, watching the lead couple do an impressive death drop. 'Those dancers – it's nearly eleven, and they're still going. And then they'll be on tour soon. Some of them are probably married or with people; others might even have kids. How do they cope with being away?'

'They just manage, I guess,' I say. It's not something I've thought about before. 'Get back when they can. You go where the work is, don't you?'

He doesn't answer for a while, and although his gaze is still directed into the studio, his eyes aren't following the dancers

11

around any more.

'Do you think we'd be OK?' he asks, turning to me. 'If one of us got a tour, I mean.'

Why is he even thinking that? Of *course* we'd be OK. Anyway, that's ages away. He's still got another year at college. And we've only been a couple for, like, three months. Why's he planning our break-up already?

'Yes, I do,' I reply cheerfully, but then I notice his knitted brow. 'Hey, what's brought this on?'

He cups my face in his hands. 'I have to tell you something, Nettie.'

Oh my God.

Why does he look so nervous?

He's going to finish with me.

He's worried about committing so close to graduating.

Urgh, why do I do that? It could be *anything*.

'OK,' I say, all calmity-calm, even though my heart is beating so loudly it could provide the bassline for *Six*. 'What is it?'

'I just –' He pushes my hair back gently, his eyes searching mine. He doesn't say anything for a moment. 'I . . . love you, Nettie.'

It's such a shock that I don't reply. Not that my response needs any thought – I've loved this boy almost a year to the day, ever since we sat opposite each other in the library and wrote the end of a song together and talked about losing people we loved. I knew it, even then. So I should be saying it back, right now. Shouldn't I?

But it just . . . I don't know – it *felt* like he was going to say something else.

'I love you too,' I say finally.

12

Fletch breathes out and lets his hands drop. This is not how I imagined this scene would play out. Granted, in my head it's probably a little *too* Kelli O'Hara and Matthew Morrison singing 'Say It Somehow' from *The Light in the Piazza*, and I totally get that basing your expectations of romance on musical theatre love songs is only going to end in plummeting disappointment, but seeing Fletch get so stressed working up to saying it and then almost dying of relief afterwards is not where I thought this moment would go. I watch him, waiting for him to speak.

'I wanted to say it weeks ago, but I was scared,' he says finally, like he knows he owes me an explanation. He takes my hands; I notice his are shaking. 'After Danny died, I shut myself off completely. Friends, my family, everyone. The idea of losing you – it terrifies me, Nettie. I'm not saying that to force you to be with me forever or anything – I'm just trying to explain how I feel.'

He doesn't need to. Since I lost Mum, there's been a low-level anxiety prickling at my stomach, pretty much constantly. Mum was the only person I'd ever loved – and she left me. I'm completely powerless to stop that happening again with Fletch, or anyone I get close to. It doesn't surprise me that Fletch feels the same after losing his brother so young.

'You know what?' I say. 'Mum would tell me the grief makes our bond stronger. She'd say we just need to be honest with each other.'

'Danny would tell me to stop being a knob,' says Fletch, and we both laugh. 'I don't know what I was waiting for. I bloody love you, Nettie.'

He tilts my head up, and our lips meet. It's the perfect *I love you* kiss – soft and tender and *definitely* worthy of a musical – *at*

13

first. His arms are around my waist, my hands are clasped behind his neck, the dancers across the road are doing a sultry Argentine tango . . . But after a few seconds, something changes. I can't put my finger on it, except that it feels like Fletch has pulled back. Not physically, but emotionally. Is it even possible to be able to *feel* that in a kiss? I know Cher thinks so, but, like, in real life?

Something in the kiss, in the space around us, in the way Fletch is holding me feels like we've gone back in time to that moment before he said he loved me. When I thought he was going to say something else.

When there was doubt in his eyes.